The Caravaners

By
Elizabeth Von Arnim
ILLUSTRATED BY
Arthur Litle

Elizabeth Von Arnim

Introduction:

Elizabeth von Arnim, born Mary Annette Beauchamp in 1866, was a British novelist known for her witty, satirical, and insightful portrayals of upper-class society. Her works often explored themes of love, marriage, gender roles, and the constraints of societal expectations on women. Despite facing personal challenges and societal pressures, von Arnim left a lasting legacy through her writing, which continues to captivate readers with its humor, charm, and keen observations of human nature.

Life:

Mary Annette Beauchamp, later known as Elizabeth von Arnim, was born on August 31, 1866, in Kirribilli Point, Sydney, Australia. She was the third of the six children of Henry Herron Beauchamp, a British barrister, and his wife Elizabeth Weiss Lassetter. Her family moved back to England when she was three years old, settling in Henley-on-Thames.

Growing up in a well-to-do family, Mary received a privileged education, attending various schools in England, Germany, and France. Her exposure to different cultures and languages would later influence her writing and worldview. Despite her comfortable upbringing, Mary's early life was marked by personal struggles, including the death of her father when she was just 14 years old.

In 1891, Mary married Count Henning August von Arnim-Schlagenthin, a Prussian aristocrat, and became known as Elizabeth von Arnim. The couple had five children together, but their marriage was not without its challenges. Von Arnim's husband was often unfaithful, and she found herself constrained by the rigid expectations placed upon her as a woman of her social standing. These experiences would later inform much of her writing, particularly her exploration of marriage and gender dynamics.

Despite her marital difficulties, von Arnim found solace and purpose in writing. Encouraged by her cousin, the famous author Katherine Mansfield, von Arnim began to pursue writing more seriously. Her early works, including "Elizabeth and Her German Garden" (1898) and "The Solitary Summer" (1899), garnered critical acclaim and established her reputation as a talented and insightful writer.

Throughout her life, von Arnim was known for her independent spirit and unconventional views. She embraced the ideals of feminism and social reform, advocating for women's rights and speaking out against the injustices of her time. Her progressive beliefs often found expression in her novels, which challenged traditional gender roles and questioned the societal norms of the day.

Despite facing personal setbacks and the demands of motherhood, von Arnim remained dedicated to her writing, producing a prolific body of work that continues to resonate with readers today. Her novels, characterized by their wit, humor, and keen psychological insight, offer timeless reflections on the complexities of human relationships and the pursuit of happiness.

Von Arnim's later years were marked by a period of travel and introspection. Following the end of her tumultuous marriage, she embarked on a journey of self-discovery, spending time in various European countries and immersing herself in nature and the arts. These experiences would inform her later works, including the semi-autobiographical novel "All the Dogs of My Life" (1936), in which she reflects on her experiences with love, loss, and the passage of time.

Elizabeth von Arnim passed away on February 9, 1941, at the age of 74. Though she may have been gone, her literary legacy endured, with her novels continuing to be celebrated for their wit, charm, and timeless insights into the human condition. Today, von Arnim is remembered as one of the foremost writers of her generation, whose work continues to captivate and inspire readers around the world.

Writing Career:

Elizabeth von Arnim's writing career spanned several decades and encompassed a wide range of genres, including novels, essays, and autobiographical works. Her distinctive voice and keen observational skills earned her a devoted following and established her as one of the leading literary figures of her time.

Von Arnim's early novels, including "Elizabeth and Her German Garden" (1898) and "The Solitary Summer" (1899), were inspired by her own experiences living in Germany and reflected her love of nature and gardening. These works were notable for their charming wit and satirical observations of upper-class society, as well as their exploration of themes such as marriage, domesticity, and female independence.

In her later novels, von Arnim continued to explore these themes with greater depth and complexity. Works such as "Vera" (1921) and "The Enchanted April" (1922) delved into the intricacies of human relationships and the quest for personal fulfillment, while also offering sharp critiques of the social mores and gender norms of the early 20th century.

One of von Arnim's most famous novels, "The Enchanted April," tells the story of four women who embark on a journey of self-discovery and transformation when they rent a villa in Italy for a month. The novel explores themes of friendship, romance, and the healing power of nature, and has been praised for its evocative prose and nuanced characterizations.

In addition to her novels, von Arnim was also a prolific essayist and diarist, and her non-fiction works offer valuable insights into her life and literary philosophy. Her essays, collected in volumes such as "The Adventures of Elizabeth in Rügen" (1904) and "The Honeywood File" (1916), cover a wide range of topics, including travel, feminism, and the joys of everyday life.

Throughout her writing career, von Arnim remained committed to exploring the complexities of human nature and the intricacies of human relationships. Her novels are characterized by their wit, intelligence, and emotional depth, and continue to be celebrated for their timeless relevance and universal appeal.

In conclusion, Elizabeth von Arnim was a trailblazing writer whose work continues to captivate and inspire readers more than a century after it was first published. Through her novels, essays, and autobiographical writings, she offered profound insights into the human condition and challenged the societal norms of her time. Von Arnim's legacy endures as a testament to the power of literature to illuminate the complexities of life and to offer solace, wisdom, and inspiration to readers of all ages.

Table of Contents

CHAPTER I 1
CHAPTER II 13
CHAPTER III 25
CHAPTER IV 39
CHAPTER V 53
CHAPTER VI 65
CHAPTER VII 75
CHAPTER VIII 87
CHAPTER IX 97
CHAPTER X 107
CHAPTER XI 119
CHAPTER XII 131
CHAPTER XIII 143
CHAPTER XIV 155
CHAPTER XV 169
CHAPTER XVI 179
CHAPTER XVII 191
CHAPTER XVIII 201
CHAPTER XIX 213
CHAPTER XX 227
CHAPTER XXI 237
POST SCRIPTUM 241

CHAPTER I

IN JUNE this year there were a few fine days, and we supposed the summer had really come at last. The effect was to make us feel our flat (which is really a very nice, well-planned one on the second floor at the corner overlooking the cemetery, and not at all stuffy) but a dull place after all, and think with something like longing of the country. It was the year of the fifth anniversary of our wedding, and having decided to mark the occasion by a trip abroad in the proper holiday season of August we could not afford, neither did we desire, to spend money on trips into the country in June. My wife, therefore, suggested that we should devote a few afternoons to a series of short excursions within a radius of, say, from five to ten miles round our town, and visit one after the other those of our acquaintances who live near enough to Storchwerder and farm their own estates. "In this way," said she, "we shall get much fresh air at little cost."

After a time I agreed. Not immediately, of course, for a reasonable man will take care to consider the suggestions made by his wife from every point of view before consenting to follow them or allowing her to follow them. Women do not reason: they have instincts; and instincts would land them in strange places sometimes if it were not that their husbands are there to illuminate the path for them and behave, if one may so express it, as a kind of guiding and very clever glow-worm. As for those who have not succeeded in getting husbands, the flotsam and jetsam, so to speak, of their sex, all I can say is, God help them.

There was nothing, however, to be advanced against Edelgard's idea in this case; on the contrary, there was much to commend it. We should get fresh air; we should be fed (well fed, and, if we chose, to excess, but of course we know how to be reasonable); and we should pay nothing. As Major of the artillery regiment stationed at Storchwerder I am obliged anyhow to keep a couple of horses (they are fed at the cost of the regiment), and I also in the natural order of things have one of the men of my battalion in my flat as servant and coachman, who costs me little more than his keep and may not give me notice. All, then, that was wanting was a vehicle, and we could, as Edelgard pointed out, easily borrow our Colonel's wagonette for a few afternoons, so there was our equipage complete, and without spending a penny.

The estates round Storchwerder are big and we found on counting up that five calls would cover the entire circle of our country acquaintance. There might have been a sixth, but for reasons with which I entirely concurred my dear wife did not choose to include it. Lines have to be drawn, and I do not think an altogether bad definition of a gentleman or a lady would be one who draws them. Indeed, Edelgard was in some doubt as to whether there should be even five, a member of the five (not in this case actually the land-owner but the brother of the widowed lady owning it, who lives with her and looks after her interests) being a person we neither of us can care much about, because he is not only unsound politically, with a decided leaning disgraceful in a man of his birth and which he hardly takes any trouble to hide toward those views the middle classes and Socialist sort of people call (God save the mark!) enlightened, but he is also either unable or unwilling—Edelgard and I could never make up our minds which—to keep his sister in order. Yet to keep the woman one is responsible for in order whether she be sister, or wife, or mother, or daughter, or even under certain favourable conditions aunt (a difficult race sometimes, as may be seen by the case of Edelgard's Aunt Bockhügel, of whom perhaps more later) is really quite easy. It is only a question of beginning in time, as you mean to go on in fact, and of being especially firm whenever you feel internally least so. It is so easy that I never could understand the difficulty. It is so easy that when my wife at this point brought me my eleven o'clock bread and ham and butter and interrupted me by looking over my shoulder, I smiled up at her, my thoughts still running on this theme, and taking the hand that put down the plate said, "Is it not, dear wife?"

"Is what not?" she asked—rather stupidly I thought, for she had read what I had written to the end; then without giving me time to reply she said, "Are you not going to write the story of our experiences in England after all, Otto?"

"Certainly," said I.

"To lend round among our relations next winter?"

"Certainly," said I.

"Then had you not better begin?"

"Dear wife," said I, "it is what I am doing."

"Then," said she, "do not waste time going off the rails."

And sitting down in the window she resumed her work of enlarging the armholes of my shirts.

This, I may remark, was tartness. Before she went to England she was never tart. However, let me continue.

I wonder what she means by rails. (I shall revise all this, of course, and no doubt will strike out portions) I wonder if she means I ought to begin with my name and address. It seems unnecessary, for I am naturally as well known to persons in Storchwerder as the postman. On the other hand this is my first attempt (which explains why I wonder at all what Edelgard may or may not mean, beginners doing well, I suppose, to be humble) at what poetic and literary and other persons of bad form call, I believe, wooing the Muse. What an expression! And I wonder what Muse. I would like to ask Edelgard whether she—but no, it would almost seem as if I were seeking her advice, which is a reversing of the proper relative positions of husband and wife. So at this point, instead of adopting a course so easily disastrous, I turned my head and said quietly:

"Dear wife, our English experiences *did* begin with our visits to the neighbours. If it had not been for those visits we would probably not last summer have seen Frau von Eckthum at all, and if we had not come within reach of her persuasive tongue we would have gone on our silver wedding journey to Italy or Switzerland, as we had so often planned, and left that accursed island across the Channel alone."

I paused; and as Edelgard said nothing, which is what she says when she is unconvinced, I continued with the patience I always show her up to the point at which it would become weakness, to explain the difference between the exact and thorough methods of men, their liking for going to the root of a matter and beginning at the real beginning, and the jumping tendencies of women, who jump to things such as conclusions without paying the least heed to all the important places they have passed over while they were, so to speak, in the air.

"But we get there first," said Edelgard.

I frowned a little. A few months ago—before, that is, our time on British soil—she would not have made such a retort. She used never to retort, and the harmony of our wedded life was consequently unclouded. I think she saw me frown but she took no notice—another novelty in her behaviour; so, after waiting a moment, I determined to continue the narrative.

But before I go straight on with it I should like to explain why we, an officer and his wife who naturally do not like spending money, should have contemplated so costly a holiday as a trip abroad. The fact is, for a long time past we had made up our minds to do so in the fifth year of our marriage, and for the following reason: Before I married Edelgard I had been a widower for one year, and before being a widower I was married for no fewer than nineteen years. This sounds as though I must be old, but I need not tell my readers who see me constantly that I am not. The best of all witnesses are the eyes; also, I began my marrying unusually young. My first wife was one of the Mecklenburg Lunewitzes, the elder (and infinitely superior) branch. If she had lived, I would last year have been celebrating our silver wedding on August 1st, and there would have been much feasting and merry-making arranged for us, and many acceptable gifts in silver from our relations, friends, and acquaintances. The regiment would have been obliged to recognize it, and perhaps our two servants would have clubbed together and expressed their devotion in a metal form. All this I feel I have missed, and through no fault of my own. I fail to see why I should be deprived of every benefit of such a celebration, for have I not, with an interruption of twelve months forced upon me, been actually married twenty-five years? And why, because my poor Marie-Luise was unable to go on living, should I have to attain to the very high number of (practically) five and twenty years' matrimony without the least notice being taken of it? I had been explaining this to Edelgard for a long time, and the nearer the date drew on which in the natural order of things I would have been reaping a silver harvest and have been put in a position to gauge the esteem in which I was held, the more emphatic did I become. Edelgard seemed at first unable to understand, but she was very teachable, and gradually found my logic irresistible. Indeed, once she grasped the point she was even more strongly of opinion than I was that something ought to be done to mark the occasion, and quite saw that if Marie-Luise failed me it was not my fault, and that I at least had done my part and gone on steadily being married ever since. From recognizing this to being indignant that our friends would probably take no notice of the anniversary was but, for her, a step; and many were the talks we had together on the subject, and many the suggestions we both of us made for bringing our friends round to our point of view. We finally decided that, however much they might ignore it, we ourselves would do what was right, and accordingly we planned a silver-honeymoon trip to the land proper to romance, Italy, beginning it on the first of August, which was the date of my marriage twenty-five years before with Marie-Luise.

I have gone into this matter at some length because I wished to explain clearly to those of our relations who will have this lent to them why we undertook a journey so, in the ordinary course of things, extravagant; and having, I hope, done this satisfactorily, will now proceed with the narrative.

We borrowed the Colonel's wagonette; I wrote five letters announcing our visit and asking (a mere formality, of course) if it would be agreeable; the answers arrived assuring us in every tone of well-bred enthusiasm that it would; I donned my parade uniform; Edelgard put on her new summer finery; we gave careful instructions to Clothilde, our cook, helping her to carry them out by locking everything up; and off we started in holiday spirits, driven by my orderly, Hermann, and watched by the whole street.

At each house we were received with becoming hospitality. They were all families of our own standing, members of that chivalrous, God-fearing and well-born band that upholds the best traditions of the Fatherland and gathers in spirit if not (owing to circumstances) in body, like a protecting phalanx around our Emperor's throne. First we had coffee and cakes and a variety of sandwiches (at one of the houses there were no sandwiches, only cakes, and we both discussed this unaccountable omission during the drive home); then I was taken to view the pigs by our host, or the cows, or whatever happened to be his special pride, but in four cases out of the five it was pigs, and while I was away Edelgard sat on the lawn or the terrace or wherever the family usually sat (only one had a terrace) and conversed on subjects interesting to women-folk, such as Clothilde and Hermann and I know not what; then, after having thoroughly exhausted the pigs and been in my turn thoroughly exhausted by them, for naturally a Prussian officer on active service cannot be expected to take the same interest in these creatures so long as they are raw as a man does who devotes his life to them, we rejoined the ladies and strolled in the lighter talk suited to our listeners about the grounds, endeavouring with our handkerchiefs to drive away the mosquitoes, till summoned to supper; and after supper, which usually consisted of one excellent hot dish and a variety of cold ones, preceded by *bouillon* in cups and followed by some elegant sweet and beautiful fruit (except at Frau von Eckthum's, our local young widow's, where it was a regular dinner of six or seven courses, she being what is known as ultra-modern, her sister having married an Englishman), after supper, I repeat, having sat a while smoking on the lawn or terrace drinking coffee and liqueurs and secretly congratulating ourselves on not having in our town to live with so many and such hungry mosquitoes, we took our leave and drove back to Storchwerder, refreshed always and sometimes pleased as well.

The last of these visits was to Frau von Eckthum and her brother Graf Flitz von Flitzburg, who, as is well known, being himself unmarried, lives with her and looks after the estate left by the deceased Eckthum, thereby stepping into shoes so comfortable that they may more properly be spoken of as slippers. All had gone well up to that, nor was I conscious till much later that that had not gone well too; for only on looking back do we see the distance we have come and the way in which the road, at first so promising, led us before we knew where we were into a wilderness plentiful in stones. During our first four visits we had naturally talked about our plan to take a trip in August in Italy. Our friends, obviously surprised, and with the expression on their faces that has its source in thoughts of legacies, first enthusiastically applauded and then pointed out that it would be hot. August, they said, would be an impossible month in Italy: go where we would we should not meet a single German. This had not struck us before, and after our first disappointment we willingly listened to their advice rather to choose Switzerland, with its excellent hotels and crowds of our countrymen. Several times in the course of these conversations did we try to explain the honeymoon nature of the journey, but were met with so much of what I strongly suspect to have been wilful obtuseness that to our chagrin we began to see there was probably nothing to be done. Edelgard said she wished it would occur to them if, owing to the unusual circumstances, they did not intend to give us actual ash-trays and match-boxes, to join together in defraying the cost of the wedding journey of such respectable silver-honeymooners; but I do not think that at any time they had the least intention of doing anything at all for us—on the contrary, they made us quite uneasy by the sums they declared we would have to disburse; and on our last visit (to Frau von Eckthum) happening to bewail the amount of good German money that was going to be dragged out of us by the rascally Swiss, she (Frau von Eckthum) said, "Why not come to England?"

At the moment I was so much engaged mentally reprobating the way in which she was lying back in a low garden chair with one foot crossed over the other and both feet encased in such thin stockings that they might just as well not have been stockings at all, that I did not immediately notice the otherwise striking expression, "Come." "Go" would of course have been the usual and expected form; but the substitution, I repeat, escaped me at the moment because of my attention being otherwise engaged. I never

I never saw such little shoes

saw such little shoes. Has a woman a right to be conspicuous at the extremities? So conspicuous—Frau von Eckthum's hands also easily become absorbing—that one is unable connectedly to follow the conversation? I doubt it: but she is an attractive lady. There sat Edelgard, straight and seemly, the perfect flower of a stricter type of virtuous German womanhood, her feet properly placed side by side on the grass and clothed, as I knew, in decent wool with the flat-heeled boots of the Christian gentlewoman, and I must say the type—in one's wife, that is—is preferable. I rather wondered whether Flitz noticed the contrast between the two ladies. I glanced at him, but his face was as usual a complete blank. I wondered whether he could or could not make his sister sit up if he had wished to; and for the hundredth time I felt I never could really like the man, for from the point of view of a brother one's sister should certainly sit up. She is, however, an attractive lady: alas that her stockings should be so persistently thin.

"England," I heard Edelgard saying, "is not, I think, a suitable place."

It was then that I consciously noticed that Frau von Eckthum had said "Come."

"Why not?" she asked; and her simple way of asking questions, or answering them with others of her own without waiting to adorn them or round them off with the title of the person addressed, has helped, I know, to make her unpopular in Storchwerder society.

"I have heard," said Edelgard cautiously, no doubt bearing in mind that to hosts whose sister had married an Englishman and was still living with him one would not say all one would like to about it, "I have heard that it is not a place to go to if the object is scenery."

"Oh?" said Frau von Eckthum. Then she added—intelligently, I thought—"But there always is scenery."

"Edelgard means lofty scenery," said I gently, for we were both holding cups of the Eckthum tea (this was the only house in which we were made to drink tea instead of our aromatic and far more filling national beverage) in our hands, and I have always held one ought to humour the persons whose hospitality one happens to be enjoying—"Or enduring," said Edelgard cleverly when, on our way home, I mentioned this to her.

"Or enduring," I agreed after a slight pause, forced on reflection to see that it is not true hospitality to oblige your visitors to go without their coffee by employing the unworthy and barbarically simple expedient of not allowing it to appear. But of course that was Flitz. He behaves, I think, much too much as though the place belonged to him.

Flitz, who knows England well, having spent several years there at our Embassy, said it was the most delightful country in the world. The unpatriotic implication contained in this assertion caused Edelgard and myself to exchange glances, and no doubt she was thinking, as I was, that it would be a sad and bad day for Prussia if many of its gentleman had sisters who made misguided marriages with foreigners, the foreign being so often the thin end of that wedge which at its thick of our right to regard ourselves as specially raised by Al occupy the first place among the nations, and a dislike (I h my own ears a man at a meeting express it) an actual dislike—I can only call it hideous—of the glorious cement of blood and iron by means of which we intend to stick there.

"But I was chiefly thinking," said Frau von Eckthum, her head well back in the cushions and her eyes fixed pensively on the summer clouds sailing over our heads, "of what you were saying about expense."

"Dear lady," I said, "I have been told by all who have done it that travelling in England is the most expensive holiday you can take. The hotels are ruinous as well as bad, the meals are uneatable as well as dear, the cabs cost you a fortune, and the inhabitants are rude."

I spoke with heat, because I was roused (justly) by Flitz's unpatriotic attitude, but it was a tempered heat owing to the undoubted (Storchwerder cannot deny it) personal attractiveness of our hostess. Why are not all women attractive? What habitual lambs our sex would become if they were.

"Dear Baron," said she in her pretty, gentle voice, "do come over and see for yourself. I would like, I think, to convert you. Look at this"—she picked up some papers lying on the grass by her chair, and spreading out one showed me a picture—"do you not think it nice? And, if you want to be economical, it only costs fourteen pounds for a whole month."

The picture she held out to me was one bearing a strong resemblance to the gipsy carts that are continually (and very rightly) being sent somewhere else by our local police; a little less gaudy perhaps, a little squarer and more solid, but undoubtedly a near relation.

"It is a caravan," said Frau von Eckthum, in answer to the question contained in my eyebrows; and turning the sheet she showed me another picture representing the same vehicle's inside.

Edelgard got up and looked over my shoulder.

What we saw was certainly very nice. Edelgard said so at once. There were flowered curtains, and a shelf with books, and a comfortable chair in a cushion near a big window, and at the end two pretty beds placed one above the other as in a ship.

"A thing like this," said Frau von Eckthum, "does away at once with hotels, waiters, and expense. It costs fourteen pounds for two persons for a whole month, and all your days are spent in the sun."

She then explained her plan, which was to hire one of these vehicles for the month of August and lead a completely free and bohemian existence during that time, wandering through the English lanes, which she described as flowery, and drawing up for the night in a secluded spot near some little streamlet, to the music of whose gentle rippling, as Edelgard always easily inclined to sentiment suggested, she would probably be lulled to sleep.

"Come too," said she, smiling up at us as we looked over her shoulder.

"Two hundred and eighty marks is fourteen pounds," said I, making mental calculations.

"For two people," said Edelgard, obviously doing the same.

"No hotels," said our hostess.

"No hotels," echoed Edelgard.

"Only lovely green fields," said our hostess.

"And no waiters," said Edelgard.

"Yes, no horrid waiters," said our hostess.

"Waiters are so expensive," said Edelgard.

"You wouldn't see one," said our hostess. "Only a nice child in a clean apron from a farm bringing eggs and cream. And you move about the whole time, and see the country in a way you never would going from place to place by train."

"But," said I shrewdly, "if we move about something must either pull or push us, and that something must also be paid for."

"Oh, yes, there has to be a horse. But think of all the railway tickets you won't buy and all the porters you won't tip," said Frau von Eckthum.

Edelgard was manifestly impressed. Indeed, we both were. If it were a question of being in England for little money or being in Switzerland for much we felt unanimously that it was better to be in England. And then to travel through it in one of these conveyances was so distinctly original that we would be objects of the liveliest interest during the succeeding winter gaieties in Storchwerder. "The von Ottringels are certainly all that is most modern," we could already hear our friends saying to each other, and could already see in our mind's eye how they would press round us at *soirées* and bombard us with questions. We should be the centre of attraction.

"And think of the nightingales!" cried Edelgard, suddenly recollecting those poetic birds.

"In August they're like Germans in Italy," said Flitz, to whom I had mentioned our reason for giving up the idea of travelling in that country.

"How so?" said Edelgard, turning to him with the slight instinctive stiffening of every really virtuous German lady when speaking to an unrelated (by blood) man.

"They're not there," said Flitz.

Well, of course the moment we were able to look in our Encyclopædia at home we knew as well as he did that they do not sing in August, but I do not see how townsfolk are to keep these odds and ends of information lying loose about in their heads. We do not have the bird in Storchwerder and are therefore unable to study its habits at first hand as Flitz can, but I know that all the pieces of poetry I have come across mention nightingales before they have done, and the consequent perfectly natural impression left on my mind was that they were always more or less about. But I do not like Flitz's tone, and never shall. It is true I have not actually seen him do it, but one feels instinctively that he is laughing at one; and there are different ways of laughing, and not all of them appear on the face. As for politics, if I were not as an officer debarred from alluding to them and were led to discuss them with him, I have no doubt that each discussion would end in a duel. That is, if he would fight. The appalling suspicion has just crossed my mind that he would not. He is one of those dreadful persons who cloak their cowardice behind the garb of philosophy. Well, well, I see I am growing angry with a man ten miles away, whom I have not seen for months—I, a man of the world sitting in the calm of my own flat, surrounded by quiet domestic objects such as my wife, my shirt, and my little meal of bread and ham. Is this reasonable? Certainly not. Let me change the subject.

The long, then, and the short of our visit to Graf Flitz and his sister in June last was that we returned home determined to join Frau von

Eckthum's party, and not a little full of pleasurable anticipations. When she does talk she has a persuasive tongue. She talked more at this time than she ever did afterward, but of course there were reasons for that which I may or may not disclose. Edelgard listened with something like rapt interest to her really picturesque descriptions, or rather prophecies, for she had not herself done it before, of the pleasures of camp life; and I wish it to be clearly understood that Edelgard, who has since taken the line of telling people it was I, was the one who was swept off her usually cautious feet and who took it upon herself without waiting for me to speak to ask Frau von Eckthum to write and hire another of the carts for us.

Frau von Eckthum laughed, and said she was sure we would like it. Flitz himself smoked in silence. And Edelgard developed a sudden eloquence in regard to natural phenomena such as moons and poppies that would have done credit to a young and sentimental girl. "Think of sitting in the shade of some mighty beech tree," she said, for instance (she actually clasped her hands), "with the beams of the sinking sun slanting through its branches, and doing one's needlework."

And she said other things of the same sort, things that made me, who knew she was going to be thirty next birthday, gaze upon her with a deep surprise.

CHAPTER II

I HAVE decided not to show Edelgard my manuscript again, and my reason is that I may have a freer hand. For the same reason I will not, as we at first proposed, send it round by itself among our relations, but will either accompany it in person or invite our relations to a cozy beer-evening, with a simple little cold something to follow, and read aloud such portions of it as I think fit, omitting of course much that I say about Edelgard and probably also a good deal that I say about everybody else. A reasonable man is not a woman, and does not willingly pander to a love of gossip. Besides, as I have already hinted, the Edelgard who came back from England is by no means the Edelgard who went there. It will wear off, I am confident, in time, and we will return to the *status quo ante*—(how naturally that came out: it gratifies me to see I still remember)—a *status quo* full of trust and obedience on the one side and of kind and wise guidance on the other. Surely I have a right to refuse to be driven, except by a silken thread? When I, noticing a tendency on Edelgard's part to attempt to substitute, if I may so express it, leather, asked her the above question, will it be believed that what she answered was Bosh?

It gave me a great shock to hear her talk like that. Bosh is not a German expression at all. It is purest English. And it amazes me with what rapidity she picked it and similar portions of the language up, adding them in quantities to the knowledge she already possessed of the tongue, a fairly complete knowledge (she having been well educated), but altogether excluding words of that sort. Of course I am aware it was all Jellaby's fault—but more of him in his proper place; I will not now dwell on later incidents while my narrative is still only at the point where everything was eager anticipation and preparation.

Our caravan had been hired; I had sent, at Frau von Eckthum's direction, the money to the owner, the price (unfortunately) having to be paid beforehand; and August the first, the very day of my wedding with poor Marie-Luise, was to see us start. Naturally there was much to do and arrange, but it was pleasurable work such as getting a suit of civilian clothes adapted to the uses it would be put to, searching for stockings to match the knickerbockers, and for a hat that would be useful in both wet weather and sunshine.

"It will be all sunshine," said Frau von Eckthum with her really unusually pretty smile (it includes the sudden appearance of two dimples) when I expressed fears as to the effect of rain on the Panama that I finally bought and which, not being a real one, made me anxious.

We saw her several times because of our need for hints as to luggage, meeting place, etc., and I found her each time more charming. When she was on her feet, too, her dress hid the shoes; and she was really helpful, and was apparently looking forward greatly to showing us the beauties of her sister's more or less native land.

As soon as my costume was ready I put it on and drove out to see her. The stockings had been a difficulty because I could not bear, accustomed as I am to cotton socks, their woollen feet. This was at last surmounted by cutting off their feet and sewing my ordinary sock feet on to the woollen legs. It answered splendidly, and Edelgard assured me that with care no portion of the sock (which was not of the same colour) would protrude. She herself had sent to Berlin to Wertheim for one of the tailor-made dresses in his catalogue, which turned out to be of really astonishing value for the money, and in which she looked very nice. With a tartan silk blouse and a little Tyrolese hat and a pheasant's feather stuck in it she was so much transformed that I declared I could not believe it was our silver wedding journey, and I felt exactly as I did twenty-five years before.

"But it is not our silver wedding journey," she said with some sharpness.

"Dear wife," I retorted surprised, "you know very well that it is mine, and what is mine is also by law yours, and that therefore without the least admissible logical doubt it *is* yours."

She made a sudden gesture with her shoulders that was almost like impatience; but I, knowing what victims the best of women are to incomprehensible moods, went out and bought her a pretty little bag with a leather strap to wear over one shoulder and complete her attire, thus proving to her that a reasonable man is not a child and knows when and how to be indulgent.

Frau von Eckthum, who was going to stay with her sister for a fortnight before they both joined us (the sister, I regretted to hear, was coming too), left in the middle of July. Flitz, at that time incomprehensibly to me, made excuses for not taking part in the caravan tour, but since then light has been thrown on his behaviour: he said, I remember, that he could not leave his pigs.

"Much better not leave his sister," said Edelgard who, I fancy, was just then a little envious of Frau von Eckthum.

"Dear wife," I said gently, "*we* shall be there to take care of her and he knows she is safe in our hands. Besides, we do not want Flitz. He is the last man I can imagine myself ever wanting."

It was perfectly natural that Edelgard should be a little envious, and I felt it was and did not therefore in any way check her. I need not remind those relatives who will next winter listen to this that the Flitzes of Flitzburg, of whom Frau von Eckthum was one, are a most ancient and still more penniless family. Frau von Eckthum and her gaunt sister (last time she was staying in Prussia both Edelgard and I were struck with her extreme gauntness) each married a wealthy man by two most extraordinary strokes of luck; for what man nowadays will marry a girl who cannot take, if not the lion's share, at least a very substantial one of the household expenses upon herself? What is the use of a father if he cannot provide his daughter with the money required suitably to support her husband and his children? I myself have never been a father, so that I am qualified to speak with perfect impartiality; that is, strictly, I was one twice, but only for so few minutes each time that they can hardly be said to count. The two von Flitz girls married so young and so well, and have been, without in any way really deserving it, so snugly wrapped in comfort ever since (Frau von Eckthum actually losing her husband two years after marriage and coming into everything) that naturally Edelgard cannot be expected to like it. Edelgard had a portion herself of six thousand marks a year besides an unusual quantity of house linen, which enabled her at last—she was twenty-four when I married her—to find a good husband; and she cannot understand by what wiles the two sisters, without a penny or a table cloth, secured theirs at eighteen. She does not see that they are—"were" is the better word in the case of the gaunt sister—attractive; but then the type is so completely opposed to her own that she would not be likely to. Certainly I agree that a married woman verging, as the sister must be, on thirty should settle down to a smooth head and at least the beginnings of a suitable embonpoint. We do not want wives like lieutenants in a cavalry regiment; and Edelgard is not altogether wrong when she says that both

Frau von Eckthum and her sister make her think of those lean and elegant young men. Your lean woman with her restlessness of limb and brain is far indeed removed from the soft amplitudes and slow movements of her who is the ideal wife of every German better-class bosom. Privately, however, I feel I can at least understand that there may have been something to be said at the time for the Englishman's conduct, and I more than understand that of the deceased Eckthum. No one can deny that his widow is undoubtedly—well, well; let me return to the narrative.

We had naturally told everybody we met what we were going to do, and it was intensely amusing to see the astonishment created. Bad health for the rest of our days was the smallest of the evils predicted. Also our digestions were much commiserated. "Oh," said I with jaunty recklessness at that, "we shall live on boiled hedgehogs, preceded by mice soup,"—for I had studied the article *Gipsies* in our Encyclopædia, and discovered that they often eat the above fare.

The faces of our friends when I happened to be in this jocose vein were a study. "God in heaven," they cried, "what will become of your poor wife?"

But a sense of humour carries a man through anything, and I did not allow myself to be daunted. Indeed it was not likely, I reminded myself sometimes when inclined to be thoughtful at night, that Frau von Eckthum, who so obviously was delicately nurtured, would consent to eat hedgehogs or risk years in which all her attractiveness would evaporate on a sofa of sickness.

"Oh, but Frau von Eckthum——!" was the invariable reply, accompanied by a shrug when I reassured the ladies of our circle by pointing this out.

I am aware Frau von Eckthum is unpopular in Storchwerder. Perhaps it is because the art of conversation is considerably developed there, and she will not talk. I know she will not go to its balls, refuses its dinners, and turns her back on its coffees. I know she is with difficulty induced to sit on its philanthropic boards, and when she finally has been induced to sit on them does not do so after all but stays at home. I know she is different from the type of woman prevailing in our town, the plain, flat-haired, tightly buttoned up, God-fearing wife and mother, who looks up to her husband and after her children, and is extremely intelligent in the kitchen and not at all intelligent out of it. I know that this is the type that has made our great nation what it is, hoisting it up on ample shoulders to the first place in the world, and I know that we would have to request heaven to help us if we ever changed it. But—she is an attractive lady.

Truly it is an excellent thing to be able to put down one's opinions on paper as they occur to one without risk of irritating interruption—I hope my hearers will not interrupt at the reading aloud—and now that I have at last begun to write a book—for years I have intended doing so—I see clearly the superiority of writing over speaking. It is the same kind of superiority that the pulpit enjoys over the (very properly) muzzled pews. When, during my stay on British soil, I said anything, however short, of the nature of the above remarks about our German wives and mothers, it was most annoying the way I was interrupted and the sort of questions that were instantly put me by, chiefly, the gaunt sister. But of that more in its place. I am still at the point where she had not yet loomed on my horizon, and all was pleasurable anticipation.

We left our home on August 1st, punctually as we had arranged, after some very hard-worked days at the end during which the furniture was beaten and strewn with napthalin (against moths), curtains, etc., taken down and piled neatly in heaps, pictures covered up in newspapers, and groceries carefully weighed and locked up. I spent these days at the Club, for my leave had begun on the 25th of July and there was nothing for me to do. And I must say, though the discomfort in our flat was intense, when I returned to it in the evening in order to go to bed I was never anything but patient with the unappetisingly heated and disheveled Edelgard. And she noticed it and was grateful. It would be hard to say what would make her grateful now. These last bad days, however, came to their natural end, and the morning of the first arrived and by ten we had taken leave, with many last injunctions, of Clothilde who showed an amount of concern at our departure that gratified us, and were on the station platform with Hermann standing respectfully behind us carrying our hand luggage in both his gloved hands, and with what he could not carry piled about his feet, while I could see by the expression on their faces that the few strangers present recognized we were people of good family or, as England would say, of the Upper Ten. We had no luggage for registration because of the new law by which every *kilo* has to be paid for, but we each had a well-filled, substantial hold-all and a leather portmanteau, and into these we had succeeded in packing most of the things Frau von Eckthum had from time to time suggested we might want. Edelgard is a good packer, and got far more in than I should have thought possible, and what was left over was stowed away in different bags and baskets. Also we took a plentiful supply of vaseline and bandages. "For," as I remarked to Edelgard when she giddily did not want to, quoting the most modern (though rightly disapproved of in Storchwerder) of English writers, "you never can possibly tell,"—besides a good sized ox-tongue, smoked specially for us by our Storchwerder butcher and which was later on to be concealed in our caravan for private use in case of need at night.

The train did not start till 10:45, but we wanted to be early in order to see who would come to see us off; and it was a very good thing we were in such good time, for hardly a quarter of an hour had elapsed before, to my dismay, I recollected that I had left my Panama at home. It was Edelgard's fault, who had persuaded me to wear a cap for the journey and carry my Panama in my hand, and I had put it down on some table and in the heat of departure forgotten it. I was deeply annoyed, for the whole point of the type of costume I had chosen would be missed without just that kind of hat, and, at my sudden exclamation and subsequent explanation of my exclamation, Edelgard showed that she felt her position by becoming exceedingly red.

There was nothing for it but to leave her there and rush off in a *droschke* to our deserted flat. Hurrying up the stairs two steps at a time and letting myself in with my latch-key I immediately found the Panama on the head of one of the privates in my own battalion, who was lolling in my chair at the breakfast-table I had so lately left being plied with our food by the miserable Clothilde, she sitting on Edelgard's chair and most shamelessly imitating her mistress's manner when she is affectionately persuading me to eat a little bit more.

The wretched soldier, I presume, was endeavouring to imitate me, for he called her a dear little hare, an endearment I sometimes apply to my wife, on Clothilde's addressing him as Edelgard sometimes does (or rather did) me in her softer moments as sweet snail. The man's imitation of me was a very poor affair, but Clothilde hit my wife off astoundingly well, and both creatures were so riotously mirthful that they neither heard nor saw me as I stood struck dumb in the door. The clock on the wall, however, chiming the half-hour recalled me to the necessity for instant action, and rushing forward I snatched the Panama off the amazed man's head, hurled a furious dismissal at Clothilde, and was out of the house and in the *droschke* before they could so much as pray for mercy. Immediately on arriving at the station I took Hermann aside and gave him instructions about the removal within an hour of Clothilde, and then, swallowing my agitation with a gulp of the man of the world, I was able to chat courteously and amiably with friends who had collected to see us off, and even to make little jokes as though nothing whatever had happened. Of course directly the last smile had died away at the carriage window and the last handkerchief had been fluttered and the last promise to send many picture postcards had been made, and our friends had become mere black and shapeless masses without bodies, parts or passions on the grey of the receding platform, I recounted the affair to Edelgard, and she was so much upset that she actually wanted to get out at the next station and give up our holiday and go back and look after her house.

Strangely enough, what upset her more than the soldier's being feasted at our expense and more than his wearing my new hat while he feasted, was the fact that I had dismissed Clothilde.

"Where and when am I to get another?" was her question, repeated with a plaintiveness that was at length wearisome. "And what will become of all our things now during our absence?"

"Would you have had me not dismiss her instantly, then?" I cried at last, goaded by this persistence. "Is every shamelessness to be endured? Why, if the woman were a man and of my own station, honour would demand that I should fight a duel with her."

"But you cannot fight a duel with a cook," said Edelgard stupidly.

"Did I not expressly say that I could not?" I retorted; and having with this reached the point where patience becomes a weakness I was obliged to put it aside and explain to her with vigour that I am not only not a fool but decline to be talked to as if I were. And when I had done, she having given no further rise to discussion, we were both silent for the rest of the way to Berlin.

This was not a bright beginning to my holiday, and I thought with some gloom of the difference between it and the start twenty-five years before with my poor Marie-Luise. There was no Clothilde then, and no Panama hat (for they were not yet the fashion), and all was peace. Unwilling, however, to send Edelgard, as the English say, any longer to Coventry—we are both good English scholars as my hearers know—when we got into the *droschke* in Berlin that was to take us across to the Potsdamer Bahnhof (from which station we departed for London *via* Flushing) I took her hand, and turning (not without effort) an unclouded face to her, said some little things which enabled her to become aware that I was willing once again to overlook and forgive.

Now I do not propose to describe the journey to London. So many of our friends know people who have done it that it is not necessary for me to dwell upon it further than to say that, being all new to us, it was not without its charm—at least, up to the moment when it became so late that there were no more meals taking place in the restaurant-car and no more attractive trays being held up to our windows at the stations on the way. About what happened later in the night I would not willingly speak: suffice it to say that I had not before realized the immense and apparently endless distance of England from the good dry land of the Continent. Edelgard, indeed, behaved the whole way up to London as if she had not yet got to England at all; and I was forced at last to comment very seriously on her conduct, for it looked as much like wilfulness as any conduct I can remember to have witnessed.

We reached London at the uncomfortable hour of 8 A.M., or thereabouts, chilled, unwell, and disordered. Although it was only the second of August a damp autumn draught pervaded the station. Shivering, we went into the sort of sheep-pen in which our luggage was searched for dutiable articles, Edelgard most inconsiderately leaving me to bear the entire burden of opening and shutting our things, while she huddled into a corner and assumed (very conveniently) the air of a sufferer. I had to speak to her quite sharply once when I could not fit the key of her portmanteau into its lock and remind her that I am not a lady's maid, but even this did not rouse her, and she continued to huddle apathetically. It is absurd for a wife to collapse at the very moment when she ought to be most helpful; the whole theory of the helpmeet is shattered by such behaviour. And what can I possibly know about Customs? She looked on quite unmoved while I struggled to replace the disturbed contents of our bags, and my glances, in turn appealing and indignant, did not make her even raise her head. There were too many strangers between us for me to be able to do more than glance, so

Edelgard most inconsiderately leaving me to bear the entire burden of opening and shutting our things

reserving what I had to say for a more private moment I got the bags shut as well as I could, directed the most stupid porter (who was also apparently deaf, for each time I said anything to him he answered perfectly irrelevantly with the first letter of the alphabet) I have ever met to conduct me and the luggage to the refreshment room, and far too greatly displeased with

Edelgard to take any further notice of her, walked on after the man leaving her to follow or not as she chose.

I think people must have detected as I strode along that I was a Prussian officer, for so many looked at me with interest. I wished I had had my uniform and spurs on, so that for once the non-martial island could have seen what the real thing is like. It was strange to me to be in a crowd of nothing but civilians. In spite of the early hour every arriving train disgorged myriads of them of both sexes. Not the flash of a button was to be seen; not the clink of a sabre to be heard; but, will it be believed? at least every third person arriving carried a bunch of flowers, often wrapped in tissue paper and always as carefully as though it had been a specially good *belegtes Brödchen*. That seemed to me very characteristic of the effeminate and non-military nation. In Prussia useless persons like old women sometimes transport bunches of flowers from one point to another—but that a man should be seen doing so, a man going evidently to his office, with his bag of business papers and his grave face, is a sight I never expected to see. The softness of this conduct greatly struck me. I could understand a packet of some good thing to eat between meals being brought, some tit-bit from the home kitchen—but a bunch of flowers! Well, well; let them go on in their effeminacy. It is what has always preceded a fall, and the fat little land will be a luscious morsel some day for muscular continental (and almost certainly German) jaws.

We had arranged to go straight that very day to the place in Kent where the caravans and Frau von Eckthum and her sister were waiting for us, leaving the sights of London for the end of our holiday, by which time our already extremely good though slow and slightly literary English (by which I mean that we talked more as the language is written than other people do, and that we were singularly pure in the matter of slang) would have developed into an up-to-date agility; and there being about an hour and a half's time before the train for Wrotham started—which it conveniently did from the same station we arrived at—our idea was to have breakfast first and then, perhaps, to wash. This we accordingly did in the station restaurant, and made the astonishing acquaintance of British coffee and butter. Why, such stuff would not be tolerated for a moment in the poorest wayside inn in Germany, and I told the waiter so very plainly;

but he only stared with an extremely stupid face, and when I had done speaking said "Eh?"

It was what the porter had said each time I addressed him, and I had already, therefore, not then knowing what it was or how it was spelt, had about as much of it as I could stand.

"Sir," said I, endeavoring to annihilate the man with that most powerful engine of destruction, a witticism, "what has the first letter of the alphabet to do with everything I say?"

"Eh?" said he.

"Suppose, sir," said I, "I were to confine my remarks to you to a strictly logical sequence, and when you say A merely reply B—do you imagine we should ever come to a satisfactory understanding?"

"Eh?" said he.

"Yet, sir," I continued, becoming angry, for this was deliberate impertinence, "it is certain that one letter of the alphabet is every bit as good as another for conversational purposes."

"Eh?" said he; and began to cast glances about him for help.

"This," said I to Edelgard, "is typical. It is what you must expect in England."

The head waiter here caught one of the man's glances and hurried up.

"This gentleman," said I, addressing the head waiter and pointing to his colleague, "is both impertinent and a fool."

"Yes, sir. German, sir," said the head waiter, flicking away a crumb.

Well, I gave neither of them a tip. The German was not given one for not at once explaining his inability to get away from alphabetical repartee and so shamefully hiding the nationality he ought to have openly rejoiced in, and the head waiter because of the following conversation:

"Can't get 'em to talk their own tongue, sir," said he, when I indignantly inquired why he had not. "None of 'em will, sir. Hear 'em putting German gentry who don't know English to the greatest inconvenience. 'Eh?' this one'll say—it's what he picks up his first week, sir. 'A thousand damns,' say the German gentry, or something to that effect. 'All right,' says the waiter—that's what he picks up his second week—and makes it worse. Then the German gentry gets really put out, and I see 'em almost foamin' at the mouth. Impatient set of people, sir——"

"I conclude," said I, interrupting him with a frown, "that the object of these poor exiled fellows is to learn the language as rapidly as possible and get back to their own country."

"Or else they're ashamed of theirs, sir," said he, scribbling down the bill. "Rolls, sir? Eight, sir? Thank you, sir——"

"Ashamed?"

"Quite right, sir. Nasty cursin' language. Not fit for a young man to get into the habit of. Most of the words got a swear about 'em somewhere, sir."

"Perhaps you are not aware," said I icily, "that at this very moment you are speaking to a German gentleman."

"Sorry, sir. Didn't notice it. No offence meant. Two coffees, four boiled eggs, eight—you did say eight rolls, sir? Compliment really, you know, sir."

"Compliment!" I exclaimed, as he whisked away with the money to the paying desk; and when he came back I pocketed, with elaborate deliberation, every particle of change.

"That is how," said I to Edelgard while he watched me, "one should treat these fellows."

To which she, restored by the hot coffee to speaking point, replied (rather stupidly I thought),

"Is it?"

CHAPTER III

SHE became, however, more normal as the morning wore on, and by about eleven o'clock was taking an intelligent interest in hop-kilns.

These objects, recurring at frequent intervals as one travels through the county of Kent, are striking and picturesque additions to the landscape, and as our guide-book described them very fully I was able to talk a good deal about them. Kent pleased me very well. It looked as if there were money in it. Many thriving villages, many comfortable farmhouses, and many hoary churches peeping slyly at us through surrounding groups of timber so ancient that its not yet having been cut down and sold is in itself a testimony to the prevailing prosperity. It did not need much imagination to picture the comfortable clergyman lurking in the recesses of his snug parsonage and rubbing his well-nourished hands at life. Well, let him rub. Some day perhaps—and who knows how soon?—we shall have a decent Lutheran pastor in his black gown preaching the amended faith in every one of those churches.

Shortly, then, Kent is obviously flowing with milk and honey and well-to-do inhabitants; and when on referring to our guide-book I found it described as the Garden of England I was not in the least surprised, and neither was Edelgard. In this county, as we knew, part at any rate of our gipsying was to take place, for the caravans were stationed at a village about three miles from Wrotham, and we were very well satisfied that we were going to examine it more closely, because though no one could call the scenery majestic it yet looked full of promise of a comfortable nature. I observed for instance that the roads seemed firm and good, which was clearly important; also that the villages were so plentiful that there would be no fear of our ever getting beyond the reach of provisions. Unfortunately, the weather was not true August weather, which I take it is properly described by the word bland. This is not bland. The remains of the violent wind that had blown us across from Flushing still hurried hither and thither, and gleams of sunshine only too frequently gave place to heavy squalls of rain and hail. It was more like a blustering October day than one in what is supposed to be the very height and ripeness of summer, and we could only both hope, as the carriage windows banged and rattled, that our caravan would be heavy enough to withstand the temptation to go on by itself during the night, urged on from behind by the relentless forces of nature. Still, each time the sun got the better of the inky clouds and the Garden of England laughed at us from out of its bravery of graceful hop-fields and ripening corn, we could not resist a feeling of holiday hopefulness. Edelgard's spirits rose with every mile, and I, having readily forgiven her on her asking me to and acknowledging she had been selfish, was quite like a boy; and when we got out of the train at Wrotham beneath a blue sky and a hot sun with the hail-clouds retreating over the hills and found we would have to pack ourselves and our many packages into a fly so small that, as I jocularly remarked in English, it was not a fly at all but an insect, Edelgard was so much entertained that for several minutes she was perfectly convulsed with laughter.

By means of the address neatly written in Latin characters on an envelope, we had no difficulty in getting the driver to start off as though he knew where he was going, but after we had been on the way for about half an hour he grew restless, and began to twist round on his box and ask me unintelligible questions. I suppose he talked and understood only *patois*, for I could not in the least make out what he meant, and when I requested him to be more clear I could see by his foolish face that he was constitutionally unable to be it. A second exhibition of the addressed envelope, however, soothed him for a time, and we continued to advance up and down chalky roads, over the hedges on each side of which leapt the wind and tried to blow our hats off. The sun was in our eyes, the dust was in our eyes, and the wind was in our faces. Wrotham, when we looked behind, had disappeared. In front was a chalky desolation. We could see nothing approaching a village, yet Panthers, the village we were bound for, was only three miles from the station, and not, observe, three full-blooded German miles, but the dwindled and anæmic English kind that are typical, as so much else is, of the soul and temper of the nation. Therefore we began to be uneasy, and to wonder whether the man were trustworthy. It occurred to me that the chalk pits we constantly met would not be bad places to take us into and rob us, and I certainly could not speak English quickly enough to meet a situation demanding rapid dialogue, nor are there any directions in my German-English Conversational Guide as to what you are to say when you are being murdered.

Still jocose, but as my hearers will notice, jocose with a tinge of grimness, I imparted these two linguistic facts to Edelgard, who shuddered and suggested renewed applications of the addressed envelope to the driver. "Also it is past dinner time," she added anxiously. "I know because *mein Magen knurrt.*"

By means of repeated calls and my umbrella I drew the driver's attention to us and informed him that I would stand no further nonsense. I told him this with great distinctness and the deliberation forced upon me by want of practice. He pulled up to hear me out, and then, merely grinning, drove on. "The youngest Storchwerder *droschke* driver," I cried indignantly to Edelgard, "would die of shame on his box if he did not know every village, nay, every house within three miles of it with the same exactitude with which he knows the inside of his own pocket."

Then I called up to the man once more, and recollecting that nothing clears our Hermann's brain at home quicker than to address him as *Esel* I said, "Ask, ass."

He looked down over his shoulder at me with an expression of great surprise.

"What?" said he.

"What?" said I, confounded by this obtuseness. "What? The way, of course."

He pulled up once more and turned right round on his box.

"Look here———" he said, and paused.

"Look where?" said I, very naturally supposing he had something to show me.

"Who are you talkin' to?" said he.

The question on the face of it was so foolish that a qualm gripped my heart lest we had to do with a madman. Edelgard felt the same, for she drew closer to me.

Luckily at that moment I saw a passer-by some way down the road, and springing out of the fly hastened to meet him in spite of Edelgard's demand that I should not leave her alone. On reaching him I took off my hat and courteously asked him to direct us to Panthers, at the same time expressing my belief that the flyman was not normal. He listened with the earnest and strained attention English people gave to my utterances, an attention caused, I believe, by the slightly unpractised pronunciation combined with the number and variety of words at my command, and then going up (quite fearlessly) to the flyman he pointed in the direction entirely opposed to the one we were following and bade him go there.

"I won't take him nowhere," said the flyman with strange passion; "he calls me a ass."

"It is not your fault," said I (very handsomely, I thought). "You are what you were made. You cannot help yourself."

"I won't take him nowhere," repeated the flyman, with, if anything, increased passion.

The passer-by looked from one to another with a faint smile.

"The expression," said he to the flyman, "is, you see, merely a term of recognition in the gentleman's country. You can't reasonably object to that, you know. Drive on like a sensible man, and get your fare."

And lifting his hat to Edelgard he continued his passing by.

Well, we did finally arrive at the appointed place—indeed, my hearers next winter will know all the time that we must have, or why should I be reading this aloud?—after being forced by the flyman to walk the last twenty minutes up a hill which, he declared, his horse would not otherwise be able to ascend. The sun shone its hottest while we slowly surmounted this last obstacle—a hard one to encounter when it is long past dinner-time. I am aware that by English clocks it was not past it, but what was that to me? My watch showed that in Storchwerder, the place our inner natures were used to, it was half-past two, a good hour beyond the time at which they are accustomed daily to be replenished, and no arbitrary theory, anyhow no perilously near approach to one, will convince a man against the evidence of his senses that he is not hungry because a foreign clock says it is not dinner-time when it is.

Panthers, we found on reaching the top of the hill and pausing to regain our composure, is but a house here and a house there scattered over a

The sun shone its hottest while we slowly surmounted this last obstacle

bleak, ungenial landscape. It seemed an odd, high up district to use as a terminus for caravans, and I looked down the steep, narrow lane we had just ascended and wondered how a caravan would get up it. Afterward I found that they never do get up it, but arrive home from the exactly opposite direction along a fair road which was the one any but an imbecile driver would have brought us. We reached our destination by, so to speak, its back door; and we were still standing on the top of the hill doing what is known as getting one's wind, for I am not what would be called an ill-covered man but rather, as I jestingly tell Edelgard, a walking compliment to her good cooking, and she herself was always of a substantial build, not exaggeratedly but agreeably so—we were standing, I say, struggling for breath when some one came out quickly from a neighbouring gate and stopped with a smile of greeting upon seeing us.

It was the gaunt sister.

We were greatly pleased. Here we were, then, safely arrived, and joined to at least a portion of our party. Enthusiastically we grasped both her hands and shook them. She laughed as she returned our greetings, and I was so much pleased to find some one I knew that though Edelgard commented afterward somewhat severely on her dress because it was so short that it nowhere touched the ground, I noticed nothing except that it seemed to be extremely neat, and as for not touching the ground

Edelgard's skirt was followed wherever she went by a cloud of chalky dust which was most unpleasant.

Now why were we so glad to see this lady again? Why, indeed, are people ever glad to see each other again? I mean people who when they last saw each other did not like each other. Given a sufficient lapse of time, and I have observed that even those who parted in an atmosphere thick with sulphur of implied cursings will smile and genially inquire how the other does. I have observed this, I say, but I cannot explain it. There had, it is true, never been any sulphur about our limited intercourse with the lady on the few occasions on which proper feeling prevailed enough to induce her to visit her flesh and blood in Prussia—our attitude toward her had simply been one of well-bred chill, of chill because no thinking German can, to start with, be anything but prejudiced against a person who commits the unpatriotism—not to call it by a harsher name—of selling her inestimable German birthright for the mess of an English marriage. Also she was personally not what Storchwerder could like, for she was entirely wanting in the graces and undulations of form which are the least one has a right to expect of a being professing to be a woman. Also she had a way of talking which disconcerted Storchwerder, and nobody likes being disconcerted. Our reasons for joining issue with her in the matter of caravans were first, that we could not help it, only having discovered she was coming when it was too late; and secondly, that it was a cheap and convenient way of seeing a new country. She with her intimate knowledge of English was to be, we privately told each other, our unpaid courier—I remember Edelgard's amusement when the consolatory cleverness of this way of looking at it first struck her.

But I am still at a loss to explain how it was that when she unexpectedly appeared at the top of the hill at Panthers we both rushed at her with an effusiveness that could hardly have been exceeded if it had been Edelgard's grandmother Podhaben who had suddenly stood before us, an old lady of ninety-two of whom we are both extremely fond, and who, as is well known, is going to leave my wife her money when she (which I trust sincerely she will not do for a long time yet) dies. I cannot explain it, I say, but there it is. Rush we did, and effusive we were, and it was reserved for a quieter moment to remember with some natural discomposure that we had showed far more enthusiasm than she had. Not that she was not pleasant, but there is a gap between pleasantness and enthusiasm, and to be the one of two persons who is most pleased is to put yourself in the position of the inferior, of the suppliant, of him who hopes, or is eager to ingratiate himself. Will it be believed that when later on I said something to this effect about some other matter in general conversation, the gaunt sister immediately cried, "Oh, but that's not generous."

"What is not generous?" I asked surprised, for it was the first day of the tour and I was not then as much used as I subsequently became to her instant criticism of all I said.

"That way of thinking," said she.

Edelgard immediately bristled—(alas, what would make her bristle now?)

"Otto is the most generous of men," she said. "Every year on Sylvester evening he allows me to invite six orphans to look at the remains of our Christmas tree and be given, before they go away, doughnuts and grog."

"What! Grog for orphans?" cried the gaunt sister, neither silenced nor impressed; and there ensued a warm discussion on, as she put it, (*a*) the effect of grog on orphans, (*b*) the effect of grog on doughnuts, (*c*) the effect of grog on combined orphans and doughnuts.

But I not only anticipate, I digress.

Inside the gate through which this lady had emerged stood the caravans and her gentle sister. I was so much pleased at seeing Frau von Eckthum again that at first I did not notice our future homes. She was looking remarkably well and was in good spirits, and, though dressed in the same way as her sister, by adding to the attire all those graces so peculiarly her own the effect she produced was totally different. At least, I thought so. Edelgard said she saw nothing to choose between them.

After the first greetings she half turned to the row of caravans, and with a little motion of the hand and a pretty smile of proprietary pride said, "There they are."

There, indeed, they were.

There were three; all alike, sober brown vehicles, easily distinguishable, as I was pleased to notice, from common gipsy carts. Clean curtains fluttered at the windows, the metal portions were bright, and the names painted prettily on them were the Elsa, the Ilsa, and the Ailsa. It was an impressive moment, the moment of our first setting eyes upon them. Under those frail roofs were we for the next four weeks to be happy, as Edelgard said, and healthy and wise—"Or," I amended shrewdly on hearing her say this, "*vice versa.*"

Frau von Eckthum, however, preferred Edelgard's prophecy, and gave her an appreciative look—my hearers will remember, I am sure, how agreeably her dark eyelashes contrast with the fairness of her hair. The gaunt sister laughed, and suggested that we should paint out the names already on the caravans and substitute in large letters Happy, Healthy, and Wise, but not considering this particularly amusing I did not take any trouble to smile.

Three large horses that were to draw them and us stood peacefully side by side in a shed being fed with oats by a weather-beaten person the gaunt sister introduced as old James. This old person, a most untidy, dusty-looking creature, touched his cap, which is the inadequate English way of showing respect to superiors—as inadequate at its end of the scale as the British army is at the other—and shuffled off to fetch in our luggage, and the gaunt sister suggesting that we should climb up and see the interior of our new home with some difficulty we did so, there being a small ladder to help us which, as a fact, did not help us either then or later, no means being discovered from beginning to end of the tour by which it could be fixed firmly at a convenient angle.

I think I could have climbed up better if Frau von Eckthum had not been looking on; besides, at that moment I was less desirous of inspecting the caravans than I was of learning when, where, and how we were going to have our delayed dinner. Edelgard, however, behaved like a girl of sixteen once she had succeeded in reaching the inside of the Elsa, and most inconsiderately kept me lingering there too while she examined every corner and cried with tiresome iteration that it was *wundervoll, herrlich,* and *putzig.*

"I knew you'd like it," said Frau von Eckthum from below, amused apparently by this kittenish conduct.

"Like it?" called back Edelgard. "But it is delicious—so clean, so neat, so miniature."

"May I ask where we dine?" I inquired, endeavouring to free the skirts of my new mackintosh from the door, which had swung to (the caravan not standing perfectly level) and jammed them tightly. I did not need to raise my voice, for in a caravan even with its door and windows shut people outside can hear what you say just as distinctly as people inside, unless you take the extreme measure of putting something thick over your head and whispering. (Be it understood I am alluding to a caravan at rest: when in motion you may shout your secrets, for the noise of crockery leaping and breaking in what we learned—with difficulty—to allude to as the pantry will effectually drown them.)

The two ladies took no heed of my question, but coming up after us—they never could have got in had they been less spare—filled the van to overflowing while they explained the various arrangements by which our miseries on the road were to be mitigated. It was chiefly the gaunt sister who talked, she being very nimble of tongue, but I must say that on this occasion Frau von Eckthum did not confine herself to the attitude I so much admired in her, the ideal feminine one of smiling and keeping quiet. I, meanwhile, tried to make myself as small as possible, which is what persons in caravans try to do all the time. I sat on a shiny yellow wooden box that ran down one side of our "room" with holes in its lid and a flap at the end by means of which it could, if needed, be lengthened and turned into a bed for a third sufferer. (On reading this aloud I shall probably substitute traveller for sufferer, and some milder word such as discomfort for the word miseries in the first sentence of the paragraph.) Inside the box was a mattress, also extra sheets, towels, etc., so that, the gaunt sister said there was nothing to prevent our having house-parties for week-ends. As I do not like such remarks even in jest I took care to show by my expression that I did not, but Edelgard, to my surprise, who used always to be the first to scent the vicinity of thin ice, laughed heartily as she continued her frantically pleased examination of the van's contents.

It is not to be expected of any man that he shall sit in a cramped position on a yellow box at an hour long past his dinner time and take an interest in puerilities. To Edelgard it seemed to be a kind of a doll's house, and she, entirely forgetting the fact of which I so often reminded her that she will be thirty next birthday, behaved in much the same way as a child who has just been presented with this expensive form of toy by some foolish and spendthrift relation. Frau von Eckthum, too, appeared to me to be less intelligent than I was accustomed to suppose her. She smiled at

Edelgard's delight as though it pleased her, chatting in a way I hardly recognized as she drew my wife's attention to the objects she had not had time to notice. Edelgard's animation amazed me. She questioned and investigated and admired without once noticing that as I sat on the lid of the wooden box I was obviously filled with sober thoughts. Why, she was so much infatuated that she actually demanded at intervals that I too should join in this exhibition of childishness; and it was not until I said very pointedly that I, at least, was not a little girl, that she was recalled to a proper sense of her behaviour.

"Poor Otto is hungry," she said, pausing suddenly in her wild career round the caravan and glancing at my face.

"Is he? Then he must be fed," said the gaunt sister, as carelessly and with as little real interest as if there were no particular hurry. "Look—aren't these too sweet?—each on its own little hook—six of them, and their saucers in a row underneath."

And so it would have gone on indefinitely if an extremely pretty, nice, kind little lady had not put her head in at the door and asked with a smile that fell like oil on the troubled water of my brain whether we were not dying for something to eat.

Never did the British absence of ceremony and introductions and preliminary phrases seem to me excellent before. I sprang up, and immediately knocked my elbow so hard against a brass bracket holding a candle and hanging on a hook in the wall that I was unable altogether to suppress an exclamation of pain. Remembering, however, what is due to society I very skilfully converted it into a rather precipitate and agonized answer to the little lady's question, and she, with a charming hospitality, pressing me to come into her adjoining garden and have some food, I accepted with alacrity, only regretting that I was unable, from the circumstance of her going first, to help her down the ladder. (As a matter of fact she had in the end to help me, because the door slammed behind me and again imprisoned the skirts of my mackintosh.)

Edelgard, absorbed in delighted contemplation of a corner beneath the so-called pantry full of brooms and dusters also hanging in rows on hooks, only shook her head when I inquired if she would not come too; so leaving her to her ecstasies I went off with my new protector, who asked me why I wore a mackintosh when there was not a cloud in the sky. I avoided giving a direct answer by retorting playfully (though wholly politely), "Why not?"—and indeed my reasons, connected with creases and other ruin attendant on confinement in a hold-all, were of too domestic and private a nature to be explained to a stranger so charming. But my counter-question luckily amused her, and she laughed as she opened a small gate in the wall and led me into her garden.

Here I was entertained with the greatest hospitality by herself and her husband. The fleet of caravans which yearly pervades that part of England is stationed when not in action on their premises. Hence departs the joyful caravaner, accompanied by kind wishes; hither he returns sobered, and is received with balm and bandages—at least, I am sure he would find them and every other kind form of solace in the little garden on the hill. I spent a very pleasant and reviving half-hour in a sheltered corner of it, enjoying my *al fresco* meal and acquiring much information. To my question as to whether my entertainers were to be of our party they replied, to my disappointment, that they were not. Their functions were restricted to this seeing that we started happy, and being prompt and helpful when we came back. From them I learned that our party was to consist, besides ourselves and Frau von Eckthum and that sister whom I have hitherto distinguished by the adjective gaunt, putting off the necessity as long as possible of alluding to her by name, she having, as my hearers perhaps remember, married a person with the unpronounceable one if you see it written and the unspellable one if you hear it said of Menzies-Legh—the party was to consist, I say, besides these four, of Menzies-Legh's niece and one of her friends; of Menzies-Legh himself; and of two young men about whom no precise information was obtainable.

"But how? But where?" said I, remembering the limited accommodations of the three caravans.

My host reassured me by explaining that the two young men would inhabit a tent by night which, by day, would be carried in one of the caravans.

"In which one?" I asked anxiously.

"You must settle that among yourselves," said he smiling.

"That's what one does all day long caravaning," said my hostess, handing me a cup of coffee.

"What does one do?" I asked, eager for information.

"Settle things among oneselves," said she. "Only generally one doesn't."

I put it down to my want of practice in the more idiomatic involutions of the language that I did not quite follow her meaning; but as one of my principles is never to let people know that I have not understood them I merely bowed slightly and, taking out my note-book, remarked that if that were so I would permit myself to make a list of our party in order to keep its various members more distinct in my mind.

The following is the way in which we were to be divided:

1. A caravan (the Elsa), containing the Baron and Baroness von Ottringel, of Storchwerder in Prussia.

2. Another caravan (the Ailsa), containing Mr. and Mrs. Menzies-Legh, of various addresses, they being ridiculously and superfluously rich.

3. Another caravan (the Ilsa), containing Frau von Eckthum, the Menzies-Legh niece, and her (as I gathered, school) friend. In this caravan the yellow box was to be used.

4. One tent, containing two young men, name and status unknown.

The ill-dressed person, old James, was coming too, but would sleep each night with the horses, they being under his special care; and all of the party (except ourselves and Frau von Eckthum and her sister who had already, as I need not say, done so) were yet to assemble. They were expected every moment, and had been expected all day. If they did not come soon our first day's march, opined my host, would not see us camping further away than the end of the road, for it was already past four o'clock. This reminded me that my luggage ought to be unpacked and stowed away, and I accordingly begged to be excused that I might go and superintend the operation, for I have long ago observed that when the controlling eye of the chief is somewhere else things are very apt to go irremediably wrong.

"Against stupidity," says some great German—it must have been Goethe, and if it was not, then no doubt it was Schiller, they having, I imagine, between them said everything there is to be said—"against stupidity the very gods struggle in vain." And I beg that this may not be taken as a reflection on my dear wife, but rather as an inference of general applicability. In any case the recollection of it sent me off with a swinging stride to the caravans.

CHAPTER IV

DARKNESS had, if not actually gathered, certainly approached within measurable distance, substantially aided by lowering storm-clouds, by the time we were ready to start. Not that we were, as a fact, ever ready to start, because the two young girls of the party, with truly British inconsideration for others, had chosen to do that which Menzies-Legh in fantastic idiom described as not turning up. I heard him say it several times before I was able, by carefully comparing it with the context, to discover his meaning. The moment I discovered it I of course saw its truth: turned up they certainly had not, and though too well-bred to say it aloud I privately applauded him every time he remarked, with an accumulating emphasis, "Bother those girls."

For the first two hours nobody had time to bother them, and to get some notion of the busy scene the yard presented my hearers must imagine a bivouac during our manoeuvres in which the soldiers shall all be recruits just joined and where there shall be no superior to direct them. I know to imagine this requires imagination, but only he who does it will be able to form an approximately correct notion of what the yard looked like and sounded like while the whole party (except the two girls who were not there) did their unpacking.

It will be obvious on a moment's reflection that portmanteaus, etc., had to be opened on the bare earth in the midst, so to speak, of untamed nature, with threatening clouds driving over them, and rude winds seizing what they could of their contents and wantoning with them about the yard. It will be equally obvious that these contents had to be handed up one by one by the person below to the person in the caravan who was putting them away and the person below having less to do would be quicker in his movements, while the person above having more to do would be—I suppose naturally but I think with a little self-control it ought not to be so—quicker in her temper; and so she was, and quite unjustifiably, because though she might have the double work of sorting and putting away I, on the other hand, had to stoop so continuously that I was very shortly in a condition of actual physical distress. The young men, who might have helped and at first did help Frau von Eckthum (though I consider they were on more than delicate ground while they did it) were prevented being of use because one had brought a bull terrier, a most dangerous looking beast, and the other—probably out of compliment to us—a white Pomeranian; and the bull terrier, without the least warning or preliminary growl such as our decent German dogs emit before proceeding to action, suddenly fixed his teeth into the Pomeranian and left them there. The howls of the Pomeranian may be imagined. The bull terrier, on the other hand, said nothing at all. At once the hubbub in the yard was increased tenfold. No efforts of its master could make the bull terrier let go. Menzies-Legh called for pepper, and the women-folk ransacked the larders in the rear of the vans, but though there were cruets there was no pepper. At length the little lady of the garden, whose special gift it seemed to appear at the right moment, judging no doubt that the sounds in the yard could not altogether be explained by caravaners unpacking, came out with a pot full, and throwing it into the bull terrier's face he was obliged to let go in order to sneeze.

During the rest of the afternoon the young men could help no one because they were engaged in the care of their dogs, the owner of the Pomeranian attending to its wounds and the owner of the bull terrier preventing a repetition of its conduct. And Menzies-Legh came up to me and said in his singularly trailing melancholy voice, did I not think they were jolly dogs and going to be a great comfort to us.

"Oh, quite," said I, unable exactly to understand what he meant.

Still less was I able to understand the attitude of the dogs' masters toward each other. Not thus would our fiery German youth have behaved. Undoubtedly in a similar situation they would have come to blows, or in any case to the class of words that can only be honourably wiped out in the blood of a duel. But these lymphatic Englishmen, both of them straggly, pale persons in clothes so shabby and so much too big that I was at a loss to conceive how they could appear in them before ladies, hung on each to his dog in perfect silence, and when it was over and the aggressor's owner, said he was sorry, the Pomeranian's owner, instead of confronting him with the fury of a man who has been wronged and owes it to his virility not to endure it, actually tried to pretend that somehow, by some means, it was all his dog's fault or his own in allowing him to be near the other, and therefore it was he who, in their jargon, was "frightfully sorry." Such is the softness of this much too rich and far too comfortable nation. Merely to see it made me blush to be a man; but I became calm again on recollecting that the variety of man I happened to be was, under God, a German. And I discovered later that neither of them ever touch an honest mug of beer, but drink instead—will it be believed?—water.

Now it must not be supposed that at this point of my holiday I had already ceased to enjoy it. On the contrary, I was enjoying myself in my quiet way very much. Not only does the study of character greatly interest me, but I am blest with a sense of humour united to that toughness of disposition which stops a man from saying, however much he may want to, die. Therefore I bore the unpacking and the arranging and the advice I got from everybody and the questions I was asked by everybody and the calls here and the calls there and the wind that did not cease a moment and the rain that pelted down at intervals, without a murmur. I had paid for my holiday, and I meant to enjoy it. But it did seem to me a strange way of taking pleasure for wealthy people like the Menzies-Leghs, who could have gone to the best hotel in the gayest resort, and who instead were bent into their portmanteaus as double as I was, doing work that their footmen would have scorned; and when during an extra sharp squall we had hastily shut our portmanteaus and all scrambled into our respective—I was going to say kennels, but I will be just and say caravans, I expressed this surprise to Edelgard, she said Mrs. Menzies-Legh had told her while I was at luncheon that both she and her sister desired for a time to remove themselves as far as possible from what she called the ministrations of menials. They wished, said Edelgard, quoting Mrs. Menzies-Legh's words, to endeavour to fulfil the Scriptures and work with their hands the things which are good; and Edelgard, who was much amused by the reference to the Scriptures, agreed with me, who was also greatly diverted, that it is a game, this working with one's hands, that only seems desirable to those so much surfeited with all that is worth having that they cease to be able to distinguish its value, and that it would be interesting to watch how long the two pampered ladies enjoyed playing it. Edelgard of course had no fears for herself, for she is a most admirably trained *hausfrau*, and the keeping of our tiny wheeled house in order would be easy enough after the keeping in order of our flat at home and the constant supervision, amounting on washing days to goading, of Clothilde. But the two sisters had not had the advantage of a husband who kept them to their work from the beginning, and Mrs. Menzies-Legh was a ne'er-do-well, spoiled, and encouraged to do nothing whatever except, so far as I could see, practise how best to pretend she was clever.

By six we were ready to start. From six to seven we bothered the girls. At seven serious consultations commenced as to what had better be done. Start we must, for kind though our host and hostess were I do not think they wanted us to camp in their front yard; if they did they did not say so, and it became every moment more apparent that a stormy night was drawing nearer across the hills. Menzies-Legh, with growing uneasiness, asked his wife I suppose a dozen times what on earth, as he put it, had become of the girls; whether she thought he had better go and look for them; whether she thought they had had an accident; whether she thought they had lost the address or themselves; to all of which she answered that she thought nothing except that they were naughty girls who would be suitably scolded when they did come.

The little lady of the garden came on the scene at this juncture with her usual happy tact, and suggested that it being late and we being new at it and therefore no doubt going to take longer arranging our camp this first night than we afterward would, we should start along the road to a bit of common about half a mile further on and there, with no attempt at anything like a march, settle for the night. We would then, she pointed out, either meet the girls or, if they came another way, she would send them round to us.

Such sensible suggestions could only, as the English say, be jumped at. In a moment all was bustle. We had been sitting disconsolately each on his ladder arguing (not without touches of what threatened to become recrimination), and we now briskly put them away and prepared to be off. With some difficulty the horses, who did not wish to go, were put in, the dogs were chained behind separate vans, the ladders slung underneath (this was no easy job, but one of the straggly young men came to our assistance just as Edelgard was about to get under our caravan and find out how to do it, and showed such unexpected skill that I put him down as being probably in the bolt and screw trade), adieux and appropriate speeches were made to our kind entertainer, and off we went.

First marched old James, leading the Ilsa's horse, with Menzies-Legh beside him, and Mrs. Menzies-Legh, her head wrapped up very curiously in yards and yards of some transparent fluttering stuff of a most unpractically feminine nature and her hand grasping a walking stick of a most aggressively masculine one, marched behind, giving me who followed (to my surprise I found it was expected of me that far from sitting as I had intended to do inside our caravan I should trudge along leading our horse) much unneeded and unasked-for advice. Her absurd head arrangement, which I afterward learned was called a motor veil, prevented my seeing anything except egregiously long eyelashes and the tip of an inquiring and strange to say not over aristocratic nose—Edelgard's, true to its many ancestors, is purest hook. Taller and gaunter than ever in her straight up and down sort of costume, she stalked beside me her head on a level with mine (and I am by no means a short man), telling me what I ought to do and what I ought not to do in the matter of leading a horse; and when she had done that *ad nauseam, ad libitum,* and *ad infinitum* (I believe I have forgotten nothing at all of my classics) she turned to my peaceful wife sitting on the Elsa's platform and announced that if she stayed up there she would probably soon be sorry.

In another moment Edelgard was sorry, for unfortunately my horse had had either too many oats or not enough exercise, and the instant the first van had lumbered through the gate and out of sight round the corner to the left he made a sudden and terrifying attempt to follow it at a gallop.

Those who know caravans know that they must never gallop: not, that is, if the contents are to remain unbroken and the occupants unbruised. They also know that no gate is more than exactly wide enough to admit of their passing through it, and that unless the passing through is calculated and carried out to a nicety the caravan that emerges will not be the caravan that went in. Providence that first evening was on my side, for I never got through any subsequent gate with an equal neatness. My heart had barely time to leap into my mouth before we were through and out in the road, and Mrs. Menzies-Legh, catching hold of the bridle, was able to prevent the beast's doing what was clearly in his eye, turn round to the left after his mate with a sharpness that would have snapped the Elsa in two.

Edelgard, rather pale, scrambled down. The sight of our caravan heaving over inequalities or lurching as it was turned round was a sight I never learned to look at without a tightened feeling about the throat. Anxiously I asked Mrs. Menzies-Legh, when the horse, having reached the rear of the Ilsa, had settled down again, what would happen if I did not get through the next gate with an equal skill.

"Everything may happen," said she, "from the scraping off of the varnish to the scraping off of a wheel."

"But this is terrible," I cried. "What would we do with one wheel too few?"

"We couldn't do anything till there was a new one."

"And who would pay——"

I stopped. Aspects of the tour were revealed to me which had not till then been illuminated. "It depends," said she, answering my unfinished question, "whose wheel it was."

"And suppose my dear wife," I inquired after a pause during which many thoughts surged within me, "should have the misfortune to break, say, a cup?"

"A new cup would have to be provided."

"And would I—but suppose cups are broken by circumstances over which I have no control?"

She snatched quickly at the bridle. "Is that the horse?" she asked.

"Is what the horse?"

"The circumstances. If I hadn't caught him then he'd have had your caravan in the ditch."

"My dear lady," I cried, nettled, "he would have done nothing of the sort. I was paying attention. As an officer you must admit that my ignorance of horses cannot be really as extensive as you are pleased to pretend you think."

"Dear Baron, when does a woman ever admit?"

A shout from behind drowned the answer that would, I was sure, have silenced her, for I had not then discovered that no answer ever did. It was from one of the pale young men, who was making signs to us from the rear.

"Run back and see what he wants," commanded Mrs. Menzies-Legh, marching on at my horse's head with Edelgard, slightly out of breath, beside her.

I found that our larder had come undone and was shedding our ox-tongue, which we had hoped to keep private, on to the road in front of the eyes of Frau von Eckthum and the two young men. This was owing to Edelgard's carelessness, and I was extremely displeased with her. At the back of each van were two lockers, one containing an oil stove and saucepans and the other, provided with air-holes, was the larder in which our provisions were to be kept. Both had doors consisting of flaps that opened outward and downward and were fastened by a padlock. With gross carelessness Edelgard, after putting in the tongue, had merely shut the larder door without padlocking it, and when a sufficient number of jolts had occurred the flap fell open and the tongue fell out. It was being followed by some private biscuits we had brought.

Naturally I was upset. Every time Edelgard is neglectful or forgetful she recedes about a year in my esteem. It takes her a year of attentiveness and diligence to regain that point in my affection on which she previously stood. She knew this, and used to be careful to try to keep proper pace, if I may so express it, with my love, and at the date at which I have arrived in the narrative had not yet given up trying, so that when by shouting I had made Mrs. Menzies-Legh understand that the Elsa was to be stopped Edelgard hurried back to inquire what was wrong, and was properly distressed when she saw the result of her negligence. Well, repentance may be a good thing, but our ox-tongue was gone forever; before he could be stopped the Ailsa's horse, following close behind, had placed his huge hoof on it and it became pulp.

"How sad," said Frau von Eckthum gazing upon this ruin. "But so nice of you, dear Baroness, to think of it. It might just have saved us all from starvation."

"Well, it can't now," said one of the young men; and he took it on the point of his stick and cast it into the ditch.

Edelgard began silently to pick up the scattered biscuits. Immediately both the young men darted forward to do it for her with a sudden awakening to energy that seemed very odd in persons who slouched along with their hands in their pockets. It made me wonder whether perhaps they thought her younger than she was. As we resumed our march, I came to the conclusion that this must be so, for such activity of assistance would otherwise be unnatural, and I resolved to take the earliest opportunity of bringing the conversation round to birthdays and then carelessly mentioning that my wife's next one would be her thirtieth. In this department of all others I am not the man to allow buds to go unnipped.

We had not been travelling ten minutes before we came to a stony turning up to the right which old James, who was a native of those parts, said was the entrance to the common. It seemed strange to camp almost within a stone's throw of our starting-place, but the rain was at that moment pelting down on our defenceless heads, and people hurrying to their snug homes stopped in spite of it to look at us with a wondering pity, so that we all wished to get off the road as soon as possible and into the privacy of furze bushes. The lane was in no sense a hill: it was a gentle incline, almost immediately reaching flat ground; but it was soft and stony, and the Ilsa's horse, after dragging his caravan for a few yards up it, could get no farther, and when Menzies-Legh put the roller behind the back wheel to prevent the Ilsa's returning thither from whence it had just come the chain of the roller snapped, the roller, released, rolled away, and the Ilsa began to move backward on top of the Elsa, which in its turn began to move backward on top of the Ailsa, which in its turn began to move backward across the road in the direction of the ditch.

It was an unnerving spectacle; for it must be borne in mind that however small the caravans seemed when you were inside them when you were outside they looked like mighty monsters, towering above hedges, filling up all but wide roads, and striking awe into the hearts even of motorists, who got out of their way with the eager politeness otherwise rude persons display when confronted by yet greater powers of being disagreeable.

Menzies-Legh and the two young men, acting on some shouted directions from old James, rushed at the stones lying about and selecting the biggest placed them, I must say with commendable promptness, behind the Ilsa's wheels, and what promised to be an appalling catastrophe was averted. I, who was reassuring Edelgard, was not able to help. She had asked me with ill-concealed anxiety whether I thought the caravans would begin to go backward in the night when we were inside them, and I was doing my best to calm her, only of course I had to point out that it was extremely windy; and quite a dirty and undesirable workman trudging by at that moment with his bag of tools on his back and his face set homeward, she stared after him and said: "Otto, how nice to be going to a house."

"Come, come," said I rallying her—but undoubtedly the weather was depressing.

We had to trace up the lane to the common. This was the first time that ominous verb fell upon my ear; how often it was destined to do so will be readily imagined by those of my countrymen who have ever visited the English county of Sussex supposing, which I doubt, that such there are. Its meaning is that you are delayed for any length of time from an hour upward at the bottom of each hill while the united horses drag one caravan after another to the top. On this first occasion the tracing chains we had brought with us behaved in the same way the roller chain had and immediately snapped, and Menzies-Legh, moved to anger, inquired severely of old James how it was that everything we touched broke; but he, being innocent, was not very voluble, and Menzies-Legh soon left him alone. Happily we had another pair of chains with us. All this, however, meant great delays, and the rain had almost left off, and the sun was setting in a gloomy bank of leaden clouds across a comfortless distance and sending forth its last pale beams through thinning raindrops, by the time the first caravan safely reached the common.

If any of you should by any chance, however remote, visit Panthers, pray go to Grib's (or Grip's—in spite of repeated inquiries I at no time discovered which it was) Common, and picture to yourselves our first night in that bleak

It was an unnerving spectacle

refuge. For it was a refuge—the alternative being to march along blindly till the next morning, which was, of course, equivalent to not being an alternative at all—but how bleak a one! Gray shadows were descending on it, cold winds were whirling round it, the grass was, naturally, dripping, and scattered in and out among the furze bushes were the empty sardine and other tins of happier sojourners. These last objects were explained by the presence of a hop-field skirting one side of the common, a hop-field luckily not yet in that state which attracts hop-pickers, or the common would hardly have been a place to which gentlemen care to take their wives. On the opposite side to the hop-field the ground fell away, and the tips of two hop-kilns peered at us over the edge. In front of us, concealed by the furze and other bushes of a prickly, clinging nature, lay the road, along which people going home to houses, as Edelgard put it, were constantly hurrying. All round, except on the hop-field side, we could see much farther than we wanted to across a cheerless stretch of country. The three caravans were drawn up in a row facing the watery sunset, because the wind chiefly came from the east (though it also came from all round) and the backs of the vans offered more resistance to its fury than any other side of them, there being only one small wooden window in that portion of them which, being kept carefully shut by us during the whole tour, would have been infinitely better away.

I hope my hearers *see* the caravans: if not it seems to me I read in vain. Square—or almost square—brown boxes on wheels, the door in front, with a big aperture at the side of it shut at night by a wooden shutter and affording a pleasant prospect (when there was one) by day, a much too good-sized window on each side, the bald back with no relief of any sort unless the larders can be regarded as such, for the little shutter window I have mentioned became invisible when shut, and inside an impression (I never use a word other than deliberately), an impression, then, I say, of snugness, produced by the green carpet, the green arras lining to the walls, the green eider-down quilts on the beds, the green portière dividing the main room from the small portion in front which we used as a dressing room, the flowered curtains, the row of gaily bound books on a shelf, and the polish of the brass candle brackets that seemed to hit me every time I moved. What became of this impression in the case of one reasonable man, too steady to be blown hither and thither by passing gusts of enthusiasm, perhaps the narrative will disclose.

Meanwhile the confusion on the common was indescribable. I can even now on calling it to mind only lift up hands of amazement. To get the three horses out was in itself no easy task for persons unaccustomed to such work, but to get the three tables out and try to unfold them and make them stand straight on the uneven turf was much worse. All things in a caravan have hinges and flaps, the idea being that they shall take up little room; but if they take up little room they take up a great deal of time, and that first night when there was not much of it these patent arrangements which made each chair and table a separate problem added considerably to the prevailing chaos. Having at length set them out on wet grass, table-cloths had to be extracted from the depths of the yellow boxes in each caravan and spread upon them, and immediately they blew away on to the furze bushes. Recaptured and respread they immediately did it again. Mrs. Menzies-Legh, when I ventured to say that I would not go and fetch them next time they did it, told me to weigh them down with the knives and forks, but nobody knew where they were, and their discovery having defied our united intelligences for an immense amount of precious time was at last the result of the merest chance, for who could have dreamed they were concealed among the bedding? As for Edelgard, I completely lost control over her. She seemed to slip through my fingers like water. She was everywhere, and yet nowhere. I do not know what she did, but I know that she left me quite unaided, and I found myself performing the most menial tasks, utterly unfit for an officer, such as fetching cups and saucers and arranging spoons in rows. Nor, if I had not witnessed it, would I ever have believed that the preparation of eggs and coffee was so difficult. What could be more frugal than such a supper? Yet it took the united efforts for nearly two hours of seven highly civilized and intelligent beings to produce it. Edelgard said that that was why it did, but I at once told her that to reason that the crude and the few are more capable than the clever and the many was childish.

When, with immense labour and infinite conversation, this meagre fare was at last placed upon the tables it was so late that we had to light our lanterns in order to be able to see it; and my hearers who have never been outside the sheltered homes of Storchwerder and know nothing about what can happen to them when they do will have difficulty in picturing us gathered round the tables in that gusty place, vainly endeavouring to hold our wraps about us, our feet in wet grass and our heads in a stormy darkness. The fitful flicker of the lanterns played over rapidly cooling eggs and grave faces. It was indeed a bad beginning, enough to discourage the stoutest holiday-maker. This was not a holiday: this was privation combined with exposure. Frau von Eckthum was wholly silent. Even Mrs. Menzies-Legh, although she tried to laugh, produced nothing but hollow sounds. Edelgard only spoke once, and that was to say that the coffee was very bad and might she make it unaided another time, a remark and a question received with a gloomy assent. Menzies-Legh was by this time extremely anxious about the girls, and though his wife still said they were naughty and would be scolded it was with an ever-fainter conviction. The two young men sat with their shoulders hunched up to their ears in total silence. No one, however, was half so much deserving of sympathy as myself and Edelgard, who had been travelling since the previous morning and more than anybody needed good food and complete rest. But there were hardly enough scrambled eggs to go round, most of them having been broken in the jolting up the lane on to the common, and after the meal, instead of smoking a cigar in the comparative quiet and actual dryness of one's caravan, I found that everybody had to turn to and—will it be believed?—wash up.

"No servants, you know—so free, isn't it?" said Mrs. Menzies-Legh, pressing a cloth into one of my hands and a fork into the other, and indicating a saucepan of hot water with a meaning motion of her forefinger.

Well, I had to. My hearers must not judge me harshly. I am aware that it was conduct unbecoming in an officer, but the circumstances were unusual. Menzies-Legh and the young men were doing it too, and I was taken by surprise. Edelgard, when she saw me thus employed, first started in astonishment and then said she would do it for me.

"No, no, let him do it," quickly interposed Mrs. Menzies-Legh, almost as though she liked me to wash up in the same saucepan as herself.

But I will not dwell on the forks. We were still engaged in the amazingly difficult and distasteful work of cleaning them when the rain suddenly descended with renewed fury. This was too much. I slipped away from Mrs. Menzies-Legh's side into the darkness, whispered to Edelgard to follow, and having found my caravan bade her climb in after me and bolt the door. What became of the remaining forks I do not know—there are limits to that which a man will do in order to have a clean one. Stealthily we undressed in the dark so that our lighted windows might not betray us—"Let them each," I said to myself with grim humour, "suppose that we are engaged helping one of the others"—and then, Edelgard having ascended into the upper berth and I having crawled into the lower, we lay listening to the loud patter of the rain on the roof so near our faces (especially Edelgard's), and marvelled that it should make a noise that could drown not only every sound outside but also our voices when we, by shouting, endeavoured to speak.

CHAPTER V

UNDER the impression that I had not closed my eyes all night I was surprised to find when I opened them in the morning that I had. I must have slept, and with some soundness; for there stood Edelgard, holding back the curtain that concealed me when in bed from the gaze of any curious should the caravan door happen to burst open, already fully dressed and urging me to get up. It is true that I had been dreaming I was still between Flushing and Queenboro', so that in my sleep I was no doubt aware of the heavings of the caravan while she dressed; for a caravan gives, so to speak, to every movement of the body, and I can only hope that if any of you ever go in one the other person in the bed above you may be a motionless sleeper. Indeed, I discovered that after all it was not an advantage to occupy the lower bed. While the rain was striking the roof with the deafening noise of unlimited and large stones I heard nothing of Edelgard, though I felt every time she moved. When, however, it left off, the creakings and crunchings of her bed and bedding (removed only a few inches from my face) every time she turned round were so alarming that disagreeable visions crossed my mind of the bed, unable longer to sustain a weight greater perhaps than what it was meant to carry, descending *in toto* in one of these paroxysms upon the helpless form (my own) stretched beneath. Clearly if it did I should be very much hurt, and would quite likely suffocate before assistance could be procured. These visions, however, in spite of my strong impression of unclosed eyes, must ultimately and mercifully have been drowned in sleep, and my bed being very comfortable and I at the end of my forces after the previous day when I did sleep I did it soundly and I also apparently did it long; for the sun was coming through the open window accompanied by appetizing smells of hot coffee when Edelgard roused me by the information that breakfast was ready, and that as everybody seemed hungry if I did not come soon I might as well not come at all.

She had put my clothes out, but had brought me no hot water because she said the two sisters had told her it was too precious, what there was being wanted for washing up. I inquired with some displeasure whether I, then, were less important than forks, and to my surprise Edelgard replied that it depended on whether they were silver; which was, of course, perilously near repartee. She immediately on delivering this left the caravan, and as I could not go to the door to call her back—as she no doubt recollected—I was left to my cold water and to my surprise. For though I had often noticed a certain talent she has in this direction (my hearers will remember instances) it had not yet been brought to bear personally on me. Repartee is not amiss in the right place, but the right place is never one's husband. Indeed, on the whole I think it is a dangerous addition to a woman, and best left alone. For is not that which we admire in woman womanliness? And womanliness, as the very sound of the word suggests, means nothing that is not round, and soft, and pliable; the word as one turns it on one's tongue has a smoothly liquid sound as of sweet oil, or precious ointment, or balm, that very well expresses our ideal. Sharp tongues, sharp wits—what are these but drawbacks and blots on the picture?

Such (roughly) were my thoughts while I washed in very little and very cold water, and putting on my clothes was glad to see that Edelgard had at least brushed them. I had to pin the curtains carefully across the windows because breakfast was going on just outside, and hurried heads kept passing to and fro in search, no doubt, of important parts of the meal that had either been forgotten or were nowhere to be found.

I confess I thought they might have waited with breakfast till I came. It is possible that Frau von Eckthum was thinking so too; but as far as the others were concerned I was dealing, I remembered, with members of the most inconsiderate nation in Europe. And besides, I reflected, it was useless to look for the courtesy we in Germany delight to pay to rank and standing among people who had neither of these things themselves. For what was Menzies-Legh? A man with much money (which is vulgar) and no title at all. Neither in the army, nor in the navy, nor in the diplomatic service, not even the younger son of a titled family, which in England, as perhaps my hearers have heard with surprise, is a circumstance sometimes sufficient to tear the title a man would have had in any other country from him and send him forth a naked Mr. into the world—Menzies-Legh, I suppose, after the fashion of our friend the fabled fox in a similar situation, saw no dignity in, nor any reason why he should be polite to, noble foreign grapes. And his wife's original good German blood had become so thoroughly undermined by the action of British microbes that I could no longer regard her as a daughter of one of our oldest families; while as for the two young men, on asking Menzies-Legh the previous evening over that damp and dreary supper of insufficient eggs who they were, being forced to do so by his not having as a German gentleman would have done given me every information at the earliest opportunity of his own accord, with details as to income, connections, etc., so that I would know the exact shade of cordiality my behaviour toward them was to be tinged with—on asking Menzies-Legh, I repeat, he merely told me that the one with the spectacles and the hollow cheeks and the bull terrier was Browne, who was going into the Church, and the other with the Pomeranian and the round, hairless face was Jellaby.

Concerning Jellaby he said no more. Who and what he was except pure Jellaby I would have been left to find out by degrees as best I could if I had not pressed him further, and inquired whether Jellaby also were going into the Church, and if not what was he going into?

Menzies-Legh replied—not with the lively and detailed interest a German gentleman would have displayed talking about the personal affairs of a friend, but with an appearance of being bored that very extraordinarily came over him whenever I endeavoured to talk to him on topics of real interest, and disappeared whenever he was either doing dull things such as marching, or cleaning his caravan, or discussing tiresome trivialities with the others such as some foolish poem lately appeared, or the best kind of kitchen ranges to put into the cottages he was building for old women on his estates—that Jellaby was not going into anything, being in already; and that what he was in was the House of Commons, where he was not only a member of the Labour Party but also a Socialist.

I need not say that I was considerably upset. Here I was going to live, as the English say, cheek by jowl for a substantial period with a Socialist member of Parliament, and it was even then plain to me that the caravan mode of life encourages, if I may so express it, a degree of cheek by jowlishness unsurpassed, nay, unattained, by any other with which I am acquainted. To descend to allegory, and taking a Prussian officer of noble family as the cheek, how terrible to him of all persons on God's earth must be a radical jowl. Since I am an officer and a gentleman it goes without saying that I am also a Conservative. You cannot be one without the others, at least not comfortably, in Germany. Like the three Graces, these other three go also hand in hand. The King of Prussia is, I am certain, in his heart passionately Conservative. So also I have every reason to believe is God Almighty. And from the Conservative point of view (which is the only right one) all Liberals are bad—bad, unworthy, and unfit; persons with whom one would never dream of either dining or talking; persons dwelling in so low a mental and moral depth that to dwell in one still lower seems almost extravagantly impossible. Yet in that lower depth, moving about like those blind monsters science tells us inhabit the everlasting darkness of the bottom of the seas, beyond the reach of light, of air, and of every Christian decency, dwells the Socialist. And who can be a more impartial critic than myself? Excluded by my profession from any opinion or share in politics I am able to look on with the undisturbed impartiality of the disinterested, and I see these persons as a danger to my country, a danger to my King, and a danger (if I had any) to my posterity. In consequence I was very cold to Jellaby when he asked me to pass him something at supper—I think it was the salt. It is true he is prevented by his nationality from riddling our Reichstag with his poisonous theories (not a day would I have endured his company if he had been a German) but the broad principle remained, and as I dressed I reflected with much ruefulness that even as it was his presence was almost compromising, and I could not but blame Frau von Eckthum for not having informed me of its imminence beforehand.

And the other—the future pastor, Browne. A pastor is necessary and even very well at a christening, a marriage, or an interment; but for mingling purposes on common social ground—no. Sometimes at public dinners in Storchwerder there has been one in the background, but he very properly remained in it; and once or twice dining with our country neighbours their pastor and his wife were present, and the pastor said grace and his wife said nothing, and they felt they were not of our class, and if they had not felt it of themselves they would very quickly have been made to feel it by others. This is all as it should be: perfectly natural and proper; and it was equally natural and proper that on finding I was required to do what the English call hobnob with a future pastor I should object. I did object strongly. And decided, while I dressed, that my attitude toward both Jellaby and Browne should be of the chilliest coolness.

Now in this narrative nothing is to be hidden, for I desire it to be a real and sincere human document, and I am the last man, having made a mistake, to pass it over in silence. My friends shall see me as I am, with all my human weaknesses and, I hope, some at least of my human strengths. Not that there is anything to be ashamed of in the matter of him Menzies-Legh spoke baldly of as Browne—rather should Menzies-Legh have been ashamed of leading me through his uncommunicativeness into a natural error; for how could I be supposed to realize that the singular nation places the Church as a profession on practically the same level as the only three that to us have a level at all, namely, the Army, the Navy, and the Service diplomatic or ministerial of the State?

To Browne, therefore, when I finally climbed down from my caravan into the soaking grass that awaited me at the bottom and found him breakfasting alone, the others being scattered about in the condition of feverish yet sterile activity that is characteristic of caravan life, I behaved in a manner perfectly suitable applied to an ordinary pastor who should begin to talk to me with an air of equality—I was, that is, exceedingly stiff.

He pushed the coffee-pot toward me: I received it with a cold bow. He talked of the rain in the night and his fears that my wife had been disturbed by it: I replied with an evasive shrug. He spoke cheerily of the brightness of the morning, and the promise it held of a pleasant day: I responded with nothing more convivial than Perhaps or Indeed—at this moment I cannot recall which. He suggested that I should partake of a thick repulsive substance he was eating which he described as porridge and as the work of Jellaby, and which was, he said, extraordinarily good stuff to march on: I sternly repressed a very witty retort that occurred to me and declined by means of a monosyllable. In a word, I was stiff.

Judge then of my vexation and dismay when I discovered not ten minutes later by the merest accident while being taken by Mrs. Menzies-Legh to a farm in order that I might carry back the vegetables she proposed to buy at it, that the young gentleman not only has a title but is the son of one of the greatest of English families. He is a younger son of the Duke of Hereford, that wealthy and well-known nobleman whose sister was not considered (on the whole) unworthy to marry our Prince of Grossburg-Niederhausen, and far from being mere Browne in the way in which Jellaby was and remained mere Jellaby, the young gentleman I had been deliberately discouraging was Browne indeed, but with the transfiguring addition of Sigismund and Lord.

Mrs. Menzies-Legh, with the same careless indifference I had observed in her husband, spoke of him briefly as Sidge. He was, it appeared, a distant cousin of her husband's. I had to question her closely and perseveringly before I could extract these details from her, she being apparently far more interested in the question as to whether the woman at the farm would not only sell us vegetables but also a large iron vessel in which to stew them. Yet it is clearly of great importance first, that one should be in good company, and secondly, that one should be told one is in it, because if one is not told how in the world is one to know? And my hearers will, I am sure, sympathize with me in the disagreeable situation in which I found myself, for never was there, I trust and believe, a more polite man than myself, a man more aware of what he owes to his own birth and breeding and those of others, a man more careful to discharge punctiliously all the little (but so important) nameless acts of courtesy where and whenever they are due, and it greatly distressed me to think I had unwittingly rejected the advances of the nephew of an aunt whom the entire German nation agrees to address on her envelopes as Serene.

While I bore back the iron vessel called a stew-pot which Mrs. Menzies-Legh had unfortunately persuaded the farmer's wife to sell her, and also a basket (in my other hand) full of big, unruly vegetables such as cabbages, and smooth, green objects, unknown to me but resembling shortened and widened cucumbers, that would not keep still and continually rolled into the road, I wished that at least I had eaten the porridge. It could not have killed me, and it was churlish to refuse. The manner of my refusal had made the original churlishness still more churlish. I made up my mind to seek out Lord Sigismund without delay and endeavour by a tactful word to set matters right between us, for one of my principles is never to be ashamed of acknowledging when I have been in the wrong; and so much preoccupied was I deciding on the exact form the tactful word was to take that I had hardly time to object to the nature and size of my burdens. Besides, I was beginning to realize that burdens were going to be my fate. There was little hope of escaping them, since the other members of the party bore similar ones and seemed to think it natural. Mrs. Menzies-Legh at that moment was herself carrying a bundle of little sticks for lighting fires, tied up in a big red handkerchief the farmer's wife had sold her, and also a parcel of butter, and she walked along perfectly indifferent to the odd figure she would cut and the wrong impression she would give should we by any chance meet any of the gentlefolk of the district. And one should always remember, I consider, when one wishes to let one's self go, that the world is very small, and that it is at least possible that the last person one would choose as a witness may be watching one through an apparently deserted hedge with his eyeglasses up. Besides, there is no pleasure in behaving as though you were a servant, and old James certainly ought to have accompanied us and carried our purchases back. Of what use is a man servant, however untidy, who is nowhere to be seen when washing up begins or shopping takes place? Being forced to pause a moment and put the stew-pot down in order to rest my hand (which ached) I inquired somewhat pointedly of my companion what she supposed the inhabitants of Storchwerder would say if they could see us at that moment.

"They wouldn't say anything," she replied—but her smile is not equal to her sister's because she has only one dimple—"they'd faint."

"Exactly," said I meaningly; adding, after a pause sufficient to point my words, "and very properly."

"Dear Baron," said she, pretending to look all innocent surprise and curling up her eyelashes, "do you think it is wrong to carry stew-pots? You mustn't carry them, then. Nobody must ever do what they think wrong. That's what is called perjuring one's soul—a dreadfully wicked thing to do. Do you suppose I would have you perjure yours for the sake of a miserable stew-pot? Put it down. Don't touch the accursed thing. Leave it in the ditch. Hang it on the hedge. I'll send Sidge for it."

Send Sidge? At once I snatched it up again, remarking that what Lord Sigismund could fetch I hoped Baron von Ottringel could carry; to which she made no answer, but a faint little sound as we resumed our journey came from behind her motor veil, whether of approval and acquiescence or disapproval and contradiction I cannot say, for there was nothing, on looking at her as she

"Dear Baron," said she, *"do you think it is wrong to carry stew-pots?"*

walked beside me, to go on except the tip of a slightly inquiring nose and the tip of a slightly defiant chin and the downward curve of the row of ridiculously long eyelashes that were on the side next to me.

When we got back to the camp we found it in precisely the same condition in which we had left it—that is, in confusion. Every one seemed to be working very hard, and nothing seemed to be different from what it was a full hour before. Indeed, hours seem to have strangely little effect in caravaning: even hours and hours have little; and it is only when you get to hours and hours and hours that you see a change. In our preparations each morning for departure it always appeared to me that they would never have ended but for a sudden desperate unanimous determination to break them off and go.

The two young girls who had not appeared the previous night when I retired to rest had at last, as Menzies-Legh would say, turned up. They had done this, I gathered, early in the morning, having slept with their governess at an inn in Wrotham, she being a discreet person who preferred not to search in rain and darkness for that which when found might not be nice. She had arrived after breakfast, handed over her charges, and taken her departure; and the young girls as I at once saw were not young girls at all, but that nondescript creature with a thick plait down its back and a disconcerting way of staring at one that we in Germany describe as *Backfisch* and the English, I am told, allude to as flapper.

Lord Sigismund was cleaning boots, seated on the edge of a table in his shirt sleeves with these two nondescripts standing in a row watching him, and I was greatly touched by observing that the boot he was actually engaged upon at the moment of our approach was one of Edelgard's.

This was magnanimity. More than ever was I sorry about the porridge. I hastily put down the stew-pot and the basket and hurried across to him.

"Pray allow me," I said, snatching up another boot that stood on the table at his side and plunging a spare brush into the blacking.

"That one's done," said he, pipe in mouth.

"Ah, yes—I beg your pardon. Are these——?"

I took up another pair, with some diffidence, for the done ones and the undone ones had a singular resemblance to each other.

"No. But you'd better take off your coat, Baron—it's hot work."

So I did. And much relieved to hear by his tone that he bore me no ill will I joined him on the edge of the table; and if any one had told me a week before that a day was at hand when I should clean boots I would, without hesitation,

Thus, as it were, with blacking, did I cement my friendship with Lord Sigismund

have challenged him to fight, the extremity of the statement's incredibleness leaving me no choice but to believe it a deliberate insult.

Thus, as it were with blacking, did I cement my friendship with Lord Sigismund. I think he thought me a thoroughly good fellow who was only, like so many people, a little stiff at breakfast, as I sat there helping him, my hat pushed back off my forehead, one leg swinging, and while I brushed and blackened chatting cheerfully about the inferior position the clergy occupy to the German eye. I am sure he was interested, for he paused several times in his work and looked at me over his spectacles with much attention. As for the two nondescripts, they never took their exceedingly round and unblinking eyes off me for an instant.

CHAPTER VI

IT was twelve o'clock before we left Grib's (or Grip's) Common, lurching off it by another grassy lane down into the road in the direction of Mereworth, and leaving, as we afterward discovered, several portions of our equipment behind us.

"What a lovely, sparkling world!" said Mrs. Menzies-Legh, coming and walking beside me.

I was struggling with the tempers of my very obstinate horse, so could only gasp a brief assent.

The road was narrow, and wound along hard and smooth between hedges she seemed to find attractive, for every few yards she stopped to pull something green out of them and take it along with her. The heavy rain in the night had naturally left things wet, and there being a bright sun the drops on the blades of grass and on the tips of the leaves could not help sparkling, but there was nothing remarkable in that, and I would not have noticed it if she had not looked round with such apparent extreme delight and sniffed in the air as if she were in a first-class perfumery shop *Unter den Linden* where there really are things worth sniffing. Also she appeared to think there was something very wonderful about the sky, which was just the ordinary blue one has a right to expect in summer sprinkled over with the usual number of white fine-weather clouds, for she gazed up at that too, and evidently with the greatest pleasure.

"*Schwärmerisch*," said I to myself; and was internally slightly amused.

My hearers will agree with me that such raptures are well enough in a young girl in a white gown, with blue eyes and the washed-out virginal appearance one does not dislike at eighteen before Love the Artist has pounced on it and painted it pink, and they will also, I think, agree that the older and married women must take care to be at all times quiet. Ejaculations of a poetic or ecstatic nature should not, as a rule, pass their lips. They may ejaculate perhaps over a young baby (if it is their own) but that is the one exception; and there is a good reason for this one, the possession of a young baby implying as a general rule a corresponding youth in its mother. I do not think, however, that it is nice when a woman ejaculates over, say, her tenth young baby. The baby, of course, will still be sufficiently young for it is a fresh one, but it is not a fresh mother, and by that time she should have stiffened into stolidity, and apart from the hours devoted to instructing her servant, silence. Indeed, the perfect woman does not talk at all. Who wants to hear her? All that we ask of her is that she shall listen intelligently when we wish, for a change, to tell her about our own thoughts, and that she should be at hand when we want anything. Surely this is not much to ask. Matches, ash-trays, and one's wife should be, so to speak, on every table; and I maintain that the perfect wife copies the conduct of the matches and the ash-trays, and combines being useful with being dumb.

These are my views, and as I drove my caravan along the gravelly road I ruminated on them. The great brute of a horse, overfed and underworked, was constantly endeavouring to pass the Ailsa which was in front of us, and as that meant in that narrow lane taking the Elsa up the bank as a preliminary, I was as constantly endeavouring to thwart him. And the sun being hot and I (if I may so put it) a very meltable man, I soon grew tired of this constant tugging and looked round for Edelgard to come and take her turn.

She was nowhere to be seen.

"Have you dropped anything?" asked Frau von Eckthum, who was walking a little way behind.

"No," said I; adding, with much readiness, "but my wife has dropped me."

"Oh!" said she.

I kept the horse back till she caught me up, while her leaner sister, who did not slacken her pace, went on ahead. Then I explained my theory about wives and matches. She listened attentively, in just the way the really clever woman knows best how to impress us favourably does, busying herself as she listened in tying some flowers she had gathered into a bunch, and not doing anything so foolish as to interrupt.

Every now and then as I warmed and drove my different points home, she just looked at me with thoughtful interest. It was delightful. I forgot the annoying horse, the heat of the sun, the chill of the wind, the bad breakfast, and all the other inconveniences, and saw how charming a caravan tour can be. "Given," I thought, "the right people and fine weather, such a holiday is bound to be agreeable."

The day was undoubtedly fine, and as for the right people they were amply represented by the lady at my side. Never had I found so good a listener. She listened to everything. She took no mean advantage of one's breath-pauses to hurry in observations of her own as so many women do. And the way she looked at me when anything struck her particularly was sufficient to show how keenly appreciative she was. After all there is nothing so enjoyable as a conversation with a thoroughly competent listener. The first five miles flew. It seemed to me that we had hardly left Grip's Common before we were pulling up at a wayside inn and sinking on to the bench in front of it and calling for drink.

What the others all drank was milk, or a gray, frothy liquid they said was ginger-beer—childish, sweet stuff, with little enough beer about it, heaven knows, and quite unfit one would think for the stomach of a real man. Jellaby brought Frau von Eckthum a glass of it, and even provided the two nondescripts with refreshments, and they took his attentions quite as a matter of course, instead of adopting the graceful German method of ministering to the wants of the sterner and therefore more thirsty sex.

The road stretched straight and white as far as one could see on either hand. On it stood the string of caravans, with old James watering the horses in the sun. Under the shadow of the inn we sat and rested, the three Englishmen, to my surprise, in their shirt-sleeves, a condition in which no German gentleman would ever show himself to a lady.

"Why? Are there so many holes in them?" asked the younger and more pink and white of the nondescripts, on hearing me remark on this difference of custom to Mrs. Menzies-Legh; and she looked at me with an air of grave interest.

Of course I did not answer, but inwardly criticized the upbringing of the English child. It is characteristic of the nation that Mrs. Menzies-Legh did not so much as say Hush to her.

On the right, the direction in which we were going to travel, the road dipped down into a valley with distant hills beyond, and the company, between their sips of milk, talked much about the blueness of this distance. Also they talked much about the greenness of the Mereworth woods rustling opposite, and the way the sun shone; as though woods in summer were ever anything but green, and as though the sun, when it was there at all, could do anything but go on shining!

I was on the point of becoming impatient at such talk and suggesting that if they would only leave off drinking milk they would probably see things differently, when Frau von Eckthum came and sat down beside me on the bench, her ginger-beer in one hand and a biscuit, also made of ginger, in the other (the thought of what they must taste like together made me shiver) and said in her attractive voice:

"I hope you are going to enjoy your holiday. I feel responsible, you know." And she looked at me with her pretty smile.

I liked to think of the gentle lady as a kind of godmother, and made the proper reply, chivalrous and sugared, and was asking myself what it is that gives other people's wives a charm one's own never did, never could, and never will possess, when the door-curtain of the Elsa was pulled aside, and Edelgard, whose absence at our *siesta* I had not noticed, stepped out on to the platform.

Lord Sigismund and Jellaby immediately got up and unhooked the steps and held them for her to come down by. Menzies-Legh also went across and offered her a hand. I alone sat still, as well I might; for not only am I her husband, but it is absurd to put false notions of her importance into a woman's head who has not had such attentions paid her since she was eighteen and what we call *appetitlich*.

Besides, I was rooted to the bench by amazement at her extraordinary appearance. No wonder she was not to be seen when duty ought to have kept her at my side helping me with the horse. She had not walked one of those five hot miles. She had been sitting in the caravan, busily cutting her skirt short, altering her hair, and transforming herself into as close a copy as she could manage of Mrs. Menzies-Legh and her sister.

Small indeed was the resemblance now to the Christian gentlewoman one wishes one's wife to seem to be. Few were the traces of Prussia. I declare I would not have recognized her had I met her casually in the road; and to think she had dared do it without a word, without asking my permission, without even asking my opinion! Her nice new felt hat with its pheasant's wing had almost disappeared beneath a gauze veil arranged after the fashion adopted by the sisters. Heaven knows where she got it, or out of what other garment, now of course ruined, she had cut and contrived it; and what is the use of having a pheasant's wing if you hide it? Her hair, up to then so tight and inconspicuous, was loosened, her skirt showed almost all of both her boots. The whole figure was strangely like that of the two sisters, a little thickened, a little emphasized.

What galled me was the implied entire indifference to my authority. My mind's indignant eye saw the snap her fingers were executing in its face. Also, one's own wife is undoubtedly a thing apart. It is proper and delightful that the wives of others should be attractive, but one's own ought to be adorned solely with the ornament of a meek and quiet spirit combined with that other ornament, an enduring desire to keep the husband God has given her comfortable and therefore happy. Without these two a wife cannot be regarded as a fit object for her husband's esteem. I plainly saw that I would find it impossible to esteem mine in that skirt. I do not know what she had done to her feet, but they looked much smaller than I had been accustomed to suppose them as she came down the steps assisted by the three gentlemen. My full beer-glass, held neglected in my hand, dripped unheeded on to the road as I stared stupidly at this apparition. Rapidly I selected the first few of the phrases I would address to her the moment we found ourselves alone. There should be an immediate stop put to this loosening of the earth round the roots of the great and sheltering tree of a husband's authority.

"Poor silly sheep," I could not help murmuring, those animals flashing into my mind as a legitimate development of the sheltering-tree image.

Then I felt there was a quotation atmosphere about them, and was sure Horace or Virgil—elusive bugbears of my boyhood—must have said something that began like that and went on appropriately if only I could remember it. I regretted that having forgotten it I was unable to quote it, to myself as it were, but yet just loud enough for the lady beside me to hear. She, however, heard what I did say, and looked at me inquiringly.

"If I were to explain, dear lady," said I, instantly responding to the look, "you would not understand."

"Oh," said she.

"I was thinking in symbols."

"Oh," said she.

"It is one of my mental tricks," I said, my gaze however contracting sternly as it fell on Edelgard's approaching form.

"Oh," said she.

Certainly she is a quiet lady. But how stimulating. Her solitary oh's are more packed with expressiveness than other women's hour-long tirades.

She too was watching Edelgard coming toward us across the sun-beaten bit of road, her head slightly turned away from me but not so much that I could not see she was smiling at my wife. Of course she must have been amused at such a slavish imitation; but with her usual kindness she made room on the bench for her and, without alluding to the transformation, suggested refreshment.

Edelgard as she sat down shot a very curious glance at me round the corner of her head-wrappings. I was surprised to see little that could be called apology in her way of sitting down, and looked in vain for the red spot that used to appear on each cheek at home when she was aware that she had done wrong and that it was not going to be passed over. She was sheltered from immediate steps on my part by Frau von Eckthum who sat between us, and when Jellaby approached her with a glass of milk she actually took it without so much as breathing the honest word beer.

This was too much. I threw back my head and laughed as heartily as I have ever seen a man laugh. Edelgard and milk! Why, I do not believe she had drunk it pure like that since the day she parted from the last of her infancy's bottles. Edelgard becoming squeamish; Edelgard posing—and what a pose; good heavens, what a pose! Edelgard, one of Prussia's daughters, one of Prussia's noblemen's daughters, accepting milk instead of beer, and accepting it at the hands of a Socialist in shirt sleeves. A vision of Storchwerder's face if it could see these things rose before me. Of course I laughed. Not, mind you, without some slight tinge of bitterness, for laughter may be bitter and hearty at the same time, but on the whole I think I did credit to my unfailing sense of humour in spite of very great provocation, and I laughed till even the horses pricked up their ears and turned their heads and stared.

Nobody else smiled. On the contrary—it cannot be true that laughter is infectious—they watched me with a serious, amusingly serious, surprise. Edelgard did not watch. She knew better than that. Carefully she concealed her face in the milk, feeling no doubt it was the best place for it, and unable to leave off drinking the stuff because of the problem of how to meet my eyes once she did. Frau von Eckthum regarded me with much the same attentive interest she had

Edelgard posing—and what a pose; good heavens, what a pose!

shown when I was explaining some of my views to her on the march—I mean, of course, my views on wives, but language is full of pitfalls. The Menzies-Legh niece (they called her Jane) paused in the middle of a banana to stare. Her friend, who answered to the singular name (let us hope it was merely a *sobriquet*) of Jumps, forgot to continue greedily pressing biscuits into her mouth, and, forgetting also that her mouth was open to receive them, left it in that condition. Mrs. Menzies-Legh got up and snap-shotted me. Menzies-Legh leaned forward when I had had my laugh nearly out and said: "Come, Baron, let us share the joke?" But his melancholy voice belied his words, and looking round at him I thought he seemed little in the mood for sharing anything. I never saw such a solemn, dull face; it shrivelled up my merriment just to see it. So I merely shrugged one of my shoulders and said it was a German joke.

"Ah," said Menzies-Legh; and did not press me further. And Jellaby, wiping his forehead (on which lay perpetually a long, lank strand of hair which he was as perpetually brushing aside with his hand, apparently desirous of not having it there, but only apparently, for five seconds with any competent barber would have rid him of it forever)—Jellaby, I say, asking Menzies-Legh in his womanish tenor voice if the green shadows in the wood opposite did not remind him of some painter friend's work, they began talking pictures as though they were as important every bit as the great objects of life—wealth, and war, and a foot on the neck of the nations.

Well, it was impossible to help contrasting their sluggishness with a party of Germans under similar conditions. Edelgard would have been greeted with one immense roar of laughter on her appearing suddenly in her new guise. She would have been assailed with questions, pelted with mocking comments, and I might have expressed my own disapproval frankly and openly and no one would have thought it anything but natural. There, however, in that hypocritical country they one and all pretended not to have seen any change at all; and there was something so depressing about so many stiff and lantern jaws whichever way I turned my head that after my one Homeric burst I found myself unable to go on. A joke soon palls if nobody else can see it. In silence I drank my beer: and realized that my opinion of the nation is low.

It was chiefly Menzies-Legh and Jellaby who sent down the mercury, I reflected, as we resumed the march. One gets impressions, one knows not how or why, nor does one know when. I had not spoken much to either, yet there the impressions were. It was not likely that I could be mistaken, for I suppose that of all people in the world a Prussian officer is the least likely to be that. He is too shrewd, too quick, of too disciplined an intelligence. It is these qualities that keep him at the top of the European tree, combined, indeed, with his power of concentrating his entire being into one noble determination to stay on it. Again descending to allegory, I can see Menzies-Legh and Jellaby and all the other slow-spoken and slow-thoughted Englishmen flapping ineffectually among the lower and more comfortable branches of the tree of nations. Yes, they are more sheltered there; they have roomier nests; less wind and sun; less distance to fly in order to fetch the waiting grub from the moss beneath; but what about the Prussian eagle sitting at the top, his beak flashing in the light, his watchful eye never off them? Some day he will swoop down on them when they are, as usual, asleep, clear out their and similar well-lined nests, and have the place to himself—becoming, as the well-known picture has it (for I too can allude to pictures), in all his glory *Enfin seul*.

The road went down straight and long and white into the flat. High dusty hedges shut us in on either side. Across the end, which looked an interminable way off, lay the blue distance the milk drinkers admired. The three caravans creaked over the loose stones. Their brown varnish glistened blindingly in the sun. The horses plodded onward with hanging heads, subdued, no doubt, by the growing number of the hours. It was half-past three, and there were no signs of camp or dinner; no signs of our doing anything but walk along like that in the dust, our feet aching, our throats parching, our eyes burning, and our stomachs empty, forever.

CHAPTER VII

A MAN who is writing a book should have a free hand. When I began my narrative I hardly realized this, but I do now. No longer is Edelgard allowed to look over my shoulder. No longer are the sheets left lying open on my desk. I put Edelgard off with the promise that she shall hear it when it is done. I lock it up when I go out. And I write straight on without wasting time considering what this or that person may like or not.

At the end, indeed, there is to be a red pencil,—an active censor running through the pages making danger signals, and whenever on our beer evenings I come across its marks I shall pause, and probably cough, till my eye has found the point at which I may safely resume the reading. Our guests will tell me that I have a cold, and I shall not contradict them; for whatever one may say to one friend at a time in confidence about, for instance, one's wife, one is bound to protect her collectively.

I hope I am clear. Sometimes I fear I am not, but language, as I read in the paper lately, is but a clumsy vehicle for thought, and on this clumsy vehicle therefore, overloaded already with all I have to say, let us lay the whole blame, using it (to descend to quaintness) as a kind of tarpaulin or other waterproof cover, and tucking it in carefully at the corners. I mean the blame. Also, let it not be forgotten that this is the maiden flight of my Muse, and that even if it were not, a gentleman cannot be expected to write with the glibness of your Jew journalist or other professional quill-driver.

We did not get into camp that first day till nearly six (much too late, my friends, if you should ever find yourselves under the grievous necessity of getting into such a thing), and we had great difficulty in finding one at all. That, indeed, is a very black side of caravaning; camps are rarely there when they are wanted, and, conversely, frequently so when they are not. Not once, nor twice, but several times have I, with the midday sun streaming vertically on my head, been obliged to labour along past a most desirable field, with just the right aspect, the sheltering trees to the north, the streamlet for the dish-washing loitering about waiting, the yard full of chickens, and cream and eggs ready to be bought, merely because it came, the others said, too early in the march and we had not yet earned our dinner. Earned our dinner? Why, long before I left the last night's camp I had earned mine, if exhaustion from overwork is what they meant, and earned it well too. I pity a pedant; I pity a mind that is made up like a bed the first thing in the morning, and goes on grimly like that all day, refusing to be unmade till a certain fixed evening hour has been reached; and I assert that it is a sign of a large way of thinking, of the intellectual pliability characteristic of the real man of the world, to have no such hard and fast determinations and to be always ready to camp. Left to myself, if I were to see the right spot ten minutes, nay, five, after leaving the last one, I would instantly pounce on it. But no man can pounce instantly on anything who shall not first have rid himself of his prejudices.

On that second day of dusty endeavouring to get to Sussex, which was and remained in the much talked of blue distance, we passed no spot at all except one that was possible. That one, however, was very possible indeed in the eyes of persons who had endured sun and starvation since the morning—a shaded farmhouse, of an appearance that pleased the ladies owing to the great profusion of flowers clambering up and down it, an orchard laden with fruit suggestive of dessert, a stream whose clear waters promised an excellent foot bath, and fat chickens in great numbers, merely to look on whom caused little rolls of bacon and dabs of bread sauce and even fragments of salad to dance delightfully before one's eyes.

But the woman was cross. Worse, she was inhuman. She was a monster of indifference to the desires of her fellow-creatures, deaf to their offers of payment, stony in regard to their pains. Arguing with her, we gave up one by one our first more succulent visions, and retreating before the curtness of her refusals let first the camp beneath the plum trees go, then the dessert, then the chickens with their *etcaeteras*, then, still further backward, and fighting over each one, egg after egg of all those many eggs we were so sure she would sell us and we wanted so badly to buy.

Audaciously she swore she had no eggs, while there beneath our very eyes walked chickens brimful of the eggs of the morrow. Where were the eggs of the morning, and where the eggs of yesterday? To this question, put by me, she replied that it was no business of mine. Accurséd British female,—certainly not lady, doubtfully even woman, but emphatically *Weib*—of twisted appearance, and a gnarled and knotty age! May you in your turn be refused rest and nourishment when hard put to it and willing to pay, and after you have marched five hours in the sun controlling, from your feet, the wayward impulses of a big, rebellious horse.

She shut the door while yet we were protesting. In silence we trooped back down the brick path between rose bushes that were tended with a care she denied humans, to where the three caravans waited hopefully in the road for the call to come in and be at rest.

We continued our way subdued. This is a characteristic of those who caravan, that in the afternoons they are subdued. So many things have happened to them by then; and, apart from that, they have daily got by then into that physical condition doctors describe as run down—or, if I may alter it better to fit this special case, walked down. Subdued, therefore, we journeyed along flat uncountrified roads, reminding one, by the frequent recurrence of villas, of the outskirts of some big town rather than the seclusion it had been and still was our aim to court, and in this way we came at last to a broad and extremely sophisticated bridge crossing a river some one murmured was Medway.

Houses and shops lined its approach on the right. On the left was a wide and barren field with two donkeys finding difficulties in collecting from the scanty herbage a sufficiency of supper. In the gutter, opposite a public house, stood a piano-organ, emitting the sounds of shrill yet unconvincing joyfulness natural to those instruments, and mingled with these was a burr of machinery at work, and a smell of so searching a nature that it provoked Frau von Eckthum into a whole sentence—a plaintive and faintly spoken one, but a long one—describing her conviction that there must be a tannery somewhere near, and that it was very disagreeable. Her plaintiveness increased a hundredfold when Menzies-Legh announced that camp we must at all costs or night would be upon us.

We drew up in the middle of the road while Lord Sigismund made active inquiries of the inhabitants as to which of them would be willing to lend us a field.

"But surely not here?" murmured Frau von Eckthum, holding her little handkerchief to her nose.

It was here, however, and in the field, said Lord Sigismund returning, containing the donkeys. For the privilege of sharing with these animals their bare and shelterless field, exposed as it was to all the social amenities of the district, including the piano-organ, the shops opposite, the smell of leather in the making, and the company as long as the light lasted of innumerable troops of children, the owner would make us a charge of half a crown per caravan for the night, but this only on condition that we did not turn out, as he appeared to have had the greatest suspicions we would turn out, to be a circus.

With a flatness of which I would not have

"But surely not here," murmured Frau von Eckthum

thought her capable Frau von Eckthum refused to spend a night in the donkey field; and Mrs. Menzies-Legh, who was absorbed in snap-shotting the ever-swelling crowd of children and loafers who were surrounding us, suddenly stamped her foot and said she would not either.

"The horses can't go another yard," remonstrated Menzies-Legh.

"I won't sleep with the donkeys," said his wife, taking another snap.

Her sister said nothing, but held her handkerchief as before.

Then Jellaby, descrying a hedge with willows beyond it at the far-away end of the field, and no doubt conscious of a parliamentary practice in persuasion, said he would get permission to go in there for the night, and disappeared. Lord Sigismund expressed doubts as to his success, for the man, he said, was apparently own brother to the female at the farm, or at any rate of the closest spiritual affinity; but Jellaby did come back after a while, during which the piano-organ's waltzes had gone on accentuating the blank dreariness of the spot, and said it was all right.

Later on I discovered that what he called all right was paying exactly twice as much per caravan for the superior exclusiveness of the willow field as what was demanded for the donkey field. Well, he did not have to pay, being Menzies-Legh's guest, so no doubt he did think it all right; but I call it monstrous that I should be asked to pay that which would have secured me a perfectly dry bedroom with no grass in it in a first-rate Berlin hotel for the use for a few hours of a gnat-haunted, nettle-infested, low-lying, swampy meadow.

The monstrosity struck me more afterward when I looked back. That evening I was too tired to be struck, and would, I truly believe, have paid five shillings just for being allowed to sink down into a sitting position, it mattered not where, and remain in it; but there was still much, I feared to do and to suffer before I could so sink down—for instance, there was the gate leading into the donkey field to be got through, the whole population watching, and the pleasant prospect before me of having to reimburse any damage done to a caravan that could only, under the luckiest circumstances, just fit in. Then there was Edelgard to be brought to reason, and suppose she refused to be brought? That is, quickly; for I had no fears as to her ultimate bringing.

Well, the gate came first, and as it would require my concentrated attention I put the other away from me till I should be more at leisure. Old

James, assisted by Menzies-Legh, got the Ailsa safely through, and away she heaved, while the onlookers cheered, over the mole heaps toward the willows on the horizon. Then Menzies-Legh, calling Jellaby, came to help me pull the Elsa through, Lord Sigismund waiting with the third horse, who had been his special charge throughout the day. It seemed all very well to help me, but any scratches to the varnish caused by the two gentlemen in their zeal would be put in my bill, not in theirs, and under my breath I called down a well-known Pomeranian curse of immense body and scope on all those fools who had helped in the making of the narrow British gates.

As I feared, there was too much of that zèle that somebody (I think he was French) advised somebody else (I expect he must have been English) not to have, and amid a hubbub of whoas—which is the island equivalent for our so much more lucid *brrr*—shouts from the onlookers, and a scream or two from Edelgard who could not listen unmoved to the crashings of our crockery, Menzies-Legh and Jellaby between them drew the brute so much to one side that it was only owing to my violent efforts that a terrible accident was averted. If they had had their way the whole thing would have charged into the right-hand gate post—with what a crashing and a parting from its wheels may be imagined—but thanks to me it was saved, although the left-hand gate post did scrape a considerable portion of varnish off the Elsa's left (so to speak) flank.

"I say," said the Socialist when it was all over, brushing his bit of hair aside, "you shouldn't have pulled that rein like that."

The barefaced audacity of putting the blame on to me left me speechless.

"No," said Menzies-Legh, "you shouldn't have pulled anything."

He too! Again I was left speechless—left, indeed, altogether, for they immediately dropped behind to help (save the mark) Lord Sigismund bring the Ilsa through.

So the Elsa in her turn heaved away, guided anxiously by me over the mole heaps, every mole heap being greeted by our pantry as we passed over it with a thunderous clapping together of its contents, as though the very cups, being English, were clapping their hands, or rather handles, in an ecstasy of spiteful pleasure at getting broken and on to my bill.

Little do you who only know cups in their public capacity, filled with liquids and standing quietly in rows, realize what they can do once they are let loose in a caravan. Sometimes I have thought—but no doubt fancifully—that so-called inanimate objects are not as inanimate as one might think, but are possessed of a character like other people, only one of an unadulterated pettiness and perversity rarely found in the human. I believe most people who had been in my place that evening last August guiding the Elsa across all the irregularities that lay between us and the willow-field in the distance, and had listened to what the cups were doing, would have been sure of it. As for me, I can only say that every time I touch a cup or other piece of crockery it seems to upset it, and frequently has such an effect on it that it breaks; and it is useless for Edelgard to tell me to be careful, and to hint (as she does when she is out of spirits) that I am clumsy, because I am careful; and as for being clumsy, everybody knows that I have the straightest eye and am the best shot in our regiment. But it is not only cups. If, while I am dressing (or undressing) I throw any portion of my clothes or other article I may be using on to a table or a chair, however carefully I aim it invariably either falls at once, or after a brief hesitation slips off on to the floor from which place, in its very helplessness, it seems to jeer at me. And the more important it is I should not be delayed the more certainly is this conduct indulged in. Fanciful? Perhaps. But let me remind you of what the English poet Shakespeare says through the mouth of Hamlet into the ears of Horatio, and express the wish that you too could have listened to the really exultant clapping of the cups in our pantry as I crossed the mole heaps.

Edelgard, feeling guilty, remained behind, so was not there as she otherwise certainly would have been making anxious sums, according to her custom, in what these noises were going to cost us. A man who has been persuaded to take a holiday because it is cheap may be pardoned for being preoccupied when he finds it is likely to be dear. Among other things I thought some very sharp ones about the owner of the field, who permitted his ground, in defiance I am sure (though not being an agriculturist I cannot give chapter and verse for my belief) of all laws of health and wholesomeness, to be so much ravaged by moles. If he had done his duty my cups would not have been smashed. The heaps of soil thrown up by these animals were so frequent that during the entire crossing at least one of the Elsa's wheels was constantly on the top of a heap, and sometimes two of her wheels simultaneously on the top of two.

It is a pity people do not know what other people think of them. Unfortunately it is rude to tell them, but if only means could be devised—perhaps by some Marconi of the mind—for letting them know without telling them, how nice and modest they would all become. That farmer was probably eating his supper in his snug parlour in bestial complacency and ignorance at the very moment that I was labouring across his field pouring on him, if he had only known it, a series of as scalding criticisms as ever made a man, if he were aware of them, shrivel and turn over a new leaf.

I found Mrs. Menzies-Legh at the farther gate, holding it open. Old James had already got his horse out, and when he saw me approaching came and laid hold of the bridle of mine and led him through. He then drew him up parallel with the Ailsa, the doors of both caravans being toward the river, and proceeded with the skill and expedition natural in an old person who had done nothing else all his life to unharness my horse and turn him loose.

Mrs. Menzies-Legh lit a cigarette and handed me her case. She then dropped down on to the long and very damp-looking grass and motioned to me to sit beside her; so we sat together, I much too weary either to refuse or to converse, while the muddy river slid sullenly along within a yard of us between fringes of willows, and myriads of gnats gyrated in the slanting sunbeams.

"Tired?" said she, after a silence that no doubt surprised her by its length.

"Too tired," said I, very shortly.

"Not really?" said she, turning her head to look at me, and affecting much surprise about the eyebrows.

This goaded me. The woman was inhuman. For beneath the affected surprise of the eyebrows I saw well enough the laughter in the eyes, and it has always been held since the introduction of Christianity that to laugh at physical incapacitation is a thing beyond all others barbarous.

I told her so. I tossed away the barely begun cigarette she had given me, not choosing to go on smoking a cigarette of hers, and told her so with as much Prussian thoroughness as is consistent with being at the same time a perfect gentleman. No woman (except of course my wife) shall ever be able to say I have not behaved to her as a gentleman should; and my hearers will be more than ever convinced of the inexplicable toughness of Mrs. Menzies-Legh's nature, of the surprising impossibility of producing the least effect upon her, when I tell them that at the end of quite a long speech on my part, not, I believe ineloquent, and yet as plainspoken as the speech of a man can be within the framework which should always surround him, the carved and gilt and—it must be added—expensive framework of gentlemanliness, she merely looked at me again and said:

"Dear Baron, why is it that men, when they have walked a little farther than they want to, or have gone hungry a little longer than they like to, are always so dreadfully cross?"

The lumbering into the field of the Ilsa with the rest of the party made an immediate reply impossible.

"Hullo," said Jellaby, on seeing us apparently at rest in the grass. "Enjoying yourselves?"

I fancy this must be a socialistic formula, for short as the period of my acquaintance with him had been he had already used it to me three times. Perhaps it is the way in which his sect reminds those outside it of the existence of its barren and joyless notions of other people's obligations. A Socialist, as far as I can make out, is a person who may never sit down. If he does, the bleak object he calls the Community immediately becomes vocal, because it considers that by sitting down he is cheating it of what he would be producing by his labour if he did not. Once I (quite good naturedly) observed to Jellaby that in a socialistic world the chair-making industry would be the first to go to the wall (or the dogs—I cannot quite recollect which I said it would go to) for want of suitable sitters, and he angrily retorted—but this occurred later in the tour, and no doubt I shall refer to it in its proper place.

Mrs. Menzies-Legh got up at once on his asking if we were enjoying ourselves, as though her conscience reproached her, and went over to the larder of her caravan and busily began pulling out pots; and I too seeing that it was expected of me prepared to rise (for English society is conducted on such artificial lines that immediately a woman begins to do anything a man must at least pretend to do something too) but found that my short stay on the grass had stiffened my over-tired limbs to such an extent that I could not.

The two nondescripts, who were passing, lingered to look.

"Can I help you?" said the one they called Jumps, as I made a second ineffectual effort, advancing and holding out a knuckly hand. "Will you take my arm?" said the other one, Jane, crooking a bony elbow.

"Thank you, thank you, dear children," I said, with bland heartiness one assumes—for no known reason—toward the offspring of strangers; and obliged to avail myself of their assistance (for want of practice makes it at all times difficult for me to get up from a flat surface, and my stiffness on this occasion turned the difficult into the impossible), I somehow was pulled on to my feet.

"Thank you, thank you," I said again, adding jestingly, "I expect I am too old to sit on the ground." ^

"Yes," said Jane.

This was so unexpected that I could not repress a slight sensation of annoyance, which found its expression in sarcasm.

"I am extremely obliged to you young ladies," I said, sweeping off my Panama, "for extending your charitable support and assistance to such a poor old gentleman."

The two nondescripts, who were passing, lingered to look.

"Oh," said Jumps earnestly, too thick-skinned to feel sarcasm, "I'm used to it. I have to help Papa about. He's very old too."

"Yet surely," said I, tingeing my sarcasm with playfulness (but they were too thick-skinned even for playfulness), "surely not so old as I?"

"About the same," said Jumps, considering me gravely.

"And how old," said I, inquiring of Jane, for Jumps annoyed me too much, "may your friend's excellent parent be?"

"Oh, about sixty, or seventy, or eighty," said she, indifferently.

CHAPTER VIII

"THE children of England———" I remarked, when they had gone their way, their arms linked together, to Lord Sigismund who was hurrying past to the river with a bucket—but he interrupted me by shouting over his shoulder:

"Will you stay and light the fire, or come with us and forage for food?"

Light the fire? Why, what are women for? Even Hermann, my servant, would rebel if he instead of Clothilde had to light fires. But, on the other hand, forage? Go back across that immense field and walk from shop to shop on feet that had for some time past been unable to walk at all? And then return weighed down with the results?

"Do you understand fires, Baron?" said Mrs. Menzies-Legh, appearing suddenly behind me.

"As much, I suppose, as intelligence unaided by experience does," said I unwillingly.

"Oh, but of course you do," said she, putting a box of matches—one of those enormous English boxes that never failed to arouse my amused contempt, for they did not light a single fire or candle more than their handy little continental brethren—into my right hand, and the red handkerchieful of sticks bought that morning into my left, "of course you do. You must have got quite used to them in the wars."

"What wars?" I asked sharply. "You surely do not imagine that I———"

"Oh, were you too young for Sedan and all that?" she asked, as she crossed over the very long and very green grass toward a distant ditch and I found that I was expected to cross with her.

"I was so young," I said, more nettled than my hearers will perhaps understand, but then I was tired out and no longer able to bear much, "so young that I had not even reached the stage of being born."

"Not really?" said she.

"Yes," said I. "I was still spending my birthdays among the angels."

This, of course, was not strictly true, but one likes to take off a few years in the presence of a woman who has left her *Gotha Almanach* at home, and it was, I felt, a picturesque notion—I mean about the birthdays and the angels.

"Not really?" said she again.

And what, I thought, as we walked on together, is all this talk about young and not young? If a man is not young in the forties when will he be? I have never concealed my age, which is about five or six and forty, with perhaps a year or two added on, but as I take little notice of birthdays it is just as likely the year or two ought to be added off, and the forties are universally acknowledged by all persons who are in them to be the very flower and prime of life, or rather the beginning of the very flower and prime, the beginning of the final unfolding of the last crumple in the last petal.

I should have thought this state of things was visible enough in me, plain enough to any ordinary onlooker. I have neither a gray hair nor a wrinkle. My moustache is as uninterruptedly blond as ever. My face is perfectly smooth. And when my hat is on there is no difference whatever between me and a person of thirty. Of course I am not a narrow man, weedy in the way in which Jellaby is weedy, and unable as he is unable to fill out my clothes; but it is laughable that just breadth should have made those two fledglings place me in the same category as an exceedingly venerable and obviously crippled old gentleman.

I expect the truth is that in England children are ill-trained and educated, and their perceptions are allowed to remain rudimentary. It must be so, for so few of them wear spectacles. Clearly education is not carried on with anything like our systematic rigor, for except on Lord Sigismund I had up to then nowhere seen these artificial aids to eyesight, and in Germany at least two-thirds of our young people, as a result of their application, wear either spectacles or *pince-nez*. They may well be proud of them. They are the visible proof of a youth spent entirely at its books, the hoisted standard of an ordered and studious life.

"The children of England———" I began vigorously to Mrs. Menzies-Legh, desirous of expressing a few of my objections to them to a lady who could not be supposed to mind, she being one of my own countrywomen—but she too interrupted me.

"This is the most sheltered place," she said, pointing to the dry ditch. "You'll find more sticks in that little wood. You will want heaps more."

And she left me.

Well, I had never made a fire in my life. I stood there for a moment in great hesitation as to how to begin. They should not say I was unwilling, those ant-like groups over by the caravans so feverishly hurrying hither and thither, but to do a thing one must begin it, and as there are no doubt several ways of lighting a fire, even as there are several ways of doing anything else in life, I stood uncertain while I asked myself which of these several ways (all of them, I must concede, unknown to me) I ought to choose.

The ditch had a hedge on its farther side, and through a gap in it I saw the wood, cleared in places and overgrown between the remaining stumps by bracken and brambles, wherein I was, as Mrs. Menzies-Legh said, to find more sticks. The first thing to be done, then, was to find the sticks, for the handkerchief contained the merest handful; and this was a hard task among brambles at the end of a dinnerless day, and likely, besides, to prove ruinous to my stockings.

The groups at the caravans were peeling the potatoes and other vegetables we had bought at the farm near Grip's Common that morning, and were doing it with an expedition that showed how hunger was triumphing over fatigue. Jellaby hurried to and fro to a small spring among the bracken fetching water. Menzies-Legh and Lord Sigismund had disappeared in the distance that led to the shops. Old James was feeding the horses. I could see the two fledglings sitting on the grass with bowed heads and flushed cheeks absorbed in the shredding of cabbages. Mrs. Menzies-Legh had begun, with immense energy, to peel potatoes. Her gentle sister—I deplored it—was engaged on an onion. Nowhere, look as I might (for I needed her assistance) could I see my wife.

Then Mrs. Menzies-Legh, raising her eyes from her potatoes, saw me standing motionless and called out that the vegetables would soon be ready for the fire, but she feared if I were not quick the fire would not soon be ready for the vegetables; and thus urged, and contrary to my first intention, I hastily emptied the sticks out of the handkerchief into the ditch and began to endeavour to light them.

But they would not light. Match after match flared an instant, then went out. It was a windy evening, and I saw no reason for supposing that any match would stay alight long enough to get even one stick to catch fire.

I went down on my knees and interposed my person between the sticks and the wind, but though the matches then burned to the end (where were my fingers) the sticks took no more notice than if they had been of iron. Losing patience I said something aloud and not, I am afraid, quite complimentary, about wives who neglect their duties and kick in shortened skirts over the traces of matrimony; and Edelgard's voice immediately responded from the other side of the hedge. "But *lieber* Otto," it said, "is it then my fault that you have forgotten the paper?"

I straightened myself and looked at her. She had already been on the search for sticks, for as she advanced to the gap and stood in it I saw she had an apronful of them. I must say I was surprised at her courage in confronting me thus alone, when she was aware I must be gravely displeased with her and could only be waiting for an opportunity to tell her so. She, however, with the cunning common to wives, called me *lieber* Otto as though nothing had happened, did not allude to my overheard exclamation and sought to soften me with sticks.

I looked at her therefore very coldly. "No," I said, "I had not forgotten the paper."

And this was true, because to forget paper (or indeed anything else) you must first of all have thought of it, and I had not.

"Perhaps," I went on, my coldness descending as I spoke below zero, which is the point in our well-arranged thermometers (either Celsius or Réaumur, but none of their foolish Fahrenheits) where freezing begins, "perhaps, since you are so clever, you will have the goodness to light the fire yourself. Any one," I continued with emphasis, "can criticize. We will now, if you please, change places, and you shall bring your unquestioned gifts to bear on this matter, while I assume the *role* suited to lesser capacity, and merely criticize."

This of course, was bitter; but was it not a justified bitterness? Unfortunately I shall have to suppress the passage I suppose at the reading aloud, so shall never hear the verdict of my friends; but even without that verdict (and I well know what it would be, for they all have wives) even without it I can honestly call my bitterness justified. Besides, it was very well put.

She listened in silence, and then just said, "Oh, Otto," and came down at once into the ditch, and

"But, lieber Otto, is it then my fault that you have forgotten the paper?"

bending over the sticks began to arrange them quickly on some stones she picked up.

    I did not like to sit down and smoke, which is what I would have done at home (supposing such a situation as the Ottringels lighting a fire out-of-doors in Storchwerder were conceivable), because Mrs. Menzies-Legh would probably have immediately left off peeling her potatoes to exclaim, and Jellaby would, I dare say, have put down his buckets and come over to inquire if I were enjoying myself. Not that I care ten *pfennings* for their opinions, and I also passionately disapprove of the whole English attitude toward women; but I am a fair-minded man, and believe in going as far as is reasonable with the well-known maxim of behaving in Rome as the Romans behave.

I therefore just stood with my back to the caravans and watched Edelgard. In less time than I take to write it she had piled up the sticks, stuffed a bit of newspaper she drew from her apron underneath them, lit them by means (as I noted) of a single match, and behold the fire, crackling and blazing and leaping upward or outward as the wind drove it.

No proof, if anything further in that way were needed, could be more convincing as to the position women are intended by nature to fill. Their instincts are all of the fire-lighting order, the order that serves and tends; while to man, the noble dreamer, is reserved the place in life where there is room, dignity, and uninterruption. Else how can he dream? And without his dreams there would be no subsequent crystallization of dreams; and all that we see of good and great and wealth-bringing was once some undisturbed man's dream.

But this is philosophy; and you, my friends, who breathe the very air handed down to you by our Hegels and our Kants, who are born into it and absorb it whether you want to or not through each one of your infancy's pores, you do not need to hear the Ottringel echo of your own familiar thoughts. We in Storchwerder speak seldom on these subjects for we take them for granted; and I will not in this place describe too minutely all that passed through my mind as I watched, in that grassy solitude, at the hour when the sun in setting lights up everything with extra splendour, my wife piling sticks on the fire.

Indeed, what did pass through it was of a mixed nature. It seemed so strange to be there; so strange that that meadow, in all its dampness, its high hedge round three sides of it, its row of willows brooding over the sulky river, its wood on the one hand, its barren expanse of mole-ridden field on the other, and for all view another meadow of exact similarity behind another row of exactly similar willows across the Medway, it seemed so strange that all this had been lying there silent and empty for heaven knows how many years, the exact spot on which Edelgard and I were standing waiting, as it were, for its prey throughout the entire period of our married life in Storchwerder and of my other married life previous to that, while we, all unconscious, went through the series of actions and thoughts that had at length landed us on it. Strange fruition of years. Stranger the elaborate leading up to it. Strangest the inability of man to escape such a destiny. Regarded as the fruition of years it was certainly paltry, it was certainly a disproportionate destiny. I had been led from Pomerania, a most remote place if measured by its distance from the Medway, in order to stand at evening with damp feet on this exact spot. A believer, you will cry, in predestination? Perhaps. Anyhow, filled with these reflections (and others of the same character) and watching my wife doing in silence that for which she is fitted and intended, my feeling toward her became softer; I began to excuse; to relent; to forgive. Indeed I have tried to do my duty. I am not hard, unless she forces me to be. I feel that no one can guide and help a wife except a husband. And I am older than she is; and am I not experienced in wives, who have had two, and one of them for the enormous (sometimes it used to seem endless) period of twenty years?

I said nothing to her at the moment of a softer nature, being well aware of the advantage of allowing time, before proceeding to forgiveness, for the firmer attitude to sink in; and Jellaby bringing the iron stew-pot Mrs. Menzies-Legh had bought that morning—or rather dragging it, for he is, as I have said, a weedy creature—across to us, spilling much of the water it contained on the way, I was obliged to help him get it on to the fire, fetching at his direction stones to support it and then considerably scorching my hands in the efforts to settle the thing safely on the stones.

"Please don't bother, Baroness," said Jellaby to Edelgard when she began to replenish the fire with more sticks. "We'll do that. You'll get the smoke in your eyes."

But would we not get the smoke in our eyes too? And would not eyes unused to kitchen work smart far more than eyes that did the kind of thing at home every day? For I suppose the fires in the kitchen of Storchwerder smoke sometimes, and Edelgard must have been perfectly inured to it.

"Oh," said Edelgard, in the pleasant little voice she manages to have when speaking to persons who are not her husband, "it is no bother. I do not mind the smoke."

"Why, what are we here for?" said Jellaby. And he took the sticks she was still holding from her hands.

Again the thought crossed my mind that Jellaby must be attracted by Edelgard; indeed, all three gentlemen. This is an example of the sort of attention that had been lavished on her ever since we started. Inconceivable as it seemed, there it was; and the most inconceivable part of it was that it was boldly done in the very presence of her husband. I, however, knowing that one should never trust a foreigner, determined to bring round the talk, as I had decided the day before, to the number of Edelgard's birthdays that very evening at supper.

But when supper, after an hour and a half's waiting, came, I was too much exhausted to care. We all were very silent. Our remaining strength had gone out of us like a flickering candle in a wind when we became aware of the really endless time the potatoes take to boil. Everything had gone into the pot together. Mrs. Menzies-Legh had declared that was the shortest, and indeed the only way, for the oil-stoves in the caravans and their small saucepans had sufficiently proved their inadequacy the previous night. Henceforth, said Mrs. Menzies-Legh, our hope was to be in the stew-pot; and as she said it she threw in the potatoes, the cabbages, the onion sliced by her tender sister, a piece of butter, a handful of salt, and the bacon her husband and Lord Sigismund had brought back with them from the village. It all went in together; but it did not all come out together, for we discovered after savoury fragrances had teased our nostrils for some time that the cabbage and the bacon were cooked, while the potatoes, in response to the proddings of divers anxious forks, remained obstinately hard.

We held a short council, gathered round the stew-pot, as to the best course to pursue. If we left the bacon and the cabbage in the pot they would be boiled certainly to a pulp, and perhaps—awful thought—altogether away, before the potatoes were ready. On the other hand, to relinquish the potatoes, the chief feature of our supper, would be impossible. We therefore, after much anxious argument, decided to take out that which was already cooked, put it carefully on plates, and at the last moment return it to the pot to be warmed up again.

This was done, and we sat round on the grass to wait. Now was the moment, now that we were all assembled silent in a circle, to direct the conversation into the birthday channel, but I found myself so much enfeebled and the rest so unresponsive that after a faltering beginning, which had no effect except to draw a few languid gazes upon me, I was obliged perforce to put it off. Indeed, our thoughts were wholly concentrated on food; and looking back it is almost incredible to me that that meagre supper should have roused so eager an interest.

We all sat without speaking, listening to the bubbling of the pot. Now and then one of the young men thrust more sticks beneath it. The sun had set long since, and the wind had dropped. The meadow seemed to grow much damper, and while our faces were being scorched by the fire our backs were becoming steadily more chilly. The ladies drew their wraps about them. The gentlemen did that for their comfort which they would not do for politeness, and put on their coats. I whose coat had never left me, fetched my mackintosh and hung it over my shoulders, careful to keep it as much as possible out of reach of the fire-glow in case it should begin to melt.

Long before, the ladies had spread the tables and cut piles of bread and butter, and one of them—I expect it was Frau von Eckthum—had concocted an uncooked pudding out of some cakes they alluded to as sponge, with some cream and raspberry jam and brandy, which, together with the bacon and excepting the brandy, were the result of the foraging expedition.

Toward these tables our glances often wandered. We were but human, and presently, overcome, our bodies wandered thither too.

We ate the bread and butter.

Then we ate the bacon and cabbage, agreeing that it was a pity to let it get any cooler.

Then we ate the pudding they spoke of—for after this they began to be able to speak—as a trifle.

And then—and it is as strange to relate as it is difficult to believe—we returned to the stew-pot and ate every one of the now ready and steaming hot potatoes; and never, I can safely say, was there anything so excellent.

Later on, entering our caravan much softened by these various experiences and by a cup of extremely good coffee made by Edelgard, but feeling justified in withdrawing, now that darkness had set in, from the confusions of the washing up, I found my wife searching in the depths of the yellow box for dishcloths.

I stood in the narrow gangway lighting a cigar, and when I had done lighting it I realized that I was close to her and alone. One is never at any time far from anything in these vehicles, but on this occasion the nearness combined with the privacy suggested that the moment had arrived for the words I had decided she must hear—kind words, not hard as I had at first intended, but needful.

I put out my arm, therefore, and proposed to draw her toward me as a preliminary to peace.

She would not, however, come.

Greatly surprised—for resentment had not till then been one of her failings—I opened my mouth to speak, but she, before I could do so, said, "Do you mind not smoking inside the caravan?"

Still more surprised, and indeed amazed (for this was petty) but determined not to be shaken out of my kindness, I gently began, "Dear wife——" and was going on when she interrupted me.

"Dear husband," she said, actually imitating me, "I know what you are going to say. I always know what you are going to say. I know all the things you ever can or ever do say."

She paused a moment, and then added in a firm voice, looking me straight in the eyes, "By heart."

And before I could in any way recover my presence of mind she was through the curtain and down the ladder and had vanished with the dishcloths in the darkness.

CHAPTER IX

THIS was rebellion.

But unconsciousness supervened before I had had time to consider how best to meet it, the unconsciousness of the profound and prolonged sleep which is the portion of caravaners. I fell into it almost immediately after her departure, dropping into my berth, a mere worn-out collection of aching and presently oblivious bones, and remaining in that condition till she had left the Elsa next morning.

Therefore I had little time for reflection on the new side of her nature the English atmosphere was bringing out, nor did I all that day find either the leisure or the privacy necessary for it. I felt, indeed, as I walked by my horse along roads broad and roads narrow, roads straight and roads winding, roads flat and convenient and roads hilly and tiresome, my eyes fixed principally on the ground, for if I looked up there were only hedges and in front of me only the broad back of the Ailsa blocking up any view there might be, I felt a numb sensation stealing over me, a kind of dull patience, such as I have observed (for I see most things) to be the leading characteristic of a team of oxen, a tendency becoming more marked with every mile toward the merely bovine.

The weather that day was disagreeable. There was a high wind and a leaden sky and the dust blew hard and gritty. When, on rising, I peeped out between the window curtains, it all looked very cold and wretched, the Medway—a most surly river—muddier than ever, the leaves of the willow trees wildly fluttering and showing their gray undersides. It seemed difficult to believe that one was really there, really about to go out into that gloom to breakfast instead of into a normal dining-room with a stove and a newspaper. But, on emerging, I found that though it looked so cold it was not intolerably so, and no rain in the night had, by drenching the long grass, added to our agonies.

They were all at breakfast beneath the willows, holding on their hats with one hand and endeavouring to eat with the other, and they all seemed very cheerful. Edelgard, who had taken the coffee under her management, was going round replenishing the cups, and was actually laughing when I came out at something some one had just said. Remembering how we parted this struck me as at least strange.

I made a point of at once asking for porridge, but luckily old James had not brought the milk in time, so there was none. Spared, I ate corned beef and jam, but my feet were still sore from the previous day's march, and I was unable to enjoy it very much. The tablecloth flapped in my face, and my mackintosh blew almost into the river when I let it go for an instant in order to grasp the milk jug, and I must say I could not quite understand why they should all be so happy. I trust I am as willing to be amused as any man, but what is there amusing in breakfasting in a draughty meadow with everything flapping and fluttering, and the coffee cold before it reaches one's mouth? Yet they were happy. Even Menzies-Legh, a gray-haired, badly-preserved man, older a good deal, I should say, than I am, was joking and then laughing at his jokes with the fledglings, and Lord Sigismund and Jellaby were describing almost with exultation how brisk they had felt after a bath they had taken at five in the morning in the Medway.

What a place to be in at five in the morning. I shivered only to hear of it. Well, that which makes one man brisk is the undoing of another, and a bath in that cold, unfriendly stream would undoubtedly have undone me. I could only conclude that, pasty and loosely put together as they outwardly were, they must be of a very great secret leatheriness.

This surprised me. Not that Jellaby should be leathery, for if he were not neither would he be a Socialist; but that the son of so noble a house as the house of Hereford should have anything but the thinnest, most sensitive of skins, really was astonishing. No doubt, however, Lord Sigismund combined, like the racehorse of purest breed, a skin thin as a woman's with a mettle and spirit nothing could daunt. Nothing was daunting him that morning, that was very clear, for he sat at the end of the table shedding such contented beams through his spectacles on the company and on the food that it was as if, unconsciously true to his future calling, he was saying a continual grace.

I think they must all have been up very early, for except the cups and plates actually in use everything was already stowed away. Even the tent and its furniture was neatly rolled up preparatory to being distributed among the three caravans. Such activity, after the previous day, was surprising; and still more so was the circumstance that I had heard nothing of the attendant inevitable bustle.

"How do you feel this morning?" I asked solicitously of Frau von Eckthum on meeting her a moment alone behind her larder; I hoped she, at least, had not been working too hard.

"Oh, very well," said she.

"Not too weary?"

"Not weary at all."

"Ah—youth, youth," said I, shaking my head playfully, for indeed she looked singularly attractive that morning.

She smiled, and mounting the steps into her caravan began to do things with a duster and to sing.

For a moment I wondered whether she too had been made brisk by early contact with the Medway (of course in some remoter pool or bay), so unusual in her was this flow of language; but the idea of such delicacy being enveloped and perhaps buffeted by that rude volume of muddy water was, I felt, an impossible one. Still, why should she feel brisk? Had she not walked the day before the entire distance in the dust? Was it possible that she too, in spite of her poetic exterior, was really inwardly leathery? I have my ideals about women, and believe there is much of the poet concealed somewhere about me; and there is a moonlight intangibleness about this lady, an etherealism amounting at times almost to indistinctness, that made the application to her of such an adjective as leathery one from which I shrank. Yet if she were not, how could she—but I put these thoughts resolutely aside, and began to prepare for our departure, moving about mechanically as one in a bleak and chilly dream.

That is a hideous bridge, that one the English have built themselves across the Medway. A great gray-painted iron structure, with the dusty highroad running over it and the dirty river running under it. I hope never to see it again, unless officially at the head of my battalion. On the other side was a place called Paddock Wood, also, it seemed to me, a dreary thing as I walked through it that morning at my horse's side. The sun came out just there, and the wind with its consequent dust increased. What an August, thought I; what a climate; what a place. An August and a climate and a place only to be found in the British Isles. In Storchwerder at that moment a proper harvest mellowness prevailed. No doubt also in Switzerland, whither we so nearly went, and certainly in Italy. Was this a reasonable way of celebrating one's silver wedding, plodding through

Paddock Wood with no one taking any notice of me, not even she who was the lawful partner of the celebration? The only answer I got as I put the question to myself was a mouthful of dust.

Nobody came to walk with me, and unless some one did my position was a very isolated one, wedged in between the Ailsa and the Ilsa, unable to leave the Elsa, who, like a wife, immediately strayed from the proper road if I did. The back of the Ailsa prevented my seeing who was with whom in front, but once at a sharp turning I did see, and what I saw was Frau von Eckthum walking with Jellaby, and Edelgard—if you please—on his other side. The young Socialist was slouching along with his hands in his pockets and his bony shoulders up to his ears listening, apparently, to Frau von Eckthum who actually seemed to be talking, for he kept on looking at her, and laughing as though at the things she said. Edelgard, I noticed, joined in the laughter as unconcernedly as if she had nothing in the world to reproach herself with. Then the Elsa followed round the corner and the scene in front was blotted out; but glancing back over my shoulder I saw how respectably Lord Sigismund, true to his lineage, remained by the Ilsa's horse's head, reflectively smoking his pipe and accompanied only by his dog.

Beyond Paddock Wood and its flat and dreary purlieus the road began to ascend and to wind, growing narrower and less draughty, with glimpses of a greener country and a hillier distance, in fact improving visibly as we neared Sussex. All this time I had walked by myself, and I was still too tired after the long march the day before to have any but dull objections. It would have been natural to be acutely indignant at Edelgard's persistent defiance, natural to be infuriated at the cleverness with which she shifted the entire charge of our caravan on to me while she, on the horizon, gesticulated with Jellaby. I realized, it is true, that the others would not have let her lead the horse even had she offered to, but she ought at least to have walked beside me and hear me, if that were my mood, grumble. However, a reasonable man knows how to wait. He does not, not being a woman, hasten and perhaps spoil a crisis by rushing at it. And if no opportunity should present itself for weeks, would there not be years in our flat in Storchwerder consisting solely of opportunities?

Besides, my feet ached. I think there must have been some clumsy darning of Edelgard's in my socks that pressed on my toes and made them feel as if the shoes were too short for them. And small stones kept on getting inside them, finding out the one place they could get in at and leaping through it with the greatest dexterity, dropping gradually by unpleasant stages down to underneath my socks, where they remained causing me discomfort till the next camp. These physical conditions, to which the endless mechanical trudging behind the Ailsa's varnished back must be added, reduced me as I said before to a condition of dull and bovine acquiescence. I ceased to make objections. I hardly thought. I just trudged.

At the top of the ascent, at a junction of four roads called Four Winds (why, when they were four roads, the English themselves I suppose best know), we met a motor.

It came scorching round a corner with an insolent shriek of its tooting apparatus, but the shriek died away as it were on its lips when it saw what was filling up the way. It hesitated, stopped, and then began respectfully to back. Pass us it could not at that point, and charge into such vast objects as the caravans was a task before which even bloodthirstiness quailed. I record this as the one pleasing incident that morning, and when it was my turn to walk by the thing I did so with squared shoulders and held-up head and a muttered (yet perfectly distinct) "Road hogs"—which is the term Menzies-Legh had applied to them the day before when relating how one had run over a woman near where he lives, and had continued its career, leaving her to suffer in the road, which she did for the space of two hours before the next passer-by passed in time to see her die. And she was a quite young woman, and a pretty one into the bargain.

("I don't see what that has to do with it," said the foolish Jellaby when, in answer to my questions, I extracted this information from Menzies-Legh.)

Therefore, remembering this shocking affair, and being as well a great personal detester of these conveyances, the property invariably of the insolent rich, who with us are chiefly Jews, I took care to be distinct as I muttered "Road hogs." The two occupants in goggles undoubtedly heard me, for they started and even their goggles seemed to shrink back and be ashamed of themselves, and I continued my way with a slight reviving of my spirits, the slight reviving of which he is generally conscious who has had the courage to say what he thinks of a bad thing.

The post whose finger we were following had Dundale inscribed on it, and as we wound downward the scenery considerably improved. Woods on our left sheltered us from the wind, and on our right were a number of pretty hills. At the bottom—a bottom only reached after care and exertion, for loose stones imperilled the safety of my horse's knees, and I had besides to spring about applying and regulating the brake—we found a farm with a hop-kiln in the hollow on the left, and opposite it a convenient, indeed attractive, field.

No other house was near. No populace. No iron bridge. No donkeys. No barrel-organ. Stretches of corn, so ripe that though the sky had clouded over they looked as if the sun were shining on them, alternated very pleasantly with the green of the hop-fields, and portions of woods climbed up between the folds of the hills. It was a sheltered spot, with a farm capable no doubt of supplying food, but I feared that because it was only one o'clock my pedantic companions, in defiance of the previous day's experience, would decline to camp. Taking therefore the law into my own hands I pulled up my caravan in front of the farm gate. The Ilsa behind me was forced to pull up too; and the Ailsa, in the very act of lumbering round the next corner, was arrested by my loud and masterful *Brrr*.

"Anything wrong?" asked Lord Sigismund, running up from the back.

"What is it?" asked Menzies-Legh, coming toward me from the front.

Strange to say they listened to reason; and yet not strange, for I have observed that whenever one makes up one's mind beforehand and unshakably other people give in. One must know what one wants—that is the whole secret; and in a world of flux and shilly-shally the infrequent rock is the only person who really gets it.

Jellaby (who seemed to think he was irresistible) volunteered to go to the farmer and get permission to camp in the field, and I was pleased to see that he made so doubtful an impression that the man came back with him before granting anything, to find out whether the party belonging to this odd emissary were respectable. I dare say he would have decided that we were not had he only seen the others, for the gentlemen were in their shirt sleeves again; but when he saw me, well and completely dressed, he had no further hesitations. Readily he let us use the field, recommending a certain lower portion of it on account of the nearness of the water, and then he prepared to go back and, as he said, finish his dinner.

But we, who wanted dinner too, could not be content with nothing more filling than a field, and began almost with one voice to talk to him of poultry.

He said he had none.

Of eggs.

He said he had none.

Of (anxiously) butter.

He said he had none. And he scratched his head and looked unintelligent for a space, and then repeating that about finishing his dinner turned away.

I went with him.

"Take the caravans into the field and I will forage," I called back, waving my hand; for the idea of accompanying a man who was going to finish his dinner exhilarated me into further masterfulness.

My rapid calculation was, as I kept step with him, he looking at me sideways, that though it was very likely true he had not enough for ten it was equally probable that he had plenty for one. Besides, he might be glad to let an interesting stranger share the finishing of his no doubt lonely meal.

In the short transit from the lane to his back door (the front door was choked with grass and weeds) I chatted agreeably and fluently about the butter and eggs we desired to buy, adopting the "Come, come, my dear fellow" tone, perhaps better described as the man to man form of appeal.

"Foreign?" said he, after I had thus flowed on, pausing on his doorstep as though intending to part from me at that point.

"Yes, and proud of it," said I, lifting my hat to my distant Fatherland.

"Ah," said he. "No accountin' for tastes."

This was disappointing after I had thought we were getting on. Also it was characteristically British. I would at once have resented it if with the opening of the door the unfinished dinner had not, in the form of a most appetizing odour, issued forth to within reach of my nostrils. To sit in a room with shut windows at a table and dine, without preliminary labours, on food that did not get cold between the plate and one's mouth, seemed to me at that moment a lot so blessed that tears almost came into my eyes.

"Do you never have—guests?" I asked, faltering but hurried, for he was about to shut the door with me still on the wrong side of it.

He stared. Red-faced and over stout his very personal safety demanded that he should not by himself finish that dinner.

"Guests?" he repeated stupidly. "No, I don't have no guests."

"Poor fellow," said I.

"I don't know about poor fellow," said he, getting redder.

"Yes. Poor fellow. And poor fellow inasmuch as I suppose in this secluded spot there are none to be had, and so you are prevented from exercising the most privileged and noble of rites."

"Oh, you're one of them Social Democrats?"

"Social Democrats?" I echoed.

"Them chaps that go about talkin' to us of rights, and wrongs too, till we all get mad and discontented—which is pretty well all we ever do get," he added with a chuckle that was at the same time scornful. And he shut the door.

Filled with the certitude that I had been misunderstood, and that if only he could be made aware that he had one of the aristocracy of the first nation in the world on his step willing to be his guest and that such a chance would never in all human probability occur again he would be too delighted to welcome me, I knocked vigorously.

"Let me in. I am hungry. You do not know who I am," I called out.

"Well," said he, opening the door a few inches after a period during which I had continued knocking and he, as I could hear, had moved about the room inside, "here's a quarter of a pound of butter for you. I ain't got no more. It's salt. I ain't got no fresh. I send it away to the market as soon as it's made. It'll be fourpence. Tell your party they can pay when they settle for the field."

And he thrust a bit of soft and oily butter lying on a piece of paper into my hand and shut the door.

"Man," I cried in desperation, rattling the handle, "you do not know who I am. I am a gentleman—an officer—a nobleman———"

He bolted the door.

When I got back I found them encamped in a corner at the far end of the field, as close into the shelter of a hedge as they could get, and my butter was greeted with a shout (led by Jellaby) of laughter. He and the fledglings at once started off on a fresh foraging expedition, on my advice in another direction, but all they bore back with them was the promise, from another farmer, of chickens next morning at six, and what is the good of chickens next morning at six? It was my turn to shout, and so I did, but I seemed to have little luck with my merriment, for the others were never merry at the moment that I was, and I shouted alone.

Jellaby, pretending he did not know why I should, looked surprised and said as usual, "Hullo, Baron, enjoying yourself?"

"Of course," said I, smartly—"is not that what I have come to England for?"

We dined that day on what was left of our bacon and some potatoes we had over. An attempt which failed was made to fry the potatoes—"as a pleasant change," said Lord Sigismund good humouredly—but the wind was so high that the fire could not be brought to frying pitch, so about three o'clock we gave it up, and boiled them and ate them with butter and the bacon, which was for some reason nobody understood half raw.

That was a bad day. I hope never to revisit Dundale. The field, which began dry and short-grassed at the top of the slope, was every bit as deep and damp by the time it got down to the corner we were obliged to camp in because of the wind as the meadow by the Medway had been. We had the hedge between us (theoretically) and the wind, but the wind took no notice of the hedge. Also we had a black-looking brook of sluggish movement sunk deep below some alders and brambles at our side, and infested, it appeared, with a virulent species of fly or other animal, for while we were wondering (at least I was) what we were going to do to pass the hours before bed time, and what (if any) supper there would be, and reflecting (at least I was) on the depressing size and greenness of the field and on the way the threatening clouds hung lower and lower over our heads, the fledgling Jumps appeared, struggling up from the brook through the blackberry bushes, and crying that she had been stung by some beast or beasts unknown, flung herself down on the grass and immediately began to swell.

Everybody was in consternation, and I must say so was I, for I have never seen anything to equal the rapidity of her swelling. Her face and hands even as she lay there became covered with large red, raised blotches, and judging from her incoherent remarks the same thing was happening over the rest of her. It occurred to me that if she could not soon be stopped from further swelling the very worst thing might be anticipated, and I expressed my fears to Menzies-Legh.

"Nonsense," said he, quite sharply; but I overlooked it because he was obviously in his heart thinking the same thing.

They got her into the Ilsa and put her, I was informed, to bed; and presently, just as I was expecting to be scattered with the other gentlemen in all directions in search of a doctor, Mrs. Menzies-Legh appeared in the doorway and said that Jumps had been able to gasp out, between her wild scratchings, that when anything stung her she always swelled, and the only thing to do was to let her scratch undisturbed until such time as she should contract to her ordinary size again.

Immensely relieved, for a search for a doctor in hedges and ditches would surely have been a thing of little profit and much fatigue, I sat down in one of the only three chairs that were at all comfortable and spent the rest of the afternoon in fitful argument with Jellaby as he came and went, and in sustained, and not, I trust, unsuccessful efforts to establish my friendship with Lord Sigismund on such a footing that an invitation to meet his Serene Aunt, the Princess of Grossburg-Niederhausen, would be the harmonious result.

The ladies were busied devising methods for the more rapid relief of the unhappy and still obstinately swollen fledgling.

There was no supper except ginger-biscuits.

"You can't expect it," said Edelgard, when I asked her (very distantly) about it, "with sickness in the house."

"What house?" I retorted, pardonably snappy.

I hope never to revisit Dundale.

CHAPTER X

LET me earnestly urge any of my hearers who may be fired by my example to follow it, never to go to Dundale. It is a desolate place, and a hungry place; and a place, moreover, greatly subject to becoming enveloped in a sort of universal gray cloud, emitting a steady though fine drizzle and accounted for—which made it none the less wet—by persons who knew everything, like Jellaby, as being a sea-mist.

I am no doubt very stupid, and therefore was unable to understand why there should be a sea-mist when there was no sea.

"Well, we're in Sussex now you know," said Jellaby, on my saying something of the sort to him.

"Indeed," said I politely, as though that explained it; but of course it did not.

Up to this point we had at least, since the first night, been dry. Now the rain began, and caravaning in rain is an experience that must be met with one's entire stock of fortitude and philosophy. This stock, however large originally, has a tendency to give out after drops have trickled down inside one's collar for some hours. At the other end, too, the wet ascends higher and higher, for is not one wading about in long and soaking grass, trying to perform one's (so to speak) household duties? And if, when the ascending wet and the descending wet meet, and the whole man is a mere and very unhappy sponge, he can still use such words as healthy and jolly, then I say that that man is either a philosopher indeed, worthy of and ripe for an immediate tub, or he is a liar and a hypocrite. I heard both those adjectives often that day, and silently divided their users into the proper categories. For myself I preferred to say nothing, thus producing private flowers of stoicism in response to the action of the rain.

For the first time I was glad to walk, glad to move on, glad of anything that was not helping dripping ladies to pack up dripping breakfast things beneath the dripping umbrella that with studious gallantry I endeavoured to hold the while over my and their dripping heads. However healthy and jolly the wet might be it undoubtedly made the company more silent than the dry, and our resumed march was almost entirely without conversation. We moved on in a southwesterly direction, the diseased fledgling still in bed and still, I was credibly informed, scratching, through pine woods full of wet bracken and deep gloom and drizzle, till at a place called Frant we turned off due south in response to some unaccountable impulse of Mrs. Menzies-Legh's, whose unaccountable impulses were the capricious rudder which swayed us hither and thither during the entire tour.

She used to study maps, and walk with one under her arm out of which she read aloud the names of the places we were supposed to be at; and just as we had settled down to believe it we would come to some flatly contradictory signpost which talked of quite different places, places we had been told were remote and in an altogether different direction.

"It doesn't matter," she would say, with a smile in which I, at least, never joined, for I have my own opinions of petticoat government—"the great thing is to go on."

So we went on; and it was she who made us suddenly turn off southward after Frant, leaving a fairly comfortable highroad for the vicissitudes of narrow and hilly lanes.

"Lanes," said she, "are infinitely prettier."

I dare say. They are also generally hillier, and so narrow that once a caravan is in one on it has to go whatever happens, trusting to luck not to meet anything else on wheels till it reaches, after many anxieties, the haven of another highroad. This lane ran deep between towering hedges and did not leave off again for five miles, and none of you would believe how long it took us to do those five miles because none of you know—how should you?—what the getting of caravans up hills by means of tracing is. We had, thanks to Mrs. Menzies-Legh's desire for the pretty (unsatisfied I am glad to say on that occasion, because the so-called sea-mist clung close round us like a wet gray cloak)—we had got into an almost mountainous lane. We were tracing the whole time, dragging each caravan up each hill in turn, leaving it solitary at the top and returning with all three horses for the next one left meanwhile at the bottom. I never saw such an endless succession of hills. If tracing does not teach a man patience what, I would like to know, will?

At first, on finding my horse removed and harnessed on to the Ailsa, I thought I would get inside the Elsa and stretch myself on the yellow box and wait there quietly smoking till the horse came back again; but I found Edelgard inside, blocking it up and preparing to mend her stockings.

This was unpleasant, for I had hardly spoken to her, and then only with the chilliest politeness, since her behaviour on the evening by the Medway; yet, determined to be master in my own (so to speak) house, I would have carried out my intention if Menzies-Legh's voice, which I thought had gone up the hill, had not been heard quite close outside asking where I was.

I warned my wife by means of a hasty enjoining finger to keep silence.

Will it be believed that she looked at me, said "Why should you not help?" opened the window, and called out that I was there?

"Come and give us a hand, Baron," said Menzies-Legh from outside. "It's a very stiff pull—we'll have to push behind as well, and want what help we've got."

"Certainly," said I, all apparent ready bustle; but I shot a very expressive brief glance at Edelgard as I went out.

She, however, pretended to be absorbed in her sewing.

"You Socialists," said I to Jellaby, next to whom I found I was expected to push, "do not believe in marriage, do you?"

"We—don't—believe—in—tyrants," he panted, so short of breath that I stared at him, I myself having quite a quantity of it; besides, what an answer!

I shrugged the shoulder nearest him and continued up in silence. At the top of the hill he was so warm and breathless that he could not speak, and so were the others, while I was perfectly cool and chatty.

"Why, gentlemen," I remarked banteringly, as I stood in the midst of these panters watching them wipe their heated brows, "you are scarcely what is known as in training."

"But you, Baron—undoubtedly are——" gasped Menzies-Legh. "You are—absolutely unruffled."

"Oh, yes," I agreed modestly, "I am in good condition. We always are in our army. Ready at any moment to——"

I stopped, for I had been on the verge of saying "eat the English," when I recollected that we may not inform the future mouthfuls of their fate.

"Ready to go in and win," finished Lord Sigismund.

"To blow up Europe," said Jellaby.

"To mobilize," said Menzies-Legh. "And very right and proper."

"Very wrong and improper," said Jellaby. "You know," he said, turning on his host with all the combativeness of these men of peace (the only really calm person is your thoroughly trained and equipped warrior)—"you know very well you agree with me that war is the most unnecessary———"

"Come, come, my young gentlemen," I interposed, broadening my chest, "do not forget that you are in the presence of one of its representatives———"

"Let us fetch up the next caravan," interrupted Menzies-Legh, thrusting my horse's bridle into my hand; and as I led it down the hill again my anxiety to prevent its stumbling and costing me heaven knows how much in the matter of mending its knees rendered me unable for the moment to continue the crushing of Jellaby.

About four o'clock in the afternoon we found ourselves, drenched and hungry, on the outskirts of a place called Wadhurst. It seemed wise to go no nearer unless we were prepared to continue on through it, for already the laurels of its villa residences dropped their rain on us over neat railings as we passed. We therefore, too worn out to attempt to get right through the place to the country beyond, selected the first possible field on the left of the brown and puddle-strewn road, a field of yellow stubble which, soaking as it was, was yet a degree less soaking than long grass, and though it had nothing but a treeless hedge to divide us from the eyes of wanderers along the road it had an unusually conveniently placed gate. The importance now of fields and gates! The importance, indeed, of everything usually unimportant—which is, in brief, the tragedy of caravaning.

This time the Menzies-Legh couple went to find the owner and crave permission. So reduced were we—and could reduction go further?—that to crave, hat in hand, for permission to occupy some wretched field for a few hours, and to crave it often of illiterate, selfish, and grossly greedy persons like my friend at Dundale, was not beneath any of our prides, while to obtain it seemed the one boon worth having.

While they were gone we waited, a melancholy string of vehicles and people in a world made up of mist and mud. Frau von Eckthum, who might have cheered me, had been invisible nearly the whole day, ministering (no doubt angelically) to the afflicted fledgling. Edelgard and the child Jane got into the Elsa during the pause and began to teach each other languages. I leaned against the gate, staring before me. Old James, a figure of dripping patience, remained at his horse's head. And Lord Sigismund and Jellaby, as though they had not had enough exercise, walked up and down the road talking.

Except the sound of their receding and advancing footsteps the stillness was broken by nothing at all. It was a noiseless rain. It did not patter. And yet, fine though it was, it streamed down the flanks of the horses, the sides of the caravans, and actually penetrated, as I later on discovered, through the green arras lining of the Elsa, making a long black streak from roof to floor.

I wonder what my friends at home would have said could they have seen me then. No shelter; no refuge; no rest. These three negatives, I take it, sum up fairly accurately a holiday in a caravan. You cannot get in, for if you do either you find it full already of your wife, or, if it is moving, Jellaby immediately springs up from nowhere and inquires at the window whether you have noticed how your horse is sweating. At every camp there is nothing but work—and oh, my friends, such work! Work undreamed of in your ordered lives, and nothing, nothing but it, for must you not eat? And without it there is no eating. And then when you have eaten, without the least pause, the least interval for the meditation so good after meals, there begins that frightful and accursed form of activity, most frightful and accursed of all known forms, the washing up. How it came about that it was not from the first left to the women I cannot understand; they are fitted by nature for such labour, and do not feel it; but I, being in a minority, was powerless to interfere. Nor did I always succeed in evading it. If we camped early, the daylight exposed my movements; and by the time it was done bed seemed the only place to go to. Now an intelligent man does not desire to go to bed at eight; yet in that cold weather—we were, they said, unusually unfortunate in the weather—even if it was dry, what pleasure was there in sitting out-of-doors? I had had enough during the day of out-of-doors; by the time evening came, out-of-doors and fresh air were things abhorrent to me. And there were only three comfortable chairs, low and easy, in which a man might stretch himself and smoke, and these, without so much as a preliminary offering of them to anybody else, were sat in by the ladies. It did seem a turning of good old customs upside down when I saw Edelgard get into one as a matter of course, so indifferent to what I might be thinking that she did not even look my way. How vividly on such occasions did I remember my easy chair at Storchwerder and how sacred it was, and how she never dared, if I were in the house, approach it, nor I firmly believe ever dared, so good was her training and so great her respect, approach it when I was out.

Well, our proverb—descriptive of a German gentleman about to start on his (no doubt) well-deserved holiday travels—"He who loves his wife leaves her at home," is as wise now as the day it was written, and about this time I began to see that by having made my bed in a manner that disregarded it I was going to have to lie on it.

The Menzies-Leghs returned wreathed in smiles—I beg you to note the reason, and all of wretchedness that it implies—because the owner of the field's wife had not been rude, and had together with the desired permission sold them two pounds of sausages, the cold potatoes left from her dinner, a jug of milk, a piece of butter, and some firewood. Also they had met a baker's cart and had bought loaves.

This, of course, as far as it went, was satisfactory, especially the potatoes that neither wanted peeling nor patience while they grew soft, but I submit that it was only a further proof of our extreme lowness in the scale of well-cared-for humanity. Here in my own home, with these events in what Menzies-Legh and Jellaby would have called the blue distance, how strange it seems that just sausages and cold potatoes should ever have been able to move me to exultation.

We at once got into the field, hugging the hedge, and in the shelter of the Ilsa (which entered last) made our fire. I was deputed (owing to the unfortunate circumstance of my being the only person who had brought one) to hold my umbrella over the frying pan while Jellaby fried the sausages on one of the stoves. It was not what I would have chosen, for while protecting the sausages I was also, in spite of every effort to the contrary, protecting Jellaby; and what an anomalous position for a gentleman of birth and breeding and filled with the aristocratic opinions, and perhaps (for I am a fair man) prejudices, incident to being born and bred—well born of course I mean, not recognizing any other form of birth—what a position, to stand there keeping the back of a British Socialist dry!

But there is no escaping these anomalies if you caravan; they crop up continually; and however much you try to dam them out, the waters of awkwardly familiar situations constantly break through and set all your finer feelings on edge. Fain would I have let the rain work its will on Jellaby's back, but what about the sausages? As they turned and twisted in the pan, obedient to his guiding fork, I could not find it in me to let a drop of rain mar that melodious fizzling. So I stood there doing my best, glad at least I was spared being compromised owing to the absence of my friends, while the two other gentlemen warmed up the potatoes over the fire preparatory to converting them into *purée*, and the ladies in the caravans were employed, judging by the fragrance, in making coffee.

In spite of the rain a small crowd had collected and was leaning on the gate. Their faces were divided between wonder and pity; but this was an expression we had now got used to, for except on fine days every face we met at once assumed it, unless the face belonged to a little boy, when it was covered instead with what seemed to be glee and was certainly animation, the animation being apparently not infrequently inspired by a train of thought which led up to, after we had passed, a calling out and a throwing of stones.

"You'll see these turn brown soon," said Jellaby, crouching over his sausages and pursuing them untiringly round and round the pan with a fork.

"Yes," said I; "and a pleasant sight too when one is hungry."

"By Jove, yes," said he; "caravaning makes one appreciate things, doesn't it?"

"Yes," said I, "whenever there are any."

In silence he continued to pursue with his fork.

"They are very pink," said I, after some minutes.

"Yes," said he.

"Do you think so much—such unceasing—exercise is good for them?"

"Well, but I must get them brown all round."

"They are, however, still altogether pink."

"Patience, my dear Baron. You'll soon see."

I watched him in a further silence of some minutes.

"Do you, Jellaby," I then inquired, "really understand how best to treat a sausage?"

"Oh, yes; they're bound to turn brown soon."

"But see how obstinately they continue pink. Would it not be wise, considering the lateness, to call my wife and desire her to cook them?"

"What! The Baroness in this wet stubble?" said he, with such energy that I deemed the moment come for the striking of the blow that had been so long impending.

"Do you, Jellaby," I then inquired, *"really understand how best to treat a sausage?"*

"When a lady," I said with great distinctness, "has cooked for fourteen years without interruption—ever since, that is, she was sixteen—one may safely at thirty leave it always in her hands."

"Monstrous," said he.

At first I thought he was in some way alluding to her age, and to the fact that he had been deceived into supposing her young.

"What is monstrous?" I inquired, as he did not add anything.

"Why should she cook for us? Why should she come out in the wet to cook for us? Why should any woman cook for fourteen years without interruption?"

"She did it joyfully, Jellaby, for the comfort and sustenance of her husband, as every virtuous woman ought."

"I think," said he, "it would choke me."

"What would choke you?"

"Food produced by the unceasing labour of my wife. Why should she be treated as a servant when she gets neither wages nor the privilege of giving notice and going away?"

"No wages? Her wages, young gentleman, are the knowledge that she has done her duty to her husband."

"Thin, thin," he murmured, digging his fork into the nearest sausage.

"And as for going away, I must say I am surprised you should connect such a thought with any respectable lady."

Indeed, what he said was so ridiculous, and so young, and so on the face of it unmarried that in my displeasure I moved the umbrella for a moment far enough to one side to allow the larger drops collected on its metal tips to fall on to his bent and practically collarless (he wore a flannel shirt with some loose apology for a collar of the same material) neck.

"Hullo," he said, "you're letting the sausages get wet."

"You talk, Jellaby," I resumed, obliged to hold the umbrella on its original position again and forcing myself to speak calmly, "in great ignorance. What can you know of marriage? Whereas I am very fully qualified to speak, for I have had, as you may not perhaps know, the families scheduled in the *Gotha Almanach* being unlikely to come within the range of your acquaintance, two wives."

I must of course have been mistaken, but I did fancy I heard him say, partly concealing it under his breath, "God help them," and naturally greatly startled I said very stiffly, "I beg your pardon?"

But he only mumbled unintelligibly over his pan, so that no doubt I had done him an injustice; and the sausages being, as he said (not without a note of defiance in his voice), ready, which meant that for some reason or other they had one and all come out of their skins (which lay still pink in limp and lifeless groups about the pan), and were now mere masses of minced meat, he rose up from his crouching attitude, ladled them by means of a spoon into a dish, requested my umbrella's continued company, and proceeded to make the round of caravans, holding them up at each window in turn while the ladies helped themselves from within.

"And us?" I said at last, for when he had been to the third he began to return once more to the first—"and us?"

"Us will get some presently," he replied—I cannot think grammatically—holding up the already sadly reduced dish at the Ilsa's window.

Frau von Eckthum, however, smiled and shook her head, and very luckily the sick fledgling, so it appeared, still turned with loathing from all nourishment. Lord Sigismund was following us round with the potato *puree*, and in return for being waited on in this manner, a manner that can only be described as hand and foot, Edelgard deigned to give us cups of coffee through her window and Mrs. Menzies-Legh slices of buttered bread through hers.

Perhaps my friends will have noted the curious insistence and patience with which we drank coffee. I can hear them say, "Why this continuous coffee?" I can hear them also inquire, "Where was the wine, then, that beverage for gentlemen, or the beer, that beverage for the man of muscle and marrow?"

The answer to that is, Nowhere. None of them drank anything more convivial than water or that strange liquid, seemingly so alert and full of promise, ginger-beer, and to drink alone was not quite what I cared for. There was Frau von Eckthum, for instance, looking on, and she had very early in the tour expressed surprise that anybody should ever want to drink what she called intoxicants.

"My dear lady," I had protested—tenderly, though—"you would not have a man drink milk?"

"Why not?" said she; but even when she is stupid she does not for an instant cease to be attractive.

On the march I often could make up for abstinences in between by going inside the inns outside which the gritless others lunched on bananas and milk, and privately drinking an honest mug of beer.

You, my friends, will naturally inquire, "Why privately?"

Well, I was in the minority, a position that tends to take the kick, at least the open kick, out of a man—in fact, since my wife's desertion I occupied the entire minority all by myself; then I am a considerate man, and do not like to go against the grain (other people's grain), remembering how much I feel it when other people go against mine; and finally (and this you will not understand, for I know you do not like her), there was always Frau von Eckthum looking on.

CHAPTER XI

THAT night the rain changed its character, threw off the pretence of being only a mist, and poured in loud cracking drops on to the roof of the caravan. It made such a noise that it actually woke me, and lighting a match I discovered that it was three o'clock and that why I had had an unpleasant dream—I thought I was having a bath—was that the wet was coming through the boarding and descending in slow and regular splashings on my head.

This was melancholy. At three o'clock a man has little initiative, and I was unable to think of putting my pillow at the bottom of the bed where there was no wet, though in the morning, when I found Edelgard had done so, it instantly occurred to me. But after all if I had thought of it one of my ends was bound in any case to get wet, and though my head would have been dry my feet (if doctors are to be believed far more sensitive organs) would have got the splashings. Besides, I was not altogether helpless in the face of this new calamity: after shouting to Edelgard to tell her I was awake and, although presumably indoors, yet somehow in the rain—for indeed it surprised me—and receiving no answer, either because she did not hear, owing to the terrific noise on the roof, or because she would not hear, or because she was asleep, I rose and fetched my sponge bag (a new and roomy one), emptied it of its contents, and placed my head inside it in their stead.

I submit this was resourcefulness. A sponge bag is but a little thing, and to remember it is also but a little thing, but it is little things such as these that have won the decisive battles of the world and are the finger-posts to the qualities in a man that would win more decisive battles if only he were given a chance. Many a great general, many a great victory, have been lost to our Empire owing to its inability to see the promise contained in some of its majors and its consequent dilatoriness in properly promoting them.

How the rain rattled. Even through the muffling sponge bag I could hear it. The thought of Jellaby in his watery tent on such a night, gradually, as the hours went on, ceasing to lie and beginning to float, would have amused me if it had not been that poor Lord Sigismund, *nolens volens*, must needs float too.

From this thought I somehow got back to my previous ones, and the longer I lay wakeful the more pronouncedly stern did they become. I am as loyal and loving a son of the Fatherland as it will ever in all human probability beget, but what son after a proper period of probation does not like the ring on the finger, the finer raiment, the paternal embrace, and the invitation to dinner? In other words (and quitting parable), what son after having served his time among such husks as majors does not like promotion to the fatted calves of colonels? For some time past I have been expecting it every day, and if it is not soon granted it is possible that my patience may be so changed to anger that I shall refuse to remain at my post and shall send in my resignation; though I must say I should like a hit at the English first.

Once embarked on these reflections I could not again close my eyes, and lay awake for the remaining hours of the night with as great a din going on as ever I heard in my life. I have described this—the effect of heavy rain when you are in a caravan—in that portion of the narrative dealing with the night on Grip's Common, so need only repeat that it resembles nothing so much as a sharp pelting with unusually hard stones. Edelgard, if she did indeed sleep, must be of an almost terrifying toughness, for the roof on which this pelting was going on was but a few inches from her head.

As the cold dawn crept in between the folds of our window-curtains and the noise had in no way abated, I began very seriously to wonder how I could possibly get up and go out and eat breakfast under such conditions. There was my mackintosh, and I also had galoshes, but I could not appear before Frau von Eckthum in the sponge bag, and yet that was the only sensible covering for my head. But what after all could galoshes avail in such a flood? The stubble field, I felt, could be nothing by then but a lake; no fire could live in it; no stove but would be swamped. Were it not better, if such was to be the weather, to return to London, take rooms in some water-tight boarding-house, and frequent the dryness of museums? Of course it would be better. Better? Must not anything in the world be better than that which is the worst?

But, alas, I had been made to pay beforehand for the Elsa, and had taken the entire responsibility for her and her horse's safe return and even if I could bring myself to throw away such a sum as I had disbursed one cannot leave a caravan lying about as though it were what our neighbours across the Vosges call a mere bagatelle. It is not a bagatelle. On the contrary, it is a huge and complicated mechanism that must go with you like the shell on the poor snail's back wherever you go. There is no escape from it, once you have started, day or night. Where was Panthers by now, Panthers with its kind and helpful little lady? Heaven alone knew, after all our zigzagging. Find it by myself I certainly could not, for not only had we zigzagged in obedience to the caprices of Mrs. Menzies-Legh, but I had walked most of the time as a man in a dream, heeding nothing particularly except my growing desire to sit down.

I wondered grimly as six o'clock drew near, the hour at which the rest of the company usually burst into activity, whether there would be many exclamations of healthy and jolly that day. There is a point, I should say, at which a thing or a condition becomes so excessively healthy and jolly that it ceases to be either. I drew the curtain of my bunk together—for a great upheaval over my head warned me that my wife was going to descend and dress—and feigned slumber. Sleep seemed to me such a safe thing. You cannot make a man rise and do what you consider his duty if he will not wake up. The only free man, I reflected with my eyes tightly shut, is the man who is asleep. Pushing my reflection a little further I saw with a slight start that real freedom and independence are only, then, to be found in the unconscious—a race (or sect; call it what you will) of persons untouched by and above the law. And one step further and I saw with another slight start that perfect freedom, perfect liberty, perfect deliverance from trammels, are only to be found in a person who is not merely unconscious but also dead.

These, of course, as I need not tell my hearers, are metaphysics. I do not often embark on their upsetting billows for I am, principally, a practical man. But on this occasion they were not as fruitless as usual, for the thought of a person dead suggested at once the thought of a person engaged in going through the sickness preliminary to being dead, and a sick man is also to a certain extent free—nobody, that is, can make him get up and go out into the rain and hold his umbrella over Jellaby's back while he concocts his terrible porridge. I decided that I would slightly exaggerate the feelings of discomfort which I undoubtedly felt, and take a day off in the haven of my bed. Let them see to it that the horse was led; a man in bed cannot lead a horse. Nor would it even be an exaggeration, for one who has been wakeful half the night cannot be said to be in normal health. Besides, if you come to that, who is in normal health? I should say no one. Certainly hardly any one. And if you appeal to youth as an instance, what could be younger and yet more convulsed with apparent torment than the newly born infant? Hardly any one, I maintain, is well without stopping during a single whole day. One forgets, by means of the anodynes of work or society or other excitement; but cut off a person's means of doing anything or seeing any one and he will soon find out that at least his head is aching.

When, therefore, Edelgard had reached the stage of tidying the caravan, arranging my clothes, and emptying the water out of the window preparatory to my dressing, I put the curtains aside and beckoned to her and made her understand by dint of much shouting (for the rain still pelted on the roof) that I was feeling very weak and could not get up.

She looked at me anxiously, and pushing up the sponge bag—at which she stared rather stupidly—laid her hand on my forehead. I thought her hand seemed hot, and hoped we were not both going to be ill at the same time. Then she felt my pulse. Then she looked down at me with a worried expression and said—I could not hear it, but knew the protesting shape her mouth assumed: "But Otto———"

I just shook my head and closed my eyes. You cannot make a man open his eyes. Shut them, and you shut out the whole worrying, hurrying world, and enter into a calm cave of peace from which, so long as you keep them shut no one can possibly pull you. I felt she stood there awhile longer looking down at me before putting on her cloak and preparing to face the elements; then the door was unbolted, a gust of wet air came in, the caravan gave a lurch, and Edelgard had jumped into the stubble.

Only for a short time was I able to reflect on her growing agility, and how four days back she could no more jump into stubble or anything else than can other German ladies of good family, and how the costume she had bought in Berlin and which had not fitted her not only without a wrinkle but also with difficulty, seemed gradually to be turning into a misfit, to be widening, to be loosening, and those parts of it which had before been smooth were changing every day into a greater bagginess—I was unable, I say, to think about these things because, worn out, I at last fell asleep.

How long I slept I do not know, but I was very roughly awakened by violent tossings and heavings, and looking hastily through my curtains saw a wet hedge moving past the window.

So we were on the march.

I lay back on my pillow and wondered who was leading my horse. They might at least have brought me some breakfast. Also the motion was extremely disagreeable, and likely to give me a headache. But presently, after a dizzy swoop round, a pause and much talking showed me we had come to a gate, and I understood that we had been getting over the stubble and were now about to rejoin the road. Once on that the motion was not unbearable—not nearly so unbearable, I said to myself, as tramping in the rain; but I could not help thinking it very strange that none of them had thought to give me breakfast, and in my wife the omission was more than strange, it was positively illegal. If love did not bring her to my bedside with hot coffee and perhaps a couple of (lightly boiled) eggs, why did not duty? A fasting man does not mind which brings her, so long as one of them does.

My impulse was to ring the bell angrily, but it died away on my recollecting that there was no bell. The rain, I could see, had now lightened and thinned into a drizzle, and I could hear cheerful talk going on between some persons evidently walking just outside. One voice seemed to be Jellaby's, but how could it be he who was cheerful after the night he must have had? And the other was a woman's—no doubt, I thought bitterly, Edelgard's, who, warmed herself and invigorated by a proper morning meal, cared nothing that her husband should be lying there within a stone's throw like a cold, neglected tomb.

Presently, instead of the hedge, the walls and gates of gardens passed the window, and then came houses, singly at first, but soon joining on to each other in an uninterrupted string, and raising myself on my elbow and putting two and two together, I decided that this must be Wadhurst.

It was. To my surprise about the middle of the village the caravan stopped, and raising myself once more on my elbow I was forced immediately to sink back again, for I encountered a row of eager faces pressed against the pane with eyes rudely staring at the contents of the caravan, which, of course, included myself as soon as I came into view from between the curtains of the berth.

This was very disagreeable. Again I instinctively and frantically sought the bell that was not there. How long was I to be left thus in the street of a village with my window-curtains unclosed and the entire population looking in? I could not get out and close them myself, for I am staunch to the night attire, abruptly terminating, that is still, thank heaven, characteristic during the hours of darkness of every honest German gentleman: in other words, I do not dress myself, as the English do, in a coat and trousers in order to go to bed. But on this occasion I wished that I did, for then I could have leaped out of my berth and drawn the curtains in an instant myself, and the German attire allows no margin for the leaping out of berths. As it was, all I could do was to lie there holding the berth-curtains carefully together until such time as it should please my dear wife to honour me with a visit.

This she did after, I should say, at least half an hour had passed, with the completely composed face of one who has no reproaches to make herself, and a cup of weak tea in one hand and a small slice of dry toast on a plate in the other, though she knows I never touch tea and that it is absurd to offer a large-framed, fine man one piece of toast with no butter on it for his breakfast.

"What are we stopping for?" I at once asked on her appearing.

"For breakfast," said she.

"What?"

"We are having it in the inn to-day because of the wet. It is so nice, Otto. Table-napkins and everything. And flowers in the middle. And nothing to wash up afterward. What a pity you can't be there! Are you better?"

"Better?" I repeated, with a note of justified wrath in my voice, for the thought of the others all enjoying themselves, sitting at a good meal on proper chairs in a room out of the reach of fresh air, naturally upset me. Why had they not told me? Why, in the name of all that was dutiful, had *she* not told me?

"I thought you were asleep," said she when I inquired what grounds she had for the omission.

"So I was, but that——"

"And I know you don't like being disturbed when you are," said she, lamely as I considered, for naturally it depends on what one is disturbed for—of course I would have got up if I had known.

"I will not drink such stuff," I said, pushing the cup away. "Why should I live on tepid water and butterless toast?"

"But—didn't you say you were ill?" she asked, pretending to be surprised. "I thought when one is ill——"

"Kindly draw those curtains," I said, for the crowd was straining every nerve to see and hear, "and remove this stuff. You had better," I added, when the faces had been shut out, "return to your own breakfast. Do not trouble about me. Leave me here to be ill or not. It does not matter. You are my wife, and bound by law to love me, but I will make no demands on you. Leave me here alone, and return to your breakfast."

"But, Otto, I couldn't stay in here with you before. The poor horse would never——"

"I know, I know. Put the horse before your husband. Put anything and anybody before your husband. Leave him here alone. Do not trouble. Go back to your own, no doubt, excellent breakfast."

"But Otto, why are you so cross?"

"Cross? When a man is ill and neglected, if he dare say a word he is cross. Take this stuff away. Go back to your breakfast. I, at least, am considerate, and do not desire your omelettes and other luxuries to become cold."

"It isn't omelettes," said Edelgard. "Why are you so unreasonable? Won't you really drink this?" And again she held out the cup of straw-coloured tea.

Then I turned my face to the wall, determined that nothing she could say or do should make me lose my temper. "Leave me," was all I said, with a backward wave of the hand.

She lingered a moment, as she had done in the morning, then went out. Somebody outside took the cup from her and helped her down the ladder, and a conviction that it was Jellaby caused such a wave of just anger to pass over me that, being now invisible to the crowd, I leaped out of my berth and began quickly and wrathfully to dress. Besides, as she opened the door a most attractive odour of I do not know what, but undoubtedly something to do with breakfast in the inn, had penetrated into my sick chamber.

"'Ere 'e is," said one of the many children in the crowd, when I emerged dressed from the caravan and prepared to descend the steps; "'ere's 'im out of the bed."

I frowned.

"Don't 'e get up late?" said another.

I frowned again.

"Ere 'e is"

"Don't 'e look different now?" said a third.

I deepened my frown.

"Takes it easy 'e do, don't 'e," said a fourth, "in spite of pretendin' to be a poor gipsy."

I got down the steps and elbowed my way sternly through them to the door of the inn. There I paused an instant on the threshold and faced them, frowning at them as individually as I could.

"I have been ill," I said briefly.

But in England they have neither reverence nor respect for an officer. In my own country if any one dared to speak to me or of me in that manner in the street I would immediately draw my sword and punish him, for he would in my person have insulted the Emperor's Majesty, whose uniform I wore; and it would be useless for him to complain, for no magistrate would listen to him. But in England if anybody wants to make a target of you, a target you become for so long as his stock of wit (heaven save the mark!) lasts. Of course the crowd in Wadhurst must have known. However much my mackintosh disguised me it was evident that I was an officer, for there is no mistaking the military bearing; but for their own purposes they pretended they did not, and when therefore turning to them with severe dignity I said: "I have been ill," what do you think they said? They said, "Yah."

For a moment I supposed, with some surprise I confess, that they were acquainted with the German tongue, but a glance at their faces showed me that the expression must be English and rude. I turned abruptly and left these boors: it is not part of my business to teach a foreign nation manners.

My frowns, however, were smoothed when I entered the comfortable breakfast-room and was greeted with a pleasant chorus of welcome and inquiries.

Frau von Eckthum made room for me beside her, and herself ministered to my wants. Mrs. Menzies-Legh laughed and praised me for my sensibleness in getting up instead of giving way. The breakfast was abundant and excellent. And I discovered that it was the ever kind and thoughtful Lord Sigismund who had helped Edelgard out of the caravan, Jellaby being harmlessly occupied writing picture postcards to (I suppose) his constituents.

By the time I had had my third cup of coffee—so beneficial is the effect of that blessed bean—I was able silently to forgive Edelgard and be ready to overlook all her conduct since the camp by the Medway and start fresh again; and when toward eleven o'clock we resumed the march, a united and harmonious band (for the child Jumps was also that day restored to health and her friends) we found the rain gone and the roads being dried up with all the efficiency and celerity of an unclouded August sun.

That was a pleasant march. The best we had had. It may have been the weather, which was also the best we had had, or it may have been the country, which was undeniably pretty in its homely unassuming way—nothing, of course, to be compared with what we would have gazed at from the topmost peak of the Rigi or from a boat on the bosom of an Italian lake, but very nice in its way—or it may have been because Frau von Eckthum walked with me, or because Lord Sigismund told me that next day being Sunday we were going to rest in the camp we got to that night till Monday, and dine on Sunday at the nearest inn, or, perhaps it was all this mingled together that made me feel so pleasant.

Take away annoyances and worry, and I am as good-natured a man as you will find. More, I can enjoy anything, and am ready with a jest about almost anything. It is the knowledge that I am really so good-humoured that principally upsets me when Edelgard or other circumstances force me into a condition of vexation unnatural to me. I do not wish to be vexed. I do not wish ever to be disagreeable. And it is, I think, down-right wrong of people to force a human being who does not wish it to be so. That is one of the reasons why I enjoyed the company of Frau von Eckthum. She brought out what was best in me, what I may be pardoned for calling the perfume of my better self, because though it contains the suggestion that my better self is a flower-like object it also implies that she was the warming and vivifying and scent-extracting sun.

There is a dew-pond at the top of one of the hills we walked up that day (at least Mrs. Menzies-Legh said it was a dew-pond, and that the water in it was not water at all but dew, though naturally I did not believe her—what sensible man would?) and by its side in the shade of an oak tree Frau von Eckthum and I sat while the three horses went down to fetch up the third caravan, nominally taking care of those already up but really resting in that pretty nook without bothering about them, for of all things in the world a horseless caravan is surely most likely to keep quiet. So we rested, and I amused her. I really do not know about what in particular, but I know I succeeded, for her oh's became quite animated, and were placed with such dexterous intelligence that each one contained volumes.

She was interested in everything, but especially so in what I said about Jellaby and his doctrines, of which I made great fun. She listened with the most earnest attention to my exposure of the fallacies with which he is riddled, and became at last so evidently convinced that I almost wished the young gentleman had been there too to hear me.

Altogether an agreeable, invigorating day; and when, about three o'clock, we found a good camping ground in a wide field sheltered to the north by a copse and rising ground, and dropping away in front of us to a most creditable and extensive view, for the second time since I left Panthers I was able to suspect that caravaning might not be entirely without its commendable points.

CHAPTER XII

WE supped that night beneath the stars with the field dropping downward from our feet into the misty purple of the Sussex Weald.

What we had for supper was chicken and rice and onions, and very excellent it was. The wind had gone, and it was cold. It was like a night in North Germany, where the wind sighs all day long and at sunset it suddenly grows coldly and clearly calm.

These are quotations from a conversation I overheard between Frau von Eckthum (oddly loquacious that night) and Jellaby, who both sat near where I was eating my supper, supposed to be eating theirs but really letting it spoil while they looked down at the Sussex Weald (I wish I knew what a Weald is: Kent had one too) and she described the extremely flat and notoriously dull country round Storchwerder.

Indeed I would not have recognized it from her description, and yet I know it every bit as well as she can. Blue air, blue sky, blue water, and the flash of white wings—that was how she described it, and poor Jellaby was completely taken in and murmured "Beautiful, beautiful" in his foolish slow voice, and forgot to eat his chicken and rice while it was hot, and little guessed that she had laughed at him with me a few hours before.

I listened, amused but tolerant. We must not keep a pretty lady too exactly to the truth. The first part of this chapter is a quotation from what I heard her say (excepting one sentence), but my hearers must take my word for it that it did not sound anything like as silly as one might suppose. Everything depends on the utterer. Frau von Eckthum's quasi-poetical way of describing the conduct of our climate had an odd attractiveness about it that I did not find, for instance, in my dear wife's utterances when she too, which she at this time began to do with increasing frequency, indulged in the quasi-poetic. Quasi-poetic I and other plain men take to be the violent tearing of such a word as rolling from its natural place and applying it to the plains and fields round Storchwerder. A ship rolls, but fields, I am glad to say, do not. You may also with perfect propriety talk about a rolling-pin in connection with the kitchen, or of a rolling stone in connection with moss. Of course I know that we all on suitable occasions make use of exclamations of an appreciative nature, such as *colossal* and *grossartig*, but that is brief and business-like, it is what is expected of us, and it is a duty quickly performed and almost perfunctory, with one eye on the waiter and the restaurant behind; but slow raptures, prolonged ones, raptures beaten out thin, are not in my way and had not till then been in Edelgard's way either. The English are flimsier than we are, thinner blooded, more feminine, more finnicking. There are no restaurants or *Bierhalle* wherever there is a good view to drown their admiration in wholesome floods of beer, and not being provided with this natural stopper it fizzles on to interminableness. Why, Jellaby I could see not only let his supper get stone cold but forgot to eat it at all in his endeavour to outdo Frau von Eckthum's style in his replies, and then Edelgard must needs join in too, and say (I heard her) that life in Storchwerder was a dusty, narrow life, where you could not see the *liebe Gott* because of other people's chimney-pots.

Greatly shocked (for I am a religious man) I saved her from further excesses by a loud call for more supper, and she got up mechanically to attend to my wants.

Jellaby, however, whose idea seemed to be that a woman is never to do anything (I wonder who is to do anything, then?) forestalled her with the sudden nimbleness he displayed on such occasions, so surprising in combination with his clothes and general slackness, and procured me a fresh helping.

I thanked him politely, but could not repress some irony in my bow as I apologized for disturbing him.

"Shall I hold your plate while you eat?" he said.

"Why, Jellaby?" I asked, mildly astonished.

"Wouldn't it be even more comfortable if I did?" he asked; and then I perceived that he was irritated, no doubt because I had got most of the cushions, and he, Quixotic as he is, had given up his to my wife, on whom it was entirely thrown away for she has always assured me she actually prefers hard seats.

Well, of course there were few things in the world quite so unimportant as Jellaby's irritation, so I just looked pleasant and at the food he had brought me; but I did not get another evening with Frau von Eckthum. She sat immovable on the edge of the slope with my wife and Jellaby, talking in tones that became more and more subdued as dusk deepened into night and stars grew hard and shiny.

They all seemed subdued. They even washed up in whispers. And afterward the very nondescripts lay stretched out quite quietly by the glowing embers of Lord Sigismund's splendid fire listening to Menzies-Legh's and Lord Sidge's talk, in which I did not join for it was on the subject they were so fond of, the amelioration of the condition of those dull and undeserving persons, the poor.

I put my plate where somebody would see it and wash it, and retired to the shelter of a hedge and the comfort of a cigar. The three figures on the edge of the hill became gradually almost mute. Not a leaf in my hedge stirred. It was so still that people talking at the distant farm where we had procured our chickens could almost be understood, and a dog barking somewhere far away down in the Weald seemed quite threateningly near. It was really extraordinarily still; and the stillest thing of all was that strange example of the Englishwoman grafted on what was originally such excellent German stock, Mrs. Menzies-Legh, sitting a yard or two away from me, her hands clasped round her knees, her face turned up as though she were studying astronomy.

I do not suppose she moved for half an hour. Her profile seemed to shine white in the dusk with lines that reminded me somehow of a cameo there is in a red velvet case lying on the table in our comfortable drawing-room at Storchwerder, and the remembrance brought a slight twinge of home-sickness with it. I shook this off, and fell to watching her, and for the amusement of an idle hour lazily reconstructed from the remnants before me what her appearance must have been ten years before in her prime, when there were at least undulations, at least suggestions that here was a woman and not a kind of elongated boy.

The line of her face is certainly quite passable; and that night in the half darkness it was quite as passable as any I have seen on a statue—objects in which I have never been able to take much interest. It is probable she used to be beautiful. Used to be beautiful? What is the value of that? Just a snap of the fingers, and nothing more. If women would but realize that once past their first youth their only chance of pleasing is to be gentle and rare of speech, tactful, deft—in one word, apologetic, they would be more likely to make a good impression on reasonable men such as myself. I did not wish to quarrel with Mrs. Menzies-Legh and yet her tongue and the way she used it put my back up (as the British say) to a height it never attains in the placid pools of feminine intercourse in Storchwerder.

To see her sit so silent and so motionless was unusual. Was she regretting, perhaps, her lost youth? Was she feeling bitter at her inability to attract me, a man within two yards of her, sufficiently for me to take the trouble to engage her in conversation? No doubt. Well—poor thing! I am sorry for women, but there is nothing to be done since Nature has decreed they shall grow old.

I got up and shook out the folds of my mackintosh—a most useful garment in those damp places—and threw away the end of my cigar. "I am now going to retire for the night," I explained, as she turned her head at my rustling, "and if you take my advice you will not sit here till you get rheumatism."

She looked at me as though she did not hear. In that light her appearance was certainly quite passable: quite as passable as that of any of the statues they make so much fuss about; and then of course with proper eyes instead of blank spaces, and eyes garnished with that speciality of hers, the ridiculously long eyelashes. But I knew what she was like in broad day, I knew how thin she was, and I was not to be imposed upon by tricks of light; so I said in a matter of fact manner, seizing the opportunity for gentle malice in order to avenge myself a little for her repeated and unjustified attacks on me, "You will not be wise to sit there longer. It is damp, and you and I are hardly as young as we were, you know."

Any normal woman, gentle as this was, would have shrivelled. Instead she merely agreed in an absent way that it was dewy, and turned up her face to the stars again.

"Looking for the Great Bear, eh?" I remarked, following her gaze as I buttoned my wrap.

She continued to gaze, motionless. "No, but—don't you see? At Christ Whose glory fills the skies," she said—both profanely and senselessly, her face in that light exactly like the sort of thing one sees in the windows of churches, and her voice as though she were half asleep.

So I hied me (poetry being the fashion) to my bed, and lay awake in it for some time being sorry for Menzies-Legh, for really no man can possibly like having a creepy wife.

But (luckily) *autres temps autres mœurs,* as our unbalanced but sometimes felicitous neighbours across the Vosges say, and next morning the poetry of the party was, thank heaven, clogged by porridge.

It always was at breakfast. They were strangely hilarious then, but never poetic. Poetry developed later in the day as the sun and their spirits sank together, and flourished at its full growth when there were stars or a moon. That morning, our first Sunday, a fresh breeze blew up from the Weald below and a cloudless sun dazzled us as it fell on the white cloth of the table set out in the middle of the field by somebody—I expect it was Mrs. Menzies-Legh—who wanted to make the most of the sun, and we had to hold on our hats with one hand and shade our eyes with the other while we ate.

Uncomfortable? Of course it was uncomfortable. Let no one who loves to be comfortable ever caravan. Neither let any one who loves order and decency do so. They may take it from me that there is never any order, and even less frequently is there any decency. I can give you an example from that Sunday morning. I was sitting at the table with the ladies, on a seat (as usual) too low for me, and that (also as usual) slanted on the uneven ground, with my feet slightly too cold in the damp grass and my head slightly too hot in the bright sun, and the general feeling of subtle discomfort and ruffledness that is one of the principal characteristics of this form of pleasure-taking, when I saw (and so did the ladies) Jellaby emerge from his tent—in his shirt sleeves if you please—and fastening up a mirror on the roof of his canvas lair proceed then and there in the middle of the field to lather his face and then to shave it.

Edelgard, of course, true to her early training, at once cast down her eyes and was careful to keep them averted during the remainder of the meal, but nobody else seemed to mind; indeed, Mrs. Menzies-Legh got out her camera and focussing him with deliberate care snap-shotted him.

Were these people getting blunted as the days passed to the refinements and necessary precautions of social intercourse? I had been stirred to much silent indignation by the habit of the gentlemen of walking in their shirt sleeves, and had not yet got used to that, but to see Jellaby dressing in an open field was a little more than I could endure in silence. For if, I asked myself rapidly, Jellaby dresses (shaving being a part of dressing) out-of-doors in the morning, what is to prevent his doing the opposite in the evening? Where is the line? Where is the logical limit? We had now been three days out, and we had already got to this. Where, I thought, should we have got to in another six? Where should we be by, say, the following Sunday?

I cannot think a promiscuous domesticity desirable, and am one of those who strongly disapprove of that worst example of it, the mixed bathing or *Familienbad* which blots with practically unclothed Jews of either sex our otherwise decent coasts. Never have I allowed Edelgard to indulge in it, nor have I done so myself. It is a deplorable spectacle. We used to sit and watch it for hours, in a condition of ever-increasing horror and disgust—it was quite difficult to find seats sometimes, so many of our friends were there being disgusted too.

But these denizens of the deep at the points where the deep was a *Familienbad* were, as I have said, chiefly Jews and their Jewesses, and what can you expect? Jellaby, however, in spite of his other infirmities, was not yet a Jew; he was everything else I think, but that crowning infamy had up to then been denied him.

But not to be one and yet to behave with the laxness of one within view of the rest of the party was very inexcusable. "Are there no hedges to this field?" I cried in indignant sarcasm, looking pointedly at each of its four hedges in turn and raising my voice so that he could hear.

"Oh, Baron dear, it's Sunday," said Mrs. Menzies-Legh, no longer a rather nice-looking if irreverent cameo in a velvet case, but full of morning militancy. "Don't be cross till to-morrow. Save it up, or what will you do on Monday?"

"Be, I trust, just as capable of distinguishing between the permitted and the non-permitted as I am to-day," was my ready retort.

"Oh, oh," said Mrs. Menzies-Legh, shaking her head and smiling as though she were talking to a child or a feeble-minded; and turning her camera on to me she took my photograph.

"Pray why," I inquired with justifiable heat, "should I be photographed without my consent?"

"Because," she said, "you look so deliciously cross. I want to have you in my scrap-book like that. You looked then exactly like a baby I know."

"Which baby?" I asked, frowning and at a loss how to meet this kind of thing conversationally. And there was Edelgard, all ears; and if a wife sees her husband being treated disrespectfully by other women is it not very likely that she soon will begin to treat him so herself? "Which baby?" I asked; but knew myself inadequate.

"Oh, a perfectly respectable baby," said Mrs. Menzies-Legh carelessly, putting her camera down and going on with her breakfast, "but irritable and exacting about things like bottles."

"But I do not see what I have to do with bottles," I said nettled.

"Oh, no—you haven't. Only it looks at its nurse just like you did then if they're late, or not full enough."

"But I did not look at its nurse," I said angrily, becoming still more so as they all (including my wife) laughed.

I rose abruptly. "I will go and smoke," I said.

Of course I saw what she meant about the nurse the moment I had spoken, but it is inexcusable to laugh at a man because he does not immediately follow the sense (or rather the senselessness) of a childishly skipping conversation. I am as ready as any one to laugh at really amusing phrases or incidents, but being neither a phrase nor an incident myself I do not see why I should be laughed at. Surely it is unworthy of grown men and women to laugh at each other in the way silly children do? It is ruin to the graces of social intercourse, to the courtliness that should uninterruptedly distinguish the well-born. But there was a childish spirit pervading the whole party (with the exception of myself) that seemed to increase as the days went by, a spirit of unreasoning glee and mischievousness which I believe is characteristic of very young and very healthy children. Even Edelgard was daily becoming more calf-like, as we say, daily descending nearer to the level occupied at first only by the two nondescripts, that level at which you begin to play idiotic and heating games like the one the English call Blind Man's Buff (an obviously foolish name, for what is buff?) and which we so much more sensibly call Blind Cow. Therefore I, having no intention at my age and in my position of joining in puerilities or even of seeming to countenance them by my presence, said abruptly, "I will smoke"—and strode away to do it.

One of the ladies called after me to inquire if I were not going to church with them, but I pretended not to hear and strode on toward the shelter of the hedge, giving Jellaby as I passed him such a look as would have caused any one not overgrown with the leather substitute for skin peculiar to persons who set order, morals, and religion at defiance, to creep confounded into his tent and stay there till his face was ready and his collar on. He, however, called out with the geniality born of brazenness, that it was a jolly morning; of which, of course, I took no notice.

In the dry ditch beneath the hedge on the east side of the field sat Lord Sigismund beside his *batterie de cuisine*, watching over, with unaccountable and certainly misplaced kindness, the porridge and the coffee that were presently to be Jellaby's. While he watched he smoked his pipe, stroked his dog, and hummed snatches of what I supposed were psalms with the pleasant humming of the good, the happy, and the well-born.

Near him lay Menzies-Legh, his dark and sinister face bent over a book. He nodded briefly in response to my lifted hat and morning salutation, while Lord Sigismund, full as ever of the graciousness of noble birth, asked me if I had had a good night.

"A good night, and an excellent breakfast, thanks to you, Lord Sidge," I replied; the touch of playfulness contained in the shortened name lightening the courteous correctness of my bow as I arranged myself next to him in the ditch.

Menzies-Legh got up and went away. It was characteristic of him that he seemed always to be doing that. I hardly ever joined him but he was reminded by my approach of something he ought to be doing and went away to do it. I mentioned this to Edelgard during the calm that divided one difference of opinion from another, and she said he never did that when she joined him.

"Dear wife," I explained, "you have less power to remind him of unperformed duties than I possess."

"I suppose I have," said Edelgard.

"And it is very natural that it should be so. Power, of whatever sort it may be, is a masculine attribute. I do not wish to see my little wife with any."

"Neither do I," said she.

"Ah—there speaks my own good little wife."

"I mean, not if it is that sort."

"What sort, dear wife?"

"The sort that reminds people whenever I come that it is time they went."

She looked at me with the odd look that I observed for the first time during our English holiday. Often have I seen it since, but I cannot recollect having seen it before. I, noticing that somehow we did not understand each other, patted her kindly on the shoulder, for, of course, she cannot always quite follow me, though I must say she manages very creditably as a rule.

"Well, well," I said, patting her, "we will not quibble. It is a good little wife, is it not?" And I raised her chin by means of my forefinger, and kissed her.

This, however, is a digression. I suppose it is because I am unfolding my literary wings for the first time that I digress so frequently. At least I am aware of it, which is in itself, I should say, a sign of literary instinct. My Muse has been, so to speak, kept in bed without stopping till middle age, and is now suddenly called upon to get up and go for a walk. Such a muse must inevitably stagger a little at first. I will, however, endeavour to curb these staggerings, for I perceive that I have already written more than can be conveniently read aloud in one evening, and though I am willing the same friends should come on two, I do not know that I care to see them on as many as three. Besides, think of all the sandwiches.

(This last portion of the narrative, from "one evening" to "sandwiches" will, of course, be omitted in public.)

I will, therefore, not describe my conversation with Lord Sigismund in the ditch beyond saying that it was extremely interesting, and conducted on his side (and I hope on mine) with the social skill of a perfect gentleman.

It was brought to an end by the arrival of Jellaby and his dog, which was immediately pounced on by Lord Sigismund's dog, who very properly resented his uninvited approach, and they remained inextricably mixed together for what seemed an eternity of yells, the yells rending the Sabbath calm and mingling with the distant church bells, and all proceeding from Jellaby's dog, while Lord Sigismund's, a true copy of his master, did that which he had to do with the silent self-possession of, if I may so express it, a dog of the world.

The entire company of caravaners, including old James, ran up with cries and whistling to try to separate them, and at last Jellaby, urged on I suppose to deeds of valour by knowing the eyes of the ladies upon him, made a mighty effort and tore them asunder, himself getting torn along his hand as the result.

Menzies-Legh helped Lord Sigismund to drag away the naturally infuriated bull-terrier, and Jellaby, looking round, asked me to hold his dog while he went and washed his hand. I thought this a fair instance of the brutal indifference to other people's tastes that characterizes the British nation. Why did he not ask old James, who was standing there doing nothing? Yet what was I to do? There were the ladies looking on, among them Edelgard, motionless, leaving me to my fate, though if either of us knows anything about dogs it is she who does. Jellaby had got the beast by the collar, so I thought perhaps holding him by the tail would do. It was true it was the merest stump, but at least it was at the other end. I therefore grasped it, though with no little trouble, for, for some unknown reason, just as my hand approached it, it began to wag.

"No, no—catch hold of the collar. He's all right, he won't do anything to you," said Jellaby, grinning and keeping his wounded hand well away from him while the nondescripts ran to fetch water.

The brute was quiet for a moment, and under the circumstances I do think Edelgard might have helped. She knows I cannot bear dogs. If she had held his head I would not have minded going on holding his tail, and at home she would have made herself useful as a matter of course. Here, however, she did nothing of the sort, but stood tearing up a perfectly good, clean handkerchief into strips in order, forsooth, to render that assistance to Jellaby which she denied her own husband. I did take the dog by the collar, there being no other course open to me, and was thankful to find that he was too tired and too much hurt to do anything to me. But I have never been a dog lover, carefully excluding them from my flat in Storchwerder, and selling the one Edelgard had had as a girl and wanted to saddle me with on her marriage. I remember how long it took, she being then still composed of very raw material, to make her understand I had married her and not her *Dachshund*. Will it be believed that her only answer to my arguments was a repeated parrot-like cry of "But he is so sweet!" A feeble plea, indeed, to set against the logic of my reasons. She shed tears, I remember, in quantities more suited to fourteen than twenty-four (as I pointed out to her), but later on did acknowledge, in answer to my repeated inquiries, that the furniture and carpets were, no doubt, the better for it, though for a long time she had a tendency which I found some difficulty in repressing, to make tiresomely plaintive allusions to the fact that the buyer (I sold the dog by auction) had chanced to be a maker of sausages and she had not happened to meet the dog since in the streets. Also, until I spoke very seriously to her about it, for months she would not touch anything potted, after always having been particularly fond of this type of food.

I soon found myself alone and unheeded with Jellaby's dog, while Jellaby himself, the flattered centre of the entire body of ladies, was having his wound dressed. My wife washed it, Jumps held the bucket, Mrs. Menzies-Legh bound it up, Frau von Eckthum provided one of her own safety pins (I saw her take it out of her blouse), and Jane lent her sash for a sling. As for Lord Sigismund, after having seen to his own dog's wounds (all made by Jellaby's dog) he came back and, with truly Christian goodness, offered to wash and doctor Jellaby's dog. His attitude, indeed, during these dog-fights was only one possible to a person of the very highest breeding. Never a word of reproach, yet it was clear that if Jellaby's dog had not been there there would have been no fighting. And he exhibited a real distress over Jellaby's wound, while Jellaby, thoroughly thick-skinned, laughed and declared he did not feel it; which, no doubt, was true, for that sort of person does not, I am convinced, feel anything like the same amount we others do.

The end of this pleasant Sabbath morning episode was that Jellaby took his dog to the nearest village containing a veterinary surgeon, and Menzies-Legh was found in the ditch almost as green as the surrounding leaves because—will it be believed?—he could never stand the sight of blood!

My hearers will, I am sure, be amused at this. Of course, many Britons must be the same, for it is unlikely that I should have chanced in those few days to meet the solitary instance, and I could hardly repress a hearty laugh at the spectacle of this specimen of England's manhood in a half fainting condition because he had seen a scratch that produced blood. What will he and his kind do on that battle-field of, no doubt, the near future, when the finest army in the world will face them? It will not be scratches that poor Menzies-Legh will have to look at then, and I greatly fear for his complexion.

Everybody ran in different directions in search of brandy. Never have I seen a man so green. He was, at least, ashamed of himself, and finding I was a moment alone with him and he not in a condition to get up and go away, I spoke an earnest word or two about the inevitably effeminating effect on a man of so much poetry-reading and art-admiring and dabbling in the concerns of the poor. Not thus, I explained, did the Spartans spend their time. Not thus did the ancient Romans, during their greatest period, behave. "You feel the situation of the poor, for instance, far more than the poor feel it themselves," I said, "and allow yourself to be worried into alleviating a wretchedness that they are used to, and do not notice. And what, after all, is art? And what, after all, is poetry? And what, if you come to that, is wretchedness? Do not weaken the muscles of your mind by feeding it so constantly on the pap of either your own sentimentality or the sentimentality of others. Pull down these artificial screens. Be robust. Accustom yourself to look at facts without flinching. Imitate the conduct of the modern Japanese, who take their children, as part of their training, to gaze on executions, and on their return cause the rice for their dinner to be served mixed with the crimson juices of the cherry, so that they shall imagine——"

But Menzies-Legh turned yet greener, and fainted away.

CHAPTER XIII

I AM accustomed punctually to discharge my obligations in what may be called celestial directions, holding it to be every man's duty not to put a millstone round a weaker vessel's neck by omitting to set a good example. Also, in the best sense of the word, I am a religious man. Did not Bismarck say, and has not the saying become part and parcel of the marrow of the nation, "We Germans fear God and nothing else in the world"? In exactly, I should say, the same way and degree as Bismarck was, am I religious. At Storchwerder, where I am known, I go to church every alternate Sunday and allow myself to be advised and cautioned by the pastor, willing to admit it is his turn to speak and recognizing that he is paid to do so, but reserving to myself the right to put him and keep him in his proper place during the fourteen secular days that divide these pious oases. Before our daily dinner also I say grace, a rare thing in households where there are no children to look on; and if I do not, as a few of the stricter households do, conduct family prayers every day, it is because I do not like them.

There is, after all, a limit at which duty must retire before a man's personal tastes. We are not solely machines for discharging obligations. I see perfectly clearly that it is most good and essential that one's cook and wife should pray together, and even one's orderly, but I do not see that they require the assistance and countenance of the gentleman of the house while they do it.

I am religious in the best and highest sense of the word, a sense that soars far above family prayers, a sense in no way to be explained, any more than other high things are explainable. The higher you get in the regions of thought the more dumb you become. Also the more quiescent. Doing, as all persons of intellect know, is a very inferior business to thinking, and much more likely to make one hot. But these cool excursions of the intellect are not to be talked about to women and the lower classes. What would happen if they too decided to prefer quiescence? For them creeds and churches are positive necessities, and the plainer and more definite they are the better. The devout poor, the devout mothers of families, how essential they are to the freedom and comfort of the rest. The less you have the more it is necessary that you should be contented, and nothing does this so thoroughly as the doctrine of resignation. It would indeed be an unthinkable calamity if all the uneducated and the feeble-minded, the lower classes and the women, should lose their piety enough to want things. Women, it is true, are fairly safe so long as they have a child once a year, which is Nature's way of keeping them quiet; but it fills me with nothing short of horror when I hear of any discontent among the male portion of the proletariat.

That these people should have a vote is the one mistake that great and peculiarly typical German, the ever-to-be-lamented Bismarck, made. To reflect that power is in the hands of such persons, any power, even the smallest shred of it, alarms me so seriously that if I think of it on a Sunday morning, when perhaps I had decided to omit going to church for once and rest at home while my wife went, I hastily seize my parade helmet and hurry off in a fever of anxiety to help uphold the pillars of society.

Indeed it is of paramount necessity that we should cling to the Church and its teaching; that we should see that our wives cling; that we should insist on the clinging of our servants; and these Sunday morning reflections occurring to me as I look back through the months to that first Sunday out of our Fatherland, I seem to feel as I write (though it is now December and sleeting) the summer breeze blowing over the grass on to my cheek, to hear the small birds (I do not know their names) twittering, and to see Frau von Eckthum coming across the field in the sun and standing before me with her pretty smile and telling me she is going to church and asking whether I will go too. Of course I went too. She really was (and is, in spite of Storchwerder) a most attractive lady.

We went, then, together, Jellaby safely away at the veterinary surgeon's, Edelgard following behind with the two fledglings, who had achieved an unusually clean appearance and had more of the budding maiden about them than I had yet observed, and Lord Sigismund and Mrs. Menzies-Legh remaining with our patient, who had recovered enough to sit in a low chair in the shade and be read aloud to. Let us hope the book was virile. But I greatly doubt it, for his wife's voice in the peculiar sing-song that seems to afflict the voice of him who reads verses, zigzagged behind us some way across the field.

After our vagrant life of the last few days it seemed odd to be walking respectably along with no horse to lead, presently joining other respectable persons bent on the same errand. They seemed to know we were the dusty caravaners who had trudged past the afternoon before, and we were well stared at. In the church, too, an imposing lady in the pew in front of us sat sideways in her corner and examined us with calm attention through her eye-glass both before the service

An imposing lady in the pew in front of us sat sideways in her corner and examined us with calm attention

began and during it whenever the sitting portions of the ritual were reached. She was, we afterward discovered, the lady of the manor or chief lady in the place, and it was in one of her fields we were camping. We heard that afternoon from the farmer that she had privately visited our camp the evening before with her bailiff and his dogs and observed us, also with the aid of her eye-glass, over the hedge as we sat absorbed round our supper, doubtful whether we were not a circus and ought not instantly to be moved on. I fancy the result of her scrutiny in church was very satisfactory. She could not fail to see that here she had to do with a gentleman of noble birth, and the ladies of the party, in pews concealing their short skirts but displaying their earrings, were seen to every advantage. I caught her eye so repeatedly that at last, quite involuntarily, and yielding to a natural instinct, I bowed—a little, not deeply, out of considerations of time and place. She did not return my bow, nor did she after that look again, but attended during the rest of the service to her somewhat neglected devotions.

My hearers will be as much surprised as I was, though not half so tired, when I tell them that during the greater part of the service I was expected to remain on my knees. We Germans are not accustomed to our knees. I had certainly never used mine for praying purposes before; and inquiry later on elicited the information that the singular nation kneels every night by its beds before getting into them, and says prayers there too.

But it was not only the kneeling that shocked me (for if you ache and stiffen how can you properly pray! As Satan no doubt very well knew when he first put it into their heads to do it)—it was the extraordinary speed at which the service was run through. We began at eleven, and by a quarter to twelve we were, so to speak, ejected shriven. No flock can fatten on such a diet. How differently are the flocks of the Fatherland fed! There they grow fat indeed on the ample extemporizations of their pastor, or have every opportunity of doing so if they want to. Does he not address them for the best part of an hour? Which is not a moment too long for a meal that is to last seven days.

The English pastor, arrayed in white with two meaningless red ribbons down his back, preached for seven minutes, providing as I rapidly calculated exactly one minute's edification for each day of the week until the following Sunday. Alas, for the sheep of England! That is to say, alas from the mere generally humane point of view, but not otherwise alas, for their disadvantage must always be our gain, and a British sheep starved into socialism and civil war is almost more valuable to us than a German sheep which shall be fat with faith.

The pastor, evidently a militant man, preached against the sin of bigotry, which would have been all very well as far as it went and listened to by me with the tolerance I am accustomed to bring to bear on pulpit utterances if he had not in the same breath—there was hardly time for more than one—called down heaven's wrath on all who attend the meetings or services of forms of faith other than the Anglican. These other forms include, as I need not point out, the Lutheran. Really I found it difficult to suppress a smile at the poor man's folly. I longed for Luther (a thing I cannot remember ever to have done before) to rise up and scatter the blinded gentleman out of his pulpit. But hardly had I got as far as this in my thoughts than a hurried benediction, a hasty hymn, a rapid passing round of the English equivalent for what we call God's box, ended the service. Genuinely shocked at this breathlessness—and you, my hearers, who know no other worship than that leisurely one in Storchwerder and throughout our beloved Prussian land (I do not allude to Roman Catholics beyond saying, in a spirit of tolerant humanity, poor things), that worship which fills the entire morning, that composed and comfortable worship during which you sit almost the whole time so that no fatigue of the feet or knees shall distract your thoughts from the matter in hand, you who join sitting in our chorales, slow and dignified settings of ancient sentiments with ample spaces between the verses for the thinking of appropriate thoughts in which you are assisted by the meditative organ, and stand, as men should who are not slaves, to pray, you will, I am sure, be shocked too—I decided that here no doubt was one of the keys to the manifest decadence of the British character. Reverence and speed can never go together. Irreverence in the treatment of its creeds is an inevitable sign that a nation is well on that downward plane which jerks it at last into the jaws of (say) Germany. Well, so be it. Though irreverence is undoubtedly an evil, and I am the first to deplore it, I cannot deplore it as much as I would if it were not going to be the cause of that ultimate jerking. And what a green and fruitful land it is! *Es wird gut schmecken,* as we men of healthy appetite say.

We walked home—an expression that used to strike me as strangely ironical when home was only grass and hedges—discussing these things. That is, I discussed and Frau von Eckthum said Oh? But the sympathy of the voice, the implied agreement with my views, the appreciation of the way I put them, the perfect mutual understanding expressed, all this I cannot describe even if I would to you prejudiced critics.

Edelgard went on ahead with the two young girls. She and I did not at this point see much of each other, but quite enough. Being human I got tired sometimes of being patient, and yet it was impossible to be anything else inside a caravan with walls so thin that the whole camp would have to hear. Nor can you be impatient in the middle of a field: to be so comfortably you must be on the other side of at least a hedge; so that on the whole it was best we should seldom be together.

With Frau von Eckthum, on the other hand, I never had the least desire to be anything but the mildest of men, and we walked home as harmoniously as usual to find when we arrived that, though we had in no way lingered, the active pastor was there before us.

With what haste he must have stripped off his ribbons and by what short cuts across ditches he had reached the camp so quickly I cannot say, but there he was, ensconced in one of the low chairs talking to the Menzies-Leghs as though he had known them all his life.

This want of ceremony, this immediate familiarity prevailing in British circles, was a thing I never got used to. With us, first of all, the pastor would not have come at all, and secondly, once come, he would still have been in the stage of ceremonious preface when we arrived, and only emerged from his preliminary apologies to enter into the series of prayers for forgiveness which would round off his visit. Thus there would be no time so much as to reach the ice, far less to break it, and I am conservative enough and aristocratic enough to like ice: it is such an excellent preservative.

Mrs. Menzies-Legh was feeding her invalid with biscuits and milk. "Have some?" said she to the pastor, holding out a cup of this attractive beverage without the least preliminary grace of speech.

He took it, for his part, without the least preliminary ceremony of polite refusal which would call forth equally polite pressure on her side and end with a tactful final yielding on his; he took it without even interrupting his talk to Menzies-Legh, and stretching out his hand helped himself to a biscuit, though nobody had offered him one.

Now what can be the possible future of a nation deliberately discarding all the barriers of good manners that keep the natural brute in us suppressed? Ought a man to be allowed to let this animal loose on somebody else's biscuit-plate? It seems to me the hedge of ceremony is very necessary if you would keep it out, and it dwells in us all alike whatever country we may belong to. In Germany, feeling how near the surface it really is, we are particular and careful down to the smallest detail. Experience having taught us that the only way to circumvent it is to make the wire-netting, so to speak, of etiquette very thick, we do make it thick. And how anxiously we safeguard our honour, keeping it first of all inside these high and thick nets of rules, and then holding ourselves ready on the least approach to it to rise up and shed either our own or (preferably) somebody else's blood in its defense. And apart from other animals, the rabbit of Socialism, with its two eldest children, Division of Property and Free Love, is kept out most effectually by this netting. Jellabies and their like, tolerated so openly in Britain, find it difficult to burrow beneath the careful and far-reaching insistence on forms and ceremonies observed in other countries. Their horrid doctrines have little effect on such an armour. Not that I am not modern enough and large minded enough to be very willing to divide my property if I may choose the person to divide it with. All those Jewish bankers in Berlin and Hamburg, for instance—when I think of a division with them I see little harm and some comfort; but to divide with my orderly, Hermann, or with the man who hangs our breakfast rolls in a bag on the handle of our back door every morning, is another matter. As for Free Love, it is not to be denied that there are various things to be said for that too, but not in this place. Let me return. Let me return from a subject which, though legitimate enough for men to discuss, is yet of a somewhat slippery complexion, to the English pastor helping himself to our biscuits, and describe shortly how the same scene would have unrolled itself in a field in the vicinity of Storchwerder, supposing it possible that a party of well-born Germans should be camping in one, that the municipal authorities had not long ago turned them out after punishing them with fines, and that the pastor of the nearest church had dared to come hot from his pulpit, and intrude on them.

Pastor, approaching Menzies-Legh and his wife (translated for the nonce into two aristocratic Germans) with deferential bows from the point at which he first caught their eyes, and hat in hand:

"I entreat the *Herrschaften* to pardon me a thousand times for thus obtruding myself upon their notice. I beg them not to take it amiss. It is in reality an unexampled shamelessness on my part, but—may I be permitted to introduce myself? My name is Schultz."

He would here bow twice or thrice each to the Menzies-Leghs, who after staring at him in some natural surprise—for what excuse could the man possibly have?—get up and greet him with solemn dignity, both bowing, but neither offering to shake hands.

Pastor, bowing again profoundly, and still holding his hat in his hand, repeats: "My name is Schultz."

Menzies-Legh (who it must be remembered is for the moment a noble German) would probably here say under his breath: "And mine, thank God, is not"—but probably not quite loud enough (being extremely correct) for the pastor to hear, and would then mention his own name, with its title, Fürst Graf, or Baron, explaining that the lady with him was his wife.

More bows from the pastor, profounder if possible than before.

Pastor: "I beseech the *Herrschaften* to forgive my thus appearing, and fervently hope they will not consider me obtrusive, or in any way take it amiss."

Mrs. Menzies-Legh (now a Gräfin at the least): "Will not the Herr Pastor seat himself?"

Pastor, with every appearance of being overcome: "Oh, a thousand thanks—the gracious lady is too good—if I may really be permitted to sit—an instant—after so shamelessly———"

He is waved by Menzies-Legh, as he still hesitates, with stately courtesy, into the third chair, into which he sinks, but not until he sees the *Herrschaften* are in the act of sinking too.

Mrs. Menzies-Legh, gracefully explaining Menzies-Legh's greenness and silence: "My husband is not very well to-day."

Pastor, with every sign of liveliest interest and compassion: "Oh, that indeed makes me sorry. Has the Herr Graf then perhaps been overexerting himself? Has he perhaps contracted a chill? Is he suffering from a depressed stomach?"

Menzies-Legh, with a stately wave of the hand, naturally unwilling to reveal the real reason why he is so green: "No—no."

Mrs. Menzies-Legh: "I was about to refresh him a little with milk. May I be permitted to pour out a droplet for the Herr Pastor?"

Pastor, again bowing profusely: "The gracious one is much too good. I could not think of permitting myself———"

Mrs. Menzies-Legh: "But I beg you, Herr Pastor—will you not drink just a little?"

Pastor: "The gracious one is really very amiable. I would not, however, be the means of depriving the *Herrschaften* of their———"

Mrs. Menzies-Legh: "But Herr Pastor, not at all. Truly not at all. Will you not allow me to pour you out even half a glassful? After the heat of your walk? And the exertion of conducting the church service?"

Pastor, struggling to get up from the low chair, bow, and take the proffered glass of milk at one and the same time: "Since the gracious one is so gracious———"

He takes the glass with a deep bow, having now reached the stage when, the preliminaries demanded by perfect courtesy being on each side fulfilled, he is at liberty to do so, but before drinking its contents turns bowing to Menzies-Legh.

Pastor: "But may I not be permitted to offer it to the Herr Graf?"

Menzies-Legh, with a stately wave of the hand: "No—no."

Pastor, letting himself down again into the chair with another bow and the necessary caution, the glass being in his hand: "I do not dare to think what the *Herrschaften's* opinion of me must be for intruding in this manner. I can only entreat them not to take it amiss. I am aware it is an unexampled example of shamelessness———"

Mrs. Menzies-Legh, advancing with the plate of biscuits: "Will the Herr Pastor perhaps eat a biscuit?"

The pastor again shows every sign of being overcome with gratitude, and is about to embark on a speech of thanks and protest before permitting himself to take one when Baron von Ottringel and party appear on the scene, and we get to the point at which they really did appear.

Now what could be more proper and graceful than the whole of the above? It will be observed that there has been no time whatever for anything but politeness, no time to embark on those seas of discussion, sometimes foolish, often unsuitable, and always sooner or later angry, on which an otherwise budding acquaintanceship so frequently comes to grief. We Germans of the upper classes do not consider it good form to talk on any subject that is likely to make us lose our tempers, so what can we talk about? There is hardly anything really safe, except to offer each other chairs. But used as I am to these gilt limits, elegant frames within which it is a pleasure to behave like a picture (my friends will have noticed and pardoned my liking for metaphor) it will easily be imagined with what disapproval I stood leaning on my umbrella watching the scene before me.

Frau von Eckthum had gone into her caravan. Edelgard and the girls had disappeared. I alone approached the party, not one of which thought it necessary to introduce me or take other notice of my arrival.

They were discussing with amusing absorption a subject alluded to as the Licensing Bill, which was, I gathered, something heating to do with beer, and were weaving into it all sorts of judgments and opinions that would have inflamed a group of Germans at once. Menzies-Legh was too much interested, I suppose, to go on being green, anyhow, his greenness was all gone; and the pastor sawed up and down with his hand, in which he clasped the biscuit no one had suggested he should take. Mrs. Menzies-Legh, sitting on the grass (a thing no lady should ever do when a gentleman she sees for the first time is present—"May she the second time?" asked Mrs. Menzies-Legh, when I laid this principle down in the course of a later conversation, to which I very properly replied that you cannot explain nuances, but only feel them), joined in just as though she were a man herself—I mean, with her usual air of unchallenged equality of intelligence, an air that would have diverted me if it had not annoyed me too much. And they treated her, too, as though she were an equal, listening attentively to what she had to say, which, of course, inflates a poor woman and makes it difficult for her to arrive at a right estimate of herself.

This is how that absurd sexlessness, the Suffragette, has been able to come into existence. I heard a good deal about her the first day of the tour, but on discovering how strongly I felt on the subject, they kept off it, not liking, I suppose, to have their views knocked out of recognition by what I said. I did not, be it understood, deign to argue on such a topic: I just said a few things which frightened them off it.

And, indeed, who can take a female Suffragette seriously? Encouraged, I maintain, to begin with by being treated too well, she is like the insolent and pampered menial of a rich and careless master, and the more she gets the more she demands. Storchwerder does not possess a single example of the species, and very few foreigners come that way to set a bad example to our decent and contented ladies. Once, I recollect, by some strange chance the makings of one did get there, an Englishwoman on some wedding journey expedition or other, a young creature next to whom I sat at a dinner given by our Colonel. I was contemplating her with unconcealed pleasure, for she was quite young and most agreeably rounded, and was turning over the collection of amusing trifles I keep stored in my mind for purposes of conversation with attractive ladies when, before I had either selected one or finished my soup, she began to talk to me in breathless German about an Education Bill our Reichstag was tearing itself to pieces over.

Her interest could not have been keener if she had been a deputy herself with the existence of her party depending on it. She had her own views about it, all cut and dried; she explained her husband's, which differed considerably; and she was anxious to hear mine. So anxious was she that she even forgot to smile when speaking to me—forgot, that is, that she was a woman and I a man able, if inclined, to admire her.

I remember staring at her a moment in unfeigned astonishment, and then, leaning back in my chair, giving myself up to uncontrollable mirth.

She watched me with surprise, which made me laugh still more. When I could speak she inquired whether any one at the table had said anything amusing, and seemed quite struck on my assuring her that it was she herself who was amusing.

"I am?" said she; and a faint flush enhanced her prettiness.

"Yes—you and the Education Bill together," said I, again overcome with laughter. "It is indeed an amusing mixture. It is like," I added, with happy readiness of compliment, "a rose in an inkpot."

"But is that amusing?" she asked, not in the least grateful for the flattery, and with a quite serious face.

She had had her little lesson, however, and she did not again talk politics. Indeed, she did not again talk at all, but turned to the gentleman on her other side, and left me nothing to look at but a sweet little curl behind a sweet little ear.

Now if she had been properly brought up to devote herself to the woman's function of pleasing, how agreeably we could have discoursed together about that curl and that ear, and kindred topics, branching off into all sorts of flowery and seductive byways of compliment and insinuation, such as the well-trained young woman thoroughly enjoys and understands. I can only trust the lesson I gave her did her good. It certainly cured her of talking politics to me.

Listening to the English pastor heating himself over the Licensing Bill which, with all politics, is surely as distinctly outside the pastoral province as it is outside the woman's, I remembered this earlier success, and not caring to stand there unnoticed any longer thought I would repeat it. I therefore began to laugh, gently at first, as though tickled by my thoughts, then more heartily.

They all stopped to look at me.

"What is the joke, Baron?" asked Menzies-Legh, scowling up.

"Forgive me, Pastor," said I, taking off my hat and bowing—he for his part only stared—"but we are accustomed in my country (which, thank God, is Germany!) never to connect clergymen with politics, the inevitable wranglings of which make them ill-suited as a study for men whose calling is purely that of peace. So firmly is this feeling rooted in our natures that it is as amusing to me to see a gentleman of your profession deeply interested in such questions as it would be to see—to see——"

I cast about for a simile, but nothing occurred to me at the moment (and they were all sitting waiting) than the rose and inkpot one, so I had to take that.

And Mrs. Menzies-Legh, just as obtusely as the little bride of years ago, asked, "But is that amusing?"

Before I could reply Menzies-Legh got up and said he must write some letters; the pastor got up too and said he must hurry off to a class; and Lord Sigismund, as I approached the vacated chair next to him, and was about to drop into it, said he felt sure Menzies-Legh had no stamps, and he must go and lend him some.

Looking up from the grass on which she still sat, Mrs. Menzies-Legh patted it and said, "Come and sit on this nice soft stuff, dear Baron. I think men are tiresome things, don't you? Always rushing off somewhere. Tell me about the rose and the inkpot. I do see, I think, that they're—they're funny. Why did the vicar remind you of them? Come and sit on the grass and tell me."

But I had no desire to sit on grass with Mrs. Menzies-Legh, as though we were a row of turtle doves, so I merely said I did not like grass, and bowing slightly, walked away.

CHAPTER XIV

THE next day one of those unfortunate incidents happened which may, of course, happen to anybody, but really need not have happened just to me.

We left our camp at twelve, after the usual feverish endeavour to start much earlier, the caravans as usual nearly capsizing getting out to the field, and breaking, also as usual, in their plungings several hitherto unbroken articles, and with the wind and dust in our faces and gray, lowering clouds over our heads we resumed our daily race after pleasure.

The Sunday had been fine throughout, and there had been dew and stars at the end of it which, together with windlessness, made us expect a fine Monday. But it was nothing of the sort. Monday provided the conditions I always now associate with caravaning—a high wind, a threatening sky, clouds of dust, and a hard white road.

The day began badly and continued badly, so that even writing about it at this distance I drop unconsciously into a fretful tone. Perhaps our dinner at the inn on the Sunday had been more than constitutions used to starvation could suddenly endure, or perhaps some of us may have eaten beyond the limits of discretion, remembering that another week was to pass before the next real meal, and these, becoming cross, had infected the rest; anyhow on Monday troubles seemed to accumulate, beginning with a bill from the farmer for the field and care of the horses of a most exorbitant nature, going on to the losing of various things in the hasty packing up, continuing with the hurting of Menzies-Legh's foot owing to his folly in placing it where the advancing hoof of my horse was bound to go and with his being in consequence unable to do his proper share of work, and ending with the unfortunate incident I referred to above and shall presently relate.

Menzies-Legh, indeed, was strangely irritable. Perhaps his foot hurt him, but he ought not to have minded that, considering, as I told him, it was nobody's fault but his own. I was leading the horse at the moment, and saw Menzies-Legh's foot but never dreamed he would not remove it in time, and you cannot, as I said to him, blame a dumb animal.

"Certainly not," agreed Menzies-Legh; but with a singular gloom.

And when I saw the exorbitance of the bill I felt bound to point out to him that strict honesty did not seem to be characteristic of his countrymen, and to enlarge on the difference between them and my own, and that seemed to irritate him too, though he said nothing.

Seeing this suppressed irritation I sought to remove it by reminding him of his wealth, and of how the rapacity of the various farmers would at the worst only mean for him one stove the less for one undeserving old woman the fewer; but even that did not cheer him—he was and remained in a bad temper. So that, vexed as I was myself at the expense of the holiday that was to have been so cheap, I could not prevent a temporary good-humour taking possession of me, which is the invariable effect produced on me by other people's crossness. Even then, with his hurt foot, Menzies-Legh was such a slave to duty that while I was in the very act of talking the recollection of something he ought to do made him struggle up from the low chair and rugs in which his wife had carefully placed him, and limp away; and I saw no more of him for a long while beyond an occasional glimpse of his sallow visage at the window in front of his van, where he sat all day in silence driving his horse.

Behold us, then, crawling along an ugly highroad with our mouths full of dust.

The weather was alternately hot and cold, but uninterruptedly windy, and rain threatened to descend on us and actually did as the afternoon wore on. My hearers must remember that in caravaning afternoons wear on and mornings merge into them with no such thing as a real meal throughout their entire length. Long before this I had realized that plums were to be my portion: plums, or bananas, or very green apples, mitigated by a biscuit unless biscuits chanced to be scarce (in which case the ladies got them), at a time of day when the rest of Europe was sitting down comfortably to its luncheon; and I had learned to acquiesce in this as I acquiesced in all the other privations, for I saw for myself that it was impossible to arrange a cooked meal except before leaving or after arriving in camp. A reasonable man is silent before the impossible; still, plums are poor things to march on. March on them, however, I had to, and Hunger (a most unpleasant and reverberating companion) came too, and marched with me every day.

Well, I was often glad at this time that my poor Marie-Luise was spared her silver wedding journey, and that a more robust and far less deserving wife went through it in her stead. Marie-Luise was a most wifely wife, with no whalebone (if I may so express it) either about her clothes or her character. All was soft, womanly, overflowing. Touch her, and you left a dimple. Bring your pressure, even the slightest, to bear anywhere on her mind, and it immediately gave way.

"But do you *like* that sort of thing?" asked Mrs. Menzies-Legh, to whom, as we plodded along that day, I was talking in this reminiscent strain for want of a better companion.

Ahead walked Edelgard, visibly slimmer, younger, moving quickly and easily in her short skirt and new activity. It was this figure—hardly now at a distance to be distinguished from the figures of the scanty sisters—walking before me that made me think with tenderness of Marie-Luise. Edelgard was behaving badly, and when I told her so at night in our caravan she did not answer. At home she used to express immediate penitence; here she either said nothing, or said short things that reminded me of Mrs. Menzies-Legh, little odd sentences quite unlike her usual style and annoyingly difficult to reply to. And the more she behaved in this manner the more did my thoughts go back regretfully to my gentle and yielding first wife. Sometimes, I recollect, those twenty years with her had seemed long; but that was because, firstly, twenty years are long, and secondly, because we are none of us perfect, and thirdly, because a wife, unless she is careful, is apt to get on to one's nerves. But how preferable is gentleness to an aggressive activity of mind and body. How annoying to see one's wife striding on ahead with an ease I could not imitate and therefore in itself a slight on her husband. A man wants a wife who sits still, and not only still but on the same chair every day so that he knows where to find her should he happen to want anything. Marie-Luise was a very calm sitter; she never moved, except to follow the then Clothilde about. Only her hands moved, in a tireless guiding of the needle through those of my under-garments which had become defective.

"But do you *like* that sort of thing?" asked Mrs. Menzies-Legh, unsympathetic as usual. Her gentle sister would have coo'd an interested Oh? and I would have felt soothed and understood.

"Like what?" I asked rather peevishly, for it occurred to me at that moment as I watched the figures in front—my wife and Jellaby and Frau von Eckthum—that I had not had a word with the latter since the walk back from church more than twenty-four hours previously, and that her sister, on the other hand, seemed never to leave my side.

"Calm sitters," said Mrs. Menzies-Legh, "and dimples all over one's mind wherever you touch it. I suppose when you used to remove the pressure they slowly filled out again. It rather makes one think of india-rubber, doesn't it?"

"A wife's first duty is to be submissive," said I, conscious that I had the Prayer-book behind me and waving side issues, such as india-rubber, resolutely aside.

"Yes, yes," agreed Mrs. Menzies-Legh, "but——"

"And I am thankful to say," I continued quickly, for she was about to add something that I was sure was going to be aggressive, "I am thankful to say I was very fortunate in my Marie-Luise."

"And very fortunate in your Edelgard," said she—they had got to Christian names the second day.

"Of course," said I.

"She is a person everybody must love," said she.

"Undoubtedly," said I.

"So adaptable and quick," continued the tactless lady.

"You are very good," said I, raising my Panama in stiff acknowledgment of these compliments.

"And so unselfish," said she.

I bowed again, more stiffly than before.

"Look how she cuts all the bread and butter."

I bowed again.

"Look how she makes the coffee."

I bowed again.

"Look how cheerful she is."

I bowed again.

"And how clever, dear Baron."

Clever? That indeed was a new way of looking at poor Edelgard. I could not at this repress a smile of amusement. "I am gratified that you should have so good an opinion of my wife," I said; and wished much to add, "But what is my wife to you that you should take it upon yourself to praise her? Is she not solely and exclusively my property?"

Mrs. Menzies-Legh, however, was absolutely rebuke-proof, and had so many answers ready that I thought it better not to bring them upon me in crowds. I did though rather cleverly turn the tables upon her, and at the same time bring the conversation to a point which really interested me, by beginning to praise her sister.

"It is good of you," I said, "to commend my family. In return permit me to praise yours."

"What—John?" she asked, with a quick look and something of a smile. (John was her ill-conditioned husband.) "Are you—do you like him so much?"

Now as I thought John a very poor thing indeed this question would have seemed difficult to answer to any one less ready.

"Like," said I, with conspicuously careful courtesy, "is not at all the word that describes my feelings toward your husband."

She looked at me sideways, then dropped her eyelashes. "Dear Baron," she murmured, "how very——"

"I was not, however," I interrupted hastily, for I felt the ice would not bear much skating on, "thinking of him. I was referring to your sister."

"Oh?" said she—almost like the charming relative herself.

"She is of course, and as you know, delightful. But of all her delightfulness do you know what strikes me as most delightful?"

"No," said Mrs. Menzies-Legh, watching me with obvious interest.

"Her conversation."

"Yes. She is a good talker," she admitted.

"What I call a perfect talker," said I enthusiastically.

"I know. Everybody says so."

"Never too much," I said meaningly.

"Oh?" said she. "You think so? I rather imagined——" She stopped.

"So extremely sympathetic," I continued.

"And so amusing," said she.

"Amusing?" said I, slightly surprised, for I must say I had not till then considered it possible to be amusing on one single note, however flute-like.

"Even more—really witty. Don't you think so?"

"Witty?" said I, with increased surprise.

She looked at me and smiled. "You evidently have not found her so," she said.

"No. Nor do I care for wit in ladies. Your sister has been everything that is perfect—sympathetic, an interested listener, one who shares one's opinions completely, and who never says a word more than is absolutely necessary; but thank goodness I have not yet observed her descend to the unwomanliness of wit."

Mrs. Menzies-Legh looked at me as though I were being funny. It was a way she had, and one which I particularly disliked; for surely few things are more offensive than to be treated as amusing when you are not. "Evidently," said she, "you have a soothing and restraining influence over Betti, dear Baron. Has she, then, never made you laugh?"

"Certainly not," said I with conviction.

"But look at Mr. Jellaby—do you see how he is laughing?"

"At his own dull jokes, I should say," I said, bestowing a momentary glance on the slouching figure in front. His face was turned toward Frau von Eckthum, and he was certainly laughing, and to an unbecoming extent.

"Oh, not a bit. He is laughing at Betti."

"I have heard your sister," said I emphatically, "talking in general company—such company, that is, as this tour affords—and she has done it invariably seriously, and rather poetically, but never has more than smiled herself, and never raised that doubtful tribute, a laugh."

"That," said Mrs. Menzies-Legh, "was because you were there, dear Baron. I tell you, you soothe and restrain."

I bowed. "I am glad," I said, "that I exert a good influence over the party."

"Oh, very," said she, her eyelashes cast down. "But what does Betti talk to you about, then? The scenery?"

"Your tactful sister, my dear lady, does not talk at all. Or rather, what she says consists entirely of one word, spoken indeed with so great a variety of expression that it expands into volumes. It is that that I admire so profoundly in her. If all ladies would take a lesson———"

"But—what word?" interrupted Mrs. Menzies-Legh, who had been listening with a growing astonishment on her face—astonishment, I suppose, that so near a relative should be also a person of tact and delicacy.

"Your sister simply says Oh. It sounds a small thing, and slightly bald stated in this manner, yet all I can say is that if every woman———"

Mrs. Menzies-Legh, however, made a little exclamation and bent down hastily.

"Dear Baron," she said, "I've got a thorn or something in my shoe. I'll wait for our caravan to come up, and get in and take it out. *Auf Wiedersehen.*"

And she fell behind.

This was the first really agreeable conversation I had had with Mrs. Menzies-Legh. I walked on alone for some miles, turning it over with pleasure. It was of course pleasant to reflect that I alone of the party had a beneficial influence over her whom her sister was entitled to describe as Betti; and it was also pleasant (though only what was to be expected) that I should exercise a good influence over the entire party. "Soothing" was Mrs. Menzies-Legh's word. Well, what was happening was that these English people were being leavened hourly and ceaselessly with German yeast; and now that it had been put into so many words I did see that I soothed them, for I had observed that whenever I approached a knot of them, however loudly it had been laughing and talking it sank into a sudden calm—it was soothed, in fact—and presently dispersed about its various duties.

But nothing occurred after this that day that was pleasant. I plodded along alone. Rain came down and mud increased, but still I plodded. It was pretended to me that we were unusually unlucky in the weather and that England does not as a rule have a summer of the sort; I, however, believe that it does, regularly every year, as a special punishment of Providence for its being there at all, or how should the thing be so very green? Mud and greenness, mud and greenness, that is all the place is made of, thought I, trudging between the wet hedges after an hour's rain had set everything dripping.

Stolidly I followed, at my horse's side, whither the others led. In the rain we passed through villages which the ladies in every tone of childish enthusiasm cried out were delightful, Edelgard joining in, Edelgard indeed loudest, Edelgard in fact falling in love in the silliest way with every thatched and badly repaired cottage that happened to have a show of flowers in its garden, and saying—I heard her with my own ears—that she would like to live in one. What new affectation was this, I asked myself? Not one of our friends who would not (very properly) leave off visiting us if we looked as poor as thatch. To get and to keep friends the very least that you must have is a handsome sofa-set in a suitably sized drawing-room. Edelgard till then had been justly proud of hers, which cost a sum so round that it seems written in velvet letters all over it. It is made of the best of everything—wood, stuffing, covers, and springs, and has a really beautiful walnut-wood table in the middle, with its carved and shapely legs resting on a square of carpet so good that many a guest has exclaimed in tones of envy as her feet sank into it, "But dearest Baroness, where and how did you secure so truly glorious a carpet? It must cost——!" And eyes and hands uplifted complete the sentence.

To think of Edelgard with this set and all that it implies in the background of her consciousness affecting a willingness to leave it, tried my patience a good deal; and about three o'clock, having all collected in a baker's shop in a wet village called Salehurst for the purpose of eating buns (no camp being in immediate prospect), I told her in a low tone how ill enthusiasms about things like thatch sit on a woman who is going to be thirty next birthday.

"Dear wife," I begged, "do endeavour not to be so calf-like. If you think these pretences pretty let me tell you you are mistaken. The others will not tell you so, because the others are not your husband. Nobody is taken in, nobody believes you. Everybody sees you are old enough to be sensible. But, not being your husband, they are obliged to be polite and feign to agree and sympathize, while they are really secretly lamenting your inability to adjust your conversation to your age."

This I said between two buns; and would have said more had not the eternal Jellaby thrust himself between us. Jellaby was always coming between man and wife, and this time he did it with a glass of fizzy lemonade. Edelgard refused it, and Jellaby (pert Socialist) thanked her earnestly for doing so, saying he would be wholly unable to respect a woman who drank fizzy lemonade.

Respect a woman? What a tone to adopt to a married lady whose husband is within ear-shot. And what could Edelgard's tone have been to him before such a one on his side came within the range of the possible?

"And I must warn you," I continued with a slightly less pronounced patience, "very seriously against the consequences likely to accrue if you allow a person of Jellaby's sex and standing to treat you with familiarity. Familiarity and disrespect are one and the same thing. They are inseparable. They are, in fact, twins. But not ordinary twins—rather that undividable sort of which there have been luckily only a few examples———"

"Dear Otto, do have another bun," said she, pointing to these articles in a pile on the counter; and as I paused to choose (by means of squeezing) the freshest, she, although aware I had not finished speaking, slipped away.

I begin to doubt as I proceed with my narrative whether any but relations had better be admitted to the readings aloud after all. Friends have certain Judas-like qualities, and might, perhaps, having listened to these sketches of Edelgard with every appearance of sympathy, go away and misrepresent me. Relations on the other hand are very sincere and never pretend (which is why one prefers friends, I sometimes think) and they have, besides, the family feeling which prevents their discussing each other to the unrelated. It is possible that I may restrict my invitations solely to them; and yet it seems a pity not to let my friends in as well. Have they not often suffered in the same way too? Have they not wives themselves? God help us all.

Continuing our march in the rain we left Salehurst (where I earnestly but vainly suggested we should camp in the back-yard of the inn) and went toward Bodiam—a ruined castle, explained Lord Sigismund coming and walking with me, of great interest and antiquity, rising out of a moat which at that time of the year would be filled with white and yellow water-lilies.

He knew it well and talked a good deal about it, its position, its preservation, and especially its lilies. But I was much too wet to care about lilies. A tight roof and a shut window would have interested me far more. However, it was agreeable to converse with him, and I soon deftly turned the conversation while at the same time linking it, as it were, on to the next subject, by remarking that his serene Aunt in Germany must also be very old. He vaguely said she was, and showed a tendency to get back to the ruins nearer at hand, which I dodged by observing that she must make a perfect picture in her castle in Thuringia, the background being so harmonious, such an appropriate setting for an old lady, for, as is well known, the castle grounds contain the most magnificent ruins in Europe. "And your august Aunt, my dear Lord Sigismund," I continued, "is, I am certain, not one whit less magnificent than the rest."

"Well, I don't think Aunt Lizzie actually crumbles yet, you know, Baron," said Lord Sigismund smiling. "You should see her going about in gaiters looking after things."

"There is nothing I would like better than to see her," I replied with enthusiasm, for this was surely almost an invitation.

He, however, made no direct answer but got back to the Bodiam ruins again, and again I broke the thread of what threatened to become a narrative by inquiring how long it took to go by train from London to his father the Duke's place in Cornwall.

"Oh, it's at the end of the world," said he.

"I know, I know. But my wife and I would not like to leave England without having journeyed thither and looked at a place so famous according to Baedeker both for its size, its splendour, and its associations. Of course, my dear Lord Sigismund," I added with the utmost courtesy, "we expect nothing. We would be content to go as the merest tourists. In spite of the length of the journey we should not hesitate to put up at the inn which is no doubt not far from the ducal gates. There should be no trading on what has become, certainly on my side and I hope and believe on yours, a warm friendship."

"My dear Baron," said Lord Sigismund heartily, "I agree entirely with you. Friendship should be as warm as one can possibly make it. Which reminds me that I haven't asked poor Menzies-Legh how his foot is getting on. That wasn't very warm of me, was it? I must go and see how he is."

And he dropped behind.

At this time I was leading the procession (by some accident of the start from the bun shop) and had general orders to go straight ahead unless signalled to from the rear. I went, accordingly, straight ahead down a road running along a high ridge, the blank space of rain and mist on either side filled in no doubt on more propitious days by a good view. Bodiam lay below somewhere in the flat, and we were going there; for Mrs. Menzies-Legh, and indeed all the others including Edelgard, wished (or pretended to wish) to see the ruins. I must decline to believe in the genuineness of such a wish when expressed, as in this case, by the hungry and the wet. Ruins are very well, no doubt, but they do come last. A man will not look at a ruin if he is honest until every other instinct, even the smallest, has been satisfied. If, not having had his dinner, he yet expresses eagerness to visit such things, then I say that that man is a hypocrite. To enjoy looking at the roofless must you not first have a roof yourself? To enjoy looking at the empty must you not first be filled? For the roofless and the empty to visit and admire other roofless and other empties seems to me as barren as for ghosts to go to tea with ghosts.

Alone I trudged through a dripping world. My thoughts from ruins and ghosts strayed naturally—for when you are seventy there must be a good deal of the ghost about you—once more to Lord Sigismund's august and aged Aunt in Thuringia, to the almost invitation (certainly encouragement) he had given me to go and behold her in princely gaiters, to the many distinct advantages of having such a lady on our visiting list, to conjecture as to the extent of the Duke her brother's hospitality should we go down and take up our abode very openly at the inn at his gates, to the pleasantness (apart from every other consideration) of staying in his castle after staying in a caravan, and to the interest of Storchwerder when it heard of it.

The hooting of a yet invisible motor interrupted these musings. It was hidden in the mist at first, but immediately loomed into view, coming down the straight road toward me at a terrific pace, coming along with a rush and a roar, the biggest, swiftest, and most obviously expensive example I had yet seen.

The road was wide, but sloped away considerably on either side from the crown of it, and on the crown of it I walked with my caravan. It was a clay road, made slippery by the rain; did these insolent vulgarians, I asked myself, suppose I was going to slide down one side in order to make room for them? Room there was plenty between me in the middle and the gutter and hedge at the sides. If there was to be sliding, why should it not be they who slid?

The motor, with the effrontery usual to its class, was right on the top of the road, in the very pick and middle of it. I perceived that here was my chance. No motor would dare dash straight on in the face of so slow and bulky an obstacle as a caravan, and I was sick of them—sick of their dust, their smell, and their vulgar ostentation. Also I felt that all the other members of our party would be on my side, for I have related their indignant comments on the slaying of a pretty young woman by one of these goggled demons. Therefore I kept on immovably, swerving not an inch from the top of the road.

The motor, seeing this and now very near, shrieked with childish rage (it had a voice like an angry woman) at my daring to thwart it. I remained firmly on my course, though I was obliged to push up the horse which actually tried of itself to make way. The motor, still shrieking, saw nothing for it but to abandon the heights to me, and endeavoured to pass on the slope. As it did it skidded violently, and after a short interval of upheaval and activity among its occupants subsided into calm and the gutter.

An old gentleman with a very red face struggled into view from among many wrappers.

I waited till he had finally emerged, and then addressed him impressively and distinctly from the top of the road. "Road hog," I said, "let this be a lesson to you."

I would have said more, he being unable to get away and I holding, so to speak, the key to the situation, if the officious Jellaby and the too kind Lord Sigismund had not come running up from behind breathlessly eager to render an assistance that was obviously not required.

The old gentleman, shaking himself free from his cloak and rising in the car, was in the act of addressing me in his turn, for his eyes were fixed on me and his mouth was opening and shutting in the spasms preliminary to heated conversation (all of which I observed calmly, leaning against my horse's shaft and feeling myself to be in the right) when Lord Sigismund and Jellaby arrived.

The old gentleman was in the act of addressing me in his turn

"I do hope you've not been hurt——" began Lord Sigismund with his usual concern for those to whom anything had happened.

The old gentleman gasped. "What? Sidge? It's your lot?" he exclaimed.

"Hullo, Dad!" was Lord Sigismund's immediate and astonished response.

It was the Duke.

Now was not that very unfortunate?

CHAPTER XV

I HAVE observed on frequent occasions in a life now long enough to have afforded many, a tendency on the part of Providence to punish the just man because he has been just. Not one to criticize Providence if I can avoid it, I do feel that this is to be deplored. It is also inexplicable. Marie-Luise died, I recollect, the very day I had had occasion to speak sharply to her, which almost looked, I remember thinking at the time, like malice. I was aware, however, that it was only Providence. My poor wife was being wielded as the instrument which was to put me in the wrong, and I need not say to you, my friends, who knew her and know me and were witness of the harmony of our married life, that her death had nothing to do with my rebukes. You all remember she was in perfect health that day, and was snatched from my side late in the afternoon by means of a passing *droschke*. The *droschke* passed over her, and left me, with incredible suddenness, a widower on the pavement. This might have happened to anybody, but what was so peculiarly unfortunate was that I had been forced, if I would do my duty, to rebuke her during the hours immediately preceding the occurrence. Of course, I could not know about the *droschke*. I could not know about it; I did my duty; and by the evening I was the most crushed of men, a prey to the crudest regrets and self-reproaches. Yet had I not acted aright? Conscience told me Yes. Alas, how little could Conscience do for my comfort then! In time I got over it, and regained the calm balance of mind that saw life would stand still if we feared to speak out because people might die. Indeed, I saw this so clearly that I not only married again within the year, but made up my mind that no past experience should intimidate me into not doing my duty by my second wife; I assumed, that is, from the first my proper position in the household as its guide and censor, and up to now I am glad to say Providence has left Edelgard alone, and has not used her (except in minor matters) as a weapon for making me regret I have done right.

But here, now, was this business with the Duke. Nothing could have been warmer and more cordial than my feelings toward him and his family. I admired and liked his son; I infinitely respected his sister; and I only asked to be allowed to admire, like, and respect himself. Such was my attitude toward him. Toward motors it was equally irreproachable. I detested their barbarous methods, and was as anxious as any other decent man to give them a lesson and help avenge their many unhappy victims. Now came Providence, stepping in between these two meritorious intentions, and frustrating both at one blow by the simple expedient of combining the Duke with the motor. It confounded me; it punished me; it put me in the wrong; and for what? For doing what I knew was right.

"No one, not even a pastor, can expect me to like that sort of thing," I complained to Mrs. Menzies-Legh, to whom I had been talking, owing to her sister's being somewhere else.

"No," said she; and looked at me reflectively as though tempted to say more. But (no doubt remembering my dislike of talkative women) she refrained.

I was sitting under one of the ruined arches of Bodiam Castle (never, my friends, go there; it is a terribly damp place), with the lean lady, while the others peered about as well as they could, being too tired to do anything but sit, and weary, too, of spirit, for I am a sensitive man, and had had a troubled day. The evening had done that which English people call drawing in. Lord Sigismund was gone—gone with his unreasonably incensed father in the motor to some place whose name I did not catch, and was not to be back till the next day. The others, including myself, had, after a prolonged search, found a very miserable camp with cows in it. It was too late to object to anything, so there we huddled round our stew-pot in an exposed field, while the wind howled and a fine rain fell. Our party was oddly silent and cheerless considering its ordinary spirits. No one said it was healthy and jolly; even the children did not speak, and sat buttoned up in mackintoshes, their hands clasped round their knees, their faces, shining with rain, set and serious. I think the way the Duke had behaved after getting out of the gutter had depressed them. It had been a disagreeable scene—I should say he was a man of a hot and uncontrolled temper—and my apologies had been useless. Then the supper took an unconscionable time preparing. For some reason the chickens would not boil (they missed Lord Sigismund's persuasive talent) and the potatoes could not because the stove on which they stood went out and nobody noticed it. How bleak and autumnal that field, bare of trees, with the rain driving over it, looked after the unsatisfactory day I cannot describe to you. Its dreariness, combined with what had gone before, and with the bad supper, made me dislike it more than any camp we had had. The thought that up there on those dank cow-ridden heights we were to spend the night, while down in Bodiam lights twinkled and happy cottagers undressed in rooms and went into normal beds instead of inserting themselves sideways into what was in reality a shelf, was curiously depressing. And when, after supper, our party was washing up by the flickering lantern-light, with the rain wetting the plates as quickly as they were dried, I could not refrain from saying as I stood looking down at them, "So this is what is called pleasure."

Nobody had anything to say to that.

In self-defense we went down later on, dark and wild though it was, to the ruins. Sit up there in the wet we could not, and it was too early to go to bed. Nor could we play at cards in each other's caravans, because of questions of decorum. Mrs. Menzies-Legh did, indeed, suggest it, but on my pointing this out to her with a severity I was prepared to increase if she had made the least opposition, the suggestion was dropped. Forced to stay out-of-doors we were forced to move, or rheumatism would certainly have claimed us for its own, so we set out once again along the muddy lanes, leaving Menzies-Legh (who was sulking terribly) to mind the camp, and trudged the two miles down to the castle.

Mrs. Menzies-Legh walked with me. Directly she saw I was alone, the others hurrying on ahead at a pace I did not care to keep up with, she loitered behind till I overtook her and walked with me.

I have made no secret of the fact that this lady seemed to mark me during the tour for her special prey. You, my hearers, must have noticed it by now, for I conceal nothing. I can safely say I was not to blame, for in no way did I encourage her. Not only must she have been over thirty, but more than once she had allowed herself to do that which can only be described as poking fun at me. Besides, I do not care for the type. I dislike the least suggestion of wiriness in woman; and there was nothing of her bodily (except wire) and far too much intellectually—I mean so far as a woman can be intellectual, which, of course, is not far at all. I therefore feel entirely conscience-clear, and carefully avoiding any comments which might give the impression of vanity on my part, merely state the bare facts that the lady was constantly at my elbow, that my elbow was reluctant, and that no other member of the party clung to it like that.

There she sat with me, for instance, in the ruins, pretending she was tired too, though of course she was not, for never was any one more active, and for want of a better listener—Frau von Eckthum had from the first melted away among the shadows—I was obliged to talk to her in the above strain. However, one cannot really *talk* to such a woman, not really converse with her. She soon reminded me of this fact (which I well knew) by inquiring whether I did not think people were very apt to call that Providence which was in reality nothing more nor less than their own selves—"Or," she added (profanely) "if they're in another mood they call it the Devil, but it is always just themselves."

Well, I had not come through the mud to Bodiam to be profane, so I gathered my wraps about me and prepared to go.

"But I do see your point," she said, noticing these preparations, and realizing, perhaps, that she had gone too far. "Things do sometimes happen very unluckily, and punishments are out of all proportion to the offence. I think, for instance, it was perfectly terrible for you that you should have been scolding your wife——"

"Not scolding. Rebuking."

"It's the same thing——"

"Certainly not."

"Rebuking her, then, up to the very moment—oh, it would have killed me!"

And she shivered.

"My dear lady," said I, slightly amused, "a man has certain duties, and he performs them. Sometimes they are unpleasant, and he still performs them. If he allowed himself to be killed each time there would be a mighty dearth of husbands in the world, and what would you all do then?"

Women however have no sense of humour, and she was unable to catch at this straw of it offered her for the purpose of lightening the conversation. On the contrary, she turned her head and looking at me gravely (pretty eyes, wasted) she said, "But how much better never, never to do your duty."

"Really——" I protested.

"Yes. If it means being unkind."

"Unkind? Is a mother unkind who rebukes her child?"

"Oh, call it by its proper name—scolding, preaching, advising, abusing—it's all unkind, wickedly unkind."

"Abusing, my dear lady?"

"Come, now, Baron, what you said to the Duke——"

"Ah. That was an unfortunate accident. I did what under any other circumstances would have been my duty, and Providence——"

"Oh, Baron dear, leave Providence alone. And leave your duty alone. A tongue doing its duty is such a terrible instrument of destruction. Why, you can almost see all the little Loves and Charities turning paler and paler and weaker and weaker the longer it wags, and shrivelling up quite at last and being snuffed out. Really I have been thankful on my knees every time I have not said what I was going to say when I've been annoyed."

"Indeed?" said I, ironically.

I might have added that no great strain could have been put upon her knees, for I could conceive no woman less likely to be silent if she wanted to speak. But, candidly, what did it matter? I have always found it quite impossible to take a woman seriously, even when I am attracted; and heaven knows I had no desire to sit on stones in that wet place while this one spread out her little stock of ill-assimilated wisdom for my (presumable) improvement.

I therefore began to button up my cloak with an unmistakable finality, determined to seek the others and suggest a return to the camp.

"You forget," I said, while I buttoned, "that an outburst of annoyance has nothing whatever to do with the calm discharge of a reasonable man's obligations."

"What, you've been quite calm and happy when you've been doing what you call rebuke?" said she, looking up at me. "Oh, Baron." And she shook her head and smiled.

"Calm, I hope and believe, but not happy. Nor did I expect to be. Duty has nothing to do with one's happiness."

"No, nor with the other one's," said she quickly.

Of course I could have scattered her reasoning to the winds if I had chosen to bring real logic to bear on it, but it would have taken time, she being very unconvinceable, and I really could not be bothered.

"Let Menzies-Legh convince her," thought I, making myself ready for the walk back in the rain, aware that I had quite enough to do convincing my own wife.

"Try praising," said Mrs. Menzies-Legh.

Not seeing the point, I buttoned in silence.

"Praising and encouraging. You'd be astonished at the results."

In silence, for I would not be at the trouble of asking what it was I was to praise and encourage, I turned up my collar and fastened the little strap across the front. She, seeing I had no further intention of talking, began to get ready too for the plunge out into the rain.

"You're not angry, Baron dear?" she asked, leaning across and looking into as much of my face as appeared above the collar.

This mode of addressing me was one that I had never in any way encouraged, but no amount of stiffening at its use discouraged it. In justice, I must remind you who have met her that her voice is not disagreeable. You will remember it is low, and so far removed from shrillness that it lends a spurious air to everything she says of being more worth listening to than it is. Edelgard described it fancifully, but not altogether badly, as being full of shadows. It vibrated, not unmusically, up and down among these shadows, and when she asked me if I were angry it took on a very fair semblance of sympathetic concern.

I, however, knew very well that the last thing she really was was sympathetic—all the aptitude for sympathy the Flitz family had produced was concentrated in her gentle sister—so I was in no way hoodwinked.

"My dear lady," I said, shaking out the folds of my cloak, "I am not a child."

"Sometimes I think," said she, getting up too, "that you are not enjoying your holiday. That it's not what you thought it would be. That perhaps we are not a very—not a very congenial party."

"You are very good," said I, with a stiffness that relegated her at once to an immense and proper distance away, for was not this a tending toward the confidential? And a man has to be careful.

She looked at me a moment at this, her head a little on one side, considering me. Her want of feminine reserve—conceive Edelgard staring at a living gentleman with the frank attention one brings to bear on an inanimate object—struck me afresh. She seemed absolutely without a vestige of that consciousness of sex, of those *arrière-pensées* (as our conquered but still intelligent neighbours say) very properly called female modesty. A well brought up German lady soon casts down her eyes when facing a gentleman. She at once recollects that she is a woman and he is a man, and continues to recollect it during the whole time they are together. I am sure in the days when Mrs. Menzies-Legh was yet a Flitz she did so, but England had blunted if not completely destroyed those finer Prussian feelings, and there she stood considering me with what I can only call a perfectly sexless detachment. What, I wondered, was she going to say that would annoy me at the end of it? But she said nothing; she just gave her head a little shake, turned suddenly, and walked away.

Well, I was not going to walk too—at least, not with her. The ruins were not my property, and she was not my guest, so I felt quite justified in letting her go alone. Chivalry, too, has its limits, and one does not care to waste any of one's stock of it. No man can be more chivalrous than I if provided with a proper object, but I do not consider that objects are proper once they have reached an age to be able to take care of themselves, neither are they so if Nature has encrusted them in an armour of unattractiveness; in this latter case Nature herself may be said to be chivalrous to them, and they can safely be left to her protection.

I therefore followed at my leisure in Mrs. Menzies-Legh's wake, desiring to return to the camp, but not desiring to do it with her. I thought I would search for Frau von Eckthum and she and I would walk back happily together; and, passing under the arch leading into what had been the banqueting hall, I immediately found the object of my search beneath an umbrella which was being held over her head by Jellaby.

When I was a child, and still in charge of my mother, she, doing her best by me, used to say, "Otto, put yourself in his place," if my judgments chanced to be ill-considered or headlong.

I did so; it became a habit; and in consequence I arrived at conclusions I would probably not otherwise have arrived at. So now, coming across my gentle friend beneath Jellaby's umbrella, I mechanically carried out my mother's injunction. At once I began to imagine what my feelings would be in her place. How, I rapidly asked myself, would I enjoy such close proximity to the boring Socialist, to the common man of the people if I were a lady of exceptionally refined moral and physical texture, the fine flower and latest blossom of an ancient, aristocratic, Conservative, and right-thinking family? Why, it would be torture; and so was this that I had providentially chanced upon torture.

"My dear friend," I cried, darting forward, "what are you doing here in the wet and darkness unprotected? Permit me to offer you my arm and conduct you to your sister, who is, I believe, preparing to return to camp. Allow me——"

And before Jellaby could frame a sentence I had drawn her hand through my arm and was leading her carefully away.

He, I regret to say, quite unable (owing to his thick skin) to see when his presence was not desired, came too, making clumsy attempts to hold his umbrella over her and chiefly succeeding, awkward as he is, in jerking the rain off its tips down my neck.

Well, I could not be rude to him before a lady and roundly tell him to take himself off, but I do not think he enjoyed his walk. To begin with I suddenly remembered that no members of our party, except Edelgard and myself, possessed umbrellas, so that I was able to say with the mildness that is sometimes so telling: "Jellaby, what umbrella is this?"

"The Baroness kindly lent it to me," he replied.

"Oh, indeed. Community of goods, eh? And what is she doing herself without one, may I inquire?"

"I took her home. She said she had some sewing to do. I think it was to mend a garment of yours."

"Very likely. Then, since it is my wife's umbrella, and therefore mine, as you will hardly deny, for if two persons become by the marriage law one flesh they must equally become one everything else, and therefore also one umbrella, may I request you instead of inserting it so persistently between my collar and my neck to hand it over to me, and allow its lawful owner to hold it for this lady?"

And I took it from him, and looked down at Frau von Eckthum and laughed, for I knew she would be amused at Jellaby's being treated as he ought to be.

She, of my own nation and class, must often have been, I think, scandalized at the way the English members of the party behaved to him, absolutely as though he were one of themselves. Her fastidiousness must often and often have been wounded by Jellaby's appearance and manner of speech, by his flannel collar, his untidy clothes, the wisp of hair forever being brushed aside from his forehead only forever to fall across it again, his slender, almost feminine frame, his round face, and the ridiculous whiteness of his skin. Really, the only way to treat this person was as a kind of joke; not to take him seriously, not to allow oneself to be, as one so often was on the verge of being, angry with him. So I gave the hand resting on my arm a slight pressure expressive of mutual understanding, and looked down at her and laughed.

The dear lady was not, however, invariably quick of comprehension. As a rule, yes; but once or twice she gave the last touch to her femininity by being divinely stupid, and on this occasion, whether it was because her little feet were wet and therefore cold, or she was not attending to the conversation, or she had had such a dose of Jellaby that her brain refused any new impression, she responded neither to my look nor to my laugh. Her eyes were fixed on the ground, and the delicate and serious outline of her nose was all that I was permitted to see.

Respecting her mood, as a tactful man naturally would, I did not again directly appeal to her, but laid myself out to amuse her on the way up the hill by talking to Jellaby in a strain of mock solemnity and endeavouring to draw him out for her entertainment. Unfortunately he resisted my well-meant efforts, and was more taciturn than I had yet seen him. He hardly spoke, and she, I fear, was very tired, for only once did she say Oh. So that the conversation ended by being a disquisition on Socialism held solely by myself, listened to by Frau von Eckthum with absorbed and silent interest, and by Jellaby with, I am sure, the greatest rage. Anyhow, I made some very good points, and he did not venture a single protest. Probably his fallacious theories had never had such a thorough pulling to pieces before, for there were two miles to go up hill and I made the pace as slow as possible. My hearers must also bear in mind that I exclusively employed that most deadly weapon for withering purposes, the double-barrelled syringe of irony and wit. Nothing can stand against the poison pumped out of these two, and I could afford to bid Jellaby the cheeriest good night as I helped the tender lady up the steps of her caravan.

He, it is amusing to relate, barely answered. But the moment he had gone Frau von Eckthum found her tongue again, for on my telling her as she was about to disappear through her doorway how greatly I had enjoyed being able to be of some slight service to her, she paused with her hand on the curtain and looking down at me, said: "What service?"

"Rescuing you from Jellaby," said I.

"Oh," said she; and drew back the curtain and went in.

CHAPTER XVI

THERE is a place about six hours' march from Bodiam called Frogs' Hole Farm, a deserted house lying low among hop-fields, a dank spot in a hollow with the ground rising abruptly round it on every side, a place of perpetual shade and astonishing solitude.

To this, led by the wayward Fate that had guided our vague movements from the beginning, we steadily journeyed during the whole of the next day. We were not, of course, aware of it—one never is, as no doubt my hearers have noticed too—but that that was the ultimate object of every one of our painful steps during an exceptionally long march, and that our little arguments at crossroads and hesitations as to which we would take were only the triflings of Fate, contemptuously willing to let us think we were choosing, dawned upon us at four o'clock exactly, when we lumbered in single file along a cart track at the edge of a hop-field and emerged one by one into the back yard of Frogs' Hole Farm.

The house stood (and very likely still does) on the other side of a dilapidated fence, in a square of rank garden. A line of shabby firs with many branches missing ran along the north side of it; a pond, green with slime, occupied the middle of what was once its lawn; and the last tenant had left in such an apparent hurry that he had not cleared up his packing materials, and the path to the front door was still littered with the straw and newspapers of his departure.

The house was square with many windows, so that in whatever corner we camped we were subject to the glassy and empty stare of two rows of them. Though it was only four o'clock when we arrived the sun was already hidden behind the big trees that crowned the hill to the west, and the place seemed to have settled down for the night. Ghostly? Very ghostly, my friends; but then even a villa of the reddest and newest type if it is not lived in is ghostly in the shiver of twilight; at least, that is what I heard Mrs. Menzies-Legh say to Edelgard, who was standing near the broken fence surveying the forlorn residence with obvious misgiving.

We had asked no one's permission to camp there, not deeming it necessary when we heard from a labourer on the turnpike road that down an obscure lane and through a hop-field we would find all we required. Space there was certainly of every kind: empty sheds, empty barns, empty oast-houses, and, if we had chosen to open one of the rickety windows, an empty house. Space there was in plenty; but an inhabited farm with milk and butter in it would have been more convenient. Besides, there did undoubtedly lie—as Mrs. Menzies-Legh said—a sort of shiver over the place, an ominously complete silence and motionlessness of leaf and bough, and nowhere round could I see either a roof or a chimney, no, not so much as a thread of smoke issuing upward from between the hills to show me that we were not alone.

Well, I am not one to mind much if leaves do not move and a place is silent. A man does not regard these matters in the way ladies do, but I must say even I—and my friends will be able to measure from that the uncanniness of our surroundings—even I remembered with a certain regret that Lord Sigismund's very savage and very watchful dog had gone with his master and was therefore no longer with us. Nor had we even Jellaby's, which, inferior as it was, was yet a dog, no doubt with some amount of practice in barking, for it was still at the veterinary surgeon's, a gentleman by now left far behind folded among the embosoming hills.

My hearers must be indulgent if my style from time to time is tinged with poetic expressions such as this about the veterinary surgeon and the hills, for they must not forget that the party I was with could hardly open any of its mouths without using words plain men like myself do not as a rule even recollect. It exuded poetry. Poetry rolled off it as naturally and as continuously as water off a duck's back. Mrs. Menzies-Legh was an especial offender in this respect, but I have heard her gloomy husband, and Jellaby too, run her very close. After a week of it I found myself rather inclined also to talk of things like embosoming hills, and writing now about the caravan tour I cannot always avoid falling into a strain so intimately, in my memory, associated with it. They were a strange set of human beings gathered together beneath those temporary and inadequate roofs. I hope my hearers *see* them.

Our march that day had been more silent than usual, for the party was greatly subject, as I was gradually discovering, to ups and downs in its spirits, and I suppose the dreary influence of Bodiam together with the defection of Lord Sigismund lay heavily upon them, for that day was undoubtedly a day of downs. The weather was autumnal. It did not rain, but sky and earth were equally leaden, and I only saw very occasional gleams of sunshine reflected in the puddles on which my eyes were necessarily fixed if I would successfully avoid them. At a place called Brede, a bleak hamlet exposed on the top of a hill, we were to have met Lord Sigismund but instead there was only an emissary from him with a letter for Mrs. Menzies-Legh, which she read in silence, handed to her husband in silence, waited while he read it in silence, and then without any comment gave the signal to resume the march. How differently Germans would have behaved I need not tell you, for news is a thing no German will omit to share with his neighbours, discussing it thoroughly, *lang und breit*, from every possible and impossible point of view, which is, I maintain, the human way, and the other way is inhuman.

"Is not Lord Sigismund coming to-day?" I asked Mrs. Menzies-Legh the first moment she came within earshot.

"I'm afraid not," said she.

"To-morrow?"

"I'm afraid not."

"What, not again at all?" I exclaimed, for this was indeed bad news.

"I'm afraid not."

And, contrary to her practice she dropped behind.

"Why is not Lord Sigismund coming back?" I shouted to Menzies-Legh, whose caravan was following mine, mine as usual being in the middle; and I walked on backward through all the puddles so as to face him, being unable to leave my horse.

"Eh?" said he.

How like an ill-conditioned carter he looked, trudging gloomily along, his coat off, his battered hat pushed back from his sullen forehead! Another week, I thought, and he would be perfectly indistinguishable from the worst example of a real one.

"Why is not Lord Sigismund coming back?" I repeated, my hands up to my mouth in order to carry my question right up to his heavy ears.

"He's prevented."

"Prevented?"

"Eh?"

"Prevented by what?"

"Eh?"

This was wilfulness: it must have been.

"What—has—prevented—him?" I roared.

"Look out—your van will be in the ditch."

And turning quickly I was just in time to pull the tiresome brute of a horse, who never could be left to himself an instant, straight again.

I walked on shrugging my shoulders. Menzies-Legh was without any doubt as ill-conditioned a specimen of manhood as I have ever come across.

At the four crossroads beyond Brede, on the party's pausing as usual to argue over the signpost while Fate, with Frogs' Hole Farm up her sleeve, laughed in the background, I laid my hand on Jellaby's arm—its thinness quite made me jump—and said, "Where is Lord Sigismund?"

"Gone home, I believe, with his father."

"Why is he not coming back?"

"He's prevented."

"But by what? Is he ill?"

"Oh, no. He's just—just prevented, you know."

And Jellaby slipped his arm out of my grasp and went to stare with the others up at the signpost.

On the road we finally decided to take, while they were all clustering round the labourer I have mentioned who directed us to the deserted farm, I approached Frau von Eckthum who stood on the outer fringe of the cluster, and said in the gentler voice I instinctively used when speaking to her, "I hear Lord Sigismund is not coming back."

Gently as my voice was, it yet made her start; she generally did start when spoken to, being unusually (it adds to her attractiveness) highly strung.

("She doesn't when I speak to her," said Edelgard, on my commenting to her on this characteristic.

"My dear, you are merely another woman," I replied—somewhat sharply, for Edelgard is really often unendurably obtuse.)

"I hear Lord Sigismund is not coming back," I said, then, very gently, to the tender lady.

"Oh?" said she.

For the first time I could have wished a wider range of speech.

"He has been prevented, I hear."

"Oh?"

"Do you know what has prevented him?"

She looked at me and then at the others absorbed by the labourer with a funny little look (altogether feminine) of helplessness, though it could not of course have been that; then, adding another letter but not unfortunately another word to her vocabulary, she said "No"—or rather "N-n-n-o," for she hesitated.

And up bustled Jellaby as I was about to press my inquiries, and taking me by the elbow (the familiarity of this sort of person!) led me aside to overwhelm me with voluble directions as to the turnings to Frogs' Hole Farm.

Well, it was undoubtedly a blow to find by far the most interesting and amiable member of the party (with the exception of Frau von Eckthum) gone, and gone without a word, without an explanation, a farewell, or a regret. It was Lord Sigismund's presence, the presence of one so unquestionably of my own social standing, of one whose relations could all bear any amount of scrutiny and were not like Edelgard's Aunt Bockhügel (of whom perhaps more presently) a dark and doubtful spot round which conversation had to make careful *détours*—it was undoubtedly,

Gentle as my voice was, it yet made her start

I say, Lord Sigismund who had given the expedition its decent air of being just an aristocratic whim, stamped it, marked it, raised it altogether above mere appearances. He was a Christian gentleman; more, he was the only one of the party who could cook. Were we, then, to be thrown for future sustenance entirely on Jellaby's porridge?

That afternoon, dining in the mud of the deserted farmyard, we had sausages; a dinner that had only been served once before, and which was a sign in itself that the kitchen resources were strained. I have already described how Jellaby cooked sausages, goading them round and round the pan, prodding them, pursuing them, giving them no rest in which to turn brown quietly—as foolish a way with a sausage as ever I have seen. For the second time during the tour we ate them pink, filling up as best we might with potatoes, a practice we had got quite used to, though to you, my hearers, who only know potatoes as an adjunct, it will seem a pitiable state of things. So it was; but when one is hungry to the point of starvation a hot potato is an attractive object, and two hot potatoes are exactly doubly so. Anyhow my respect for them has increased tenfold since my holiday, and I insist now on their being eaten in much larger quantities than they used to be in our kitchen, for do I not know how thoroughly they fill? And servants quarrel if they have too much meat.

"That is poor food for a man like you, Baron," said Menzies-Legh, suddenly addressing me from the other end of the table.

He had been watching me industriously scraping—picture, my friends, Baron von Ottringel thus reduced—scraping, I say, the last remnants of the potatoes out of the saucepan after the ladies had gone, accompanied by Jellaby, to begin washing up.

It was so long since he had spoken to me of his own accord that I paused in my scraping to stare at him. Then, with my natural readiness at that sort of thing, I drew his attention to his bad manners earlier in the afternoon by baldly answering "Eh?"

"I wonder you stand it," he said, taking no notice of the little lesson.

"Pray will you tell me how it is to be helped?" I inquired. "Roast goose does not, I have observed, grow on the hedges in your country." (This, I felt, was an excellent retort.)

"But it flourishes in London and other big towns," said he—a foolish thing to say to a man sitting in the back yard of Frogs' Hole Farm. "Have a cigarette," he added; and he pushed his case toward me.

I lit one, slightly surprised at the change for the better in his behaviour, and he got up and came and sat on the vacant camp-stool beside me.

"Hunger," said I, continuing the conversation, "is the best sauce, and as I am constantly hungry it follows that I cannot complain of not having enough sauce. In fact, I am beginning to feel that gipsying is a very health-giving pursuit."

"Damp—damp," said Menzies-Legh, shaking his head and screwing up his mouth in a disapproval that astonished me.

"What?" I said. "It may be a little damp if the weather is damp, but one must get used to hardships."

"Only to find," said he, "that one's constitution has been undermined."

"What?" said I, unable to understand this change of attitude.

"Undermined for life," said he, impressively.

"My dear sir, I have heard you myself, under the most adverse circumstances, repeatedly remark that it was healthy and jolly."

"My dear Baron," said he, "I am not like you. Neither Jellaby, nor I, nor Browne either, for that matter, has your physique. We are physically, compared to you—to be quite frank—mere weeds."

"Oh, come now, my dear sir, I cannot permit you—you undervalue—of slighter build, perhaps, but hardly——"

"It is true. Weeds. Mere weeds. And my point is that we, accordingly, are not nearly so likely as you are to suffer in the long run from the privations and exposure of a bad-weather holiday like this."

"Well now, you must pardon me if I entirely fail to see——"

"Why, my dear Baron, it's as plain as daylight. Our constitutions will not be undermined for the shatteringly good reason that we have none to undermine."

My hearers will agree that, logically, the position was incontrovertible, and yet I doubted.

Observing my silence, and probably guessing its cause, he took up an empty glass and poured some tea into it from the teapot at which Frau von Eckthum had been slaking her thirst in spite of my warnings (I had, alas, no right to forbid) that so much tea drinking would make her still more liable to start when suddenly addressed.

"Look here," said he.

I looked.

"You can see this tea."

"Certainly."

"Clear, isn't it? A beautiful clear brown. A tribute to the spring water here. You can see the house and all its windows through it, it is so perfectly transparent."

And he held it up, and shutting one eye stared through it with the other.

"Well?" I inquired.

"Well, now look at this."

And he took another glass and set it beside the first one, and poured both tea and milk into it.

"Look there," he said.

I looked.

"Jellaby," said he.

I stared.

Then he took another glass, and poured both tea and milk into it, setting it in a line with the first two.

"Browne," said he.

I stared.

Then he took a fourth glass, and filled it in the same manner as the second and third and placed it at the end of the line.

"Myself," said he.

I stared.

"Can you see through either of those three?" he asked, tapping them one after the other.

"No," said I.

"Now if I put a little more milk into them"—he did—"it makes no difference. They were muddy and thick before, and they remain muddy and thick. *But*"—and he held the milk jug impressively over the first glass—"if I put the least drop into this one"—he did—"see how visible it is. The admirable clearness is instantaneously dimmed. The pollution spreads at once. The entire glass, owing to that single drop, is altered, muddied, ruined."

"Well?" I inquired, as he paused and stared hard at me.

"Well?" said he. "Do you not see?"

"See what?" said I.

"My point. It's as clear as the first glass was before I put milk into it. The first glass, my dear Baron, is you, with your sound and perfect constitution."

I bowed.

"Your splendid health."

I bowed.

"Your magnificent physique."

I bowed.

"The other three are myself, and Jellaby, and Browne."

He paused.

"And the drop of milk," he said slowly, "is the caravan tour."

I was confounded; and you, my hearers, will admit that I had every reason to be. Here was an example of what is rightly called irresistible logic, and a reasonable man dare not refuse, once he recognizes it, to bow in silence. Yet I felt very well. I said I did, after a pause during which I was realizing how unassailable Menzies-Legh's position was, and endeavouring to reconcile its unassailableness with my own healthful sensations.

"You can't get away from facts," he answered. "There they are."

And he indicated with his cigarette the four glasses and the milk jug.

"But," I repeated, "except for a natural foot-soreness I undoubtedly do feel very well."

"My dear Baron, it is obvious beyond all argument that the more absolutely well a person is the more easily he must be affected by the smallest upset, by the smallest variation in the environment to which he has got accustomed. Paradox, which plays so large a part in all truths, is rampant here. Those in perfect health are nearer than anybody else to being seriously ill. To keep well you must never be quite so."

He paused.

"When," he continued, seeing that I said nothing, "we began caravaning we could not know how persistently cold and wet it was going to be, but now that we do I must say I feel the responsibility of having persuaded you—or of my sister-in-law's having persuaded you—to join us."

"But I feel very well," I repeated.

"And so you will, up to the moment when you do not."

Of course that was true.

"Rheumatism, now," he said, shaking his head; "I greatly fear rheumatism for you in the coming winter. And rheumatism once it gets hold of a man doesn't leave him till it has ravaged each separate organ, including, as everybody knows, that principal organ of all, the heart."

This was gloomy talk, and yet the man was right. The idea that a holiday, a thing planned and looked forward to with so much pleasure, was to end by ravaging my organs did not lighten the leaden atmosphere that surrounded and weighed upon Frogs' Hole Farm.

"I cannot alter the weather," I said at last—irritably, for I felt ruffled.

"No. But I wouldn't risk it for too long if I were you," said he.

"Why, I have paid for a month," I exclaimed, surprised that he should overlook this clinching fact.

"That, set against an impaired constitution, is a very inconsiderable trifle," said he.

"Not inconsiderable at all," said I sharply.

"Money is money, and I am not one to throw it away. And what about the van? You cannot abandon an entire van at a great distance from the place it belongs to."

"Oh," said he quickly, "we would see to that."

I got up, for the sight of the glasses full of what I was forced to acknowledge was symbolic truth irritated me. The one representing myself, into which he had put but one drop of milk, was miserably discoloured. I did not like to think of such discolouration being my probable portion, and yet having paid for a month's caravaning what could I do?

The afternoon was chilly and very damp, and I buttoned my wraps carefully about my throat. Menzies-Legh watched me.

"Well," said he, getting up and looking first at me and then at the glasses and then at me again, "what do you think of doing, Baron?"

"Going for a little stroll," I said.

And I went.

CHAPTER XVII

THIS was a singular conversation.

I passed round the back of the house and along a footpath I found there, turning it over in my mind. Less than ever did I like Menzies-Legh. In spite of the compliments about my physique I liked him less than ever. And how very annoying it is when a person you do not like is right; bad enough if you do like him, but intolerable if you do not. As I proceeded along the footpath with my eyes on the ground I saw at every step those four glasses of tea, particularly my one, the one that sparkled so brilliantly at first and was afterward so easily ruined. Absorbed in this contemplation I did not notice whither my steps were tending till I was pulled up suddenly by a church door. The path had led me to that, and then, as I saw, skirted along a fringe of tombstones to a gate in a wall beyond which appeared the chimneys of what was no doubt the parsonage.

The church door was open, and I went in—for I was tired, and here were pews; ruffled, and here was peace. The droning of a voice led me to conclude (rightly) that a service was in progress, for I had learned by this time that in England the churches constantly burst out into services, regardless of the sort of day it is—whether, I mean, it is a Sunday or not. I entered, and selecting a pew with a red cushion along its seat and a comfortable footstool sat down.

The pastor was reading the Scriptures out of a Bible supported, according to the unaccountable British custom, on the back of a Prussian eagle. This prophetic bird—the first swallow, as it were, of that summer which I trust will not long be delayed, when Luther's translation will rest on its back and be read aloud by a German pastor to a congregation forced to understand by the simple methods we bring to bear on our Polish (also acquired) subjects—eyed me with a human intelligence. We eyed each other, in fact, as old friends might who meet after troublous experiences in an alien land.

Except for this bird, who seemed to me quite human in his expression of alert sympathy, the pastor and I were alone in the building; and I sat there marvelling at the wasteful folly that pays a man to read and pray daily to a set of empty pews. Ought he not rather to stay at home and keep an eye on his wife? To do, indeed, anything sooner than conduct a service which nobody evidently wants? I call it heathenism; I call it idolatry; and so would any other plain man who heard and saw empty pews, things of wood and cushions, being addressed as brethren, and dearly beloved ones into the bargain.

When he had done at the eagle he crossed over to another place and began reciting something else; but very soon, after only a few words, he stopped dead and looked at me.

I wondered why, for I had not done anything. Even, however, with that innocence of conscience in the background, it does make a man uncomfortable when a pastor will not go on but fixes his eyes on you sitting harmless in your pew, and I found myself unable to return his gaze. The eagle was staring at me with a startling expression of comprehension, almost as if he too were thinking that a pastor officiating has such an undoubted advantage over the persons in the pews that it is cowardice to use it. My discomfort increased considerably when I saw the pastor descend from his place and bear down on me, his eyes still fixing me, his white clothing fluttering out behind him. What, I asked myself greatly perturbed, could the creature possibly want? I soon found out, for thrusting an open Prayer-book toward me he pointed to a verse of what appeared to be a poem, and whispered:

"Will you kindly stand up and take your part in the service?"

Even had I known how, surely I had no part nor lot in such a form of worship.

"Sir," I said, not heeding the outstretched book, but feeling about in my breast-pocket, "permit me to present you with my card. You will then see———"

He, however, in his turn refused to heed the outstretched card. He did not so much as look at it.

"I cannot *oblige* you to," he whispered, as though our conversation were unfit for the eagle's ears; and leaving the open book on the little shelf in the front of the pew he strode back again to his place and resumed his reading, doing what he called my part as well as his own with a severity of voice and manner ill-suited to one presumably addressing the *liebe Gott*.

Well, being there and very comfortable I did not see why I should go. I was behaving quite inoffensively, sitting still and holding my tongue, and the comfort of being in a building with no fresh air in it was greater than you, my friends, who only know fresh air at intervals and in properly limited quantities, will be able to understand. So I stayed till the end, till he, after a profusion of prayers, got up from his knees and walked away into some obscure portion of the church where I could no longer observe his movements, and then, not desiring to meet him, I sought the path that had led me thither and hurriedly descended the hill to our melancholy camp. Once I thought I heard footsteps behind me and I hastened mine, getting as quickly round a bend that would conceal me from any one following me as a tired man could manage, and it was not till I had reached and climbed into the Elsa that I felt really safe.

The three caravans were as usual drawn up in a parallel line with mine in the middle, and their door ends facing the farm. To be in the middle is a most awkward situation, for you cannot speak the least word of caution (or forgiveness, as the case may be) to your wife without running grave risk of being overheard. Often I used carefully to shut all the windows and draw the door curtain, hoping thus to obtain a greater freedom of speech, though this was of little use with the Ilsa and the Ailsa on either side, their windows open, and perhaps a group of caravaners sitting on the ground immediately beneath.

My wife was mending, and did not look up when I came in. How differently she behaved at home. She not only used to look up when I came in, she got up, and got up quickly too, hastening at the first sound of my return to meet me in the passage, and greeting me with the smiles of a dutiful and accordingly contented wife.

Shutting the Elsa's windows I drew her attention to this.

"But there isn't a passage," said she, still with her head bent over a sock.

Really Edelgard should take care to be specially feminine, for she certainly will never shine on the strength of her brains.

"Dear wife," I began—and then the complete futility of trying to thresh any single subject out in that airy, sound-carrying dwelling stopped me. I sat down on the yellow box instead, and remarked that I was extremely fatigued.

"So am I," said she.

"My feet ache so," I said, "that I fear there may be something serious the matter with them."

"So do mine," said she.

This, I may observe, was a new and irritating habit she had got into: whatever I complained of in the way of unaccountable symptoms in divers portions of my frame, instead of sympathizing and suggesting remedies she said hers (whatever it was) did it too.

"Your feet cannot possibly," said I, "be in the terrible condition mine are in. In the first place mine are bigger, and accordingly afford more scope for disorders. I have shooting pains in them resembling neuralgia, and no doubt traceable to some nervous source."

"So have I," said she.

"I think bathing might do them good," I said, determined not to become angry. "Will you get me some hot water, please?"

"Why?" said she.

She had never said such a thing to me before. I could only gaze at her in a profound surprise.

"Why?" I repeated at length, keeping studiously calm. "What an extraordinary question. I could give you a thousand reasons if I chose, such as that I desire to bathe them; that hot water—rather luckily for itself—has no feet, and therefore has to be fetched; and that a wife has to do as she is told. But I will, my dear Edelgard, confine myself to the counter inquiry, and ask why not?"

"I, too, my dear Otto," said she—and she spoke with great composure, her head bent over her mending, "could give you a thousand answers to that if I chose, such as that I desire to get this sock finished—yours, by the way; that I have walked exactly as far as you have; that I see no reason why you should not, as there are no servants here, fetch your own hot water; and that your wishing or not wishing to bathe your feet has really, if you come to think of it, nothing to do with me. But I will confine myself just to saying that I prefer not to go."

It can be imagined with what feelings—not mixed but unmitigated—I listened to this. And after five years! Five years of patience and guidance.

"Is this my Edelgard?" I managed to say, recovering speech enough for those four words but otherwise struck dumb.

"Your Edelgard?" she repeated musingly as she continued to mend, and not even looking at me. "Your boots, your handkerchief, your gloves, your socks—yes——"

I confess I could not follow, and could only listen amazed.

"But not your Edelgard. At least, not more than you are my Otto."

"But—my boots?" I repeated, really dazed.

"Yes," she said, folding up the finished sock, "they really are yours. Your property. But you should not suppose that I am a kind of living boot, made to be trodden on. I, my dear Otto, am a human being, and no human being is another human being's property."

A flash of light illuminated my brain. "Jellaby!" I cried.

"Hullo?" was the immediate answer from outside. "Want me, Baron?"

"No, no! No, *no*! No, NO!" I cried leaping up and dragging the door curtain to, as though that could possibly deaden our conversation. "He has been infecting you," I continued, in a whisper so much charged with indignation that it hissed, "with his poisonous——"

Then I recollected that he could probably hear every word, and muttering an imprecation on caravans I relapsed on to the yellow box and said with forced calm as I scrutinized her face:

"Dear wife, you have no idea how exactly you resemble your Aunt Bockhügel when you put on that expression."

For the first time this failed to have an effect. Up to then to be told she looked like her Aunt Bockhügel had always brought her back with a jerk to smiles; even if she had to wrench a smile into position she did so, for the Aunt Bockhügel is the sore point in Edelgard's family, the spot, the smudge across its brightness, the excrescence on its tree, the canker in its bud, the worm destroying its fruit, the night frost paralyzing its blossoms. She cannot be suppressed. She cannot be explained. Everybody knows she is there. She was one of the reasons that made me walk about my room the whole of the night before I proposed marriage to Edelgard, a prey to doubts as to how far a man may go in recklessness in the matter of the aunts he fastens upon his possible children. The Ottringels can show no such relatives; at least there is one, but she looms almost equal to the rest owing to the mirage created by fogs of antiquity and distance. But Edelgard's aunt is contemporary and conspicuous. Of a vulgar soul at her very birth, as soon as she came of age she deliberately left the ranks of the nobility and united herself to a dentist. We go there to be treated for toothache, because they take us (owing to the relationship) on unusually favourable terms; otherwise we do not know them. There is however an undoubted resemblance to Edelgard in her less pleasant moods, a thickened, heavier, and older Edelgard, and my wife, well aware of it (for I help her to check it as much as possible by pointing it out whenever it occurs) has been on each occasion eager to readjust her features without loss of time. On this one she was not. Nay, she relaxed still more, and into a profounder likeness.

"It's true," she said, not even looking at me but staring out of the window; "it's true about the boots."

"Aunt Bockhügel! Aunt Bockhügel!" I cried softly, clapping my hands.

She actually took no notice, but continued to stare abstractedly out of the window; and feeling how impossible it was to talk really naturally to her with Jellaby just outside, I chose the better part and with a movement I could not wholly suppress of impatience got up and left her.

Jellaby, as I suspected, was sitting on the ground leaning against one of our wheels as though it were a wheel belonging to his precious community and not ours, hired and paid for. Was it possible that he selected this wheel out of the twelve he could have chosen from because it was my wife's wheel?

"Do you want anything?" he asked, looking up and taking his pipe out of his mouth; and I just had enough self-control to shake my head and hurry on, for I felt if I had stopped I would have fallen upon him and rattled him about as a terrier rattles a rat.

But what terrible things caravans are when you have to share one with a person with whom you have reason to be angry! Of all their sides this is beyond doubt the worst; worse than when the rain comes in on to your bed, worse than when the wind threatens to blow them over during the night, or half of them sinks into the mud and has to be dug out laboriously in the morning. It may be imagined with what feelings I wandered forth into the chill evening, homeless, bearing as I felt a strong resemblance to that Biblical dove which was driven forth from the shelter of the ark and had no idea what to do next. Of course I was not going to fetch the hot water and return with it, as it were (to pursue my simile), in my beak. Every husband throughout Germany will understand the impossibility of doing that—picture Edelgard's triumph if I had! Yet I could not at the end of a laborious day wander indefinitely out-of-doors; besides, I might meet the pastor.

The rest of the party were apparently in their caravans, judging from the streams of conversation issuing forth, and there was no one but old James reclining on a sack in the corner of a distant shed to offer me the solace of companionship. With a sudden mounting to my head of a mighty wave of indignation and determination not to be shut out of my own caravan, I turned and quickly retraced my steps.

"Hullo, Baron," said Jellaby, still propped against my wheel. "Had enough of it already?"

"More than enough of some things," I said, eyeing him meaningly as I made my way, much impeded by my mackintosh, up the ladder at an oblique angle (it never could or would stand straight) against our door.

"For instance?" he inquired.

"I am unwell," I answered shortly, evading a quarrel—for why should I allow myself to be angered by a wisp like that?—and entering the Elsa drew the curtain sharply to on his expressions of conventional regret.

Edelgard had not changed her position. She did not look up.

I pulled off my outer garments and flung them on the floor, and sitting down with emphasis on the yellow box unlaced and kicked off my boots and pulled off my stockings.

Edelgard raised her head and fixed her eyes on me with a careful imitation of surprise.

"What is it, Otto?" she said. "Have you been invited out to dine?"

I suppose she considered this amusing, but of course it was not, and I jerked myself free of my braces without answering.

"Won't you tell me what it is?" she asked again.

For all answer I crawled into my berth and pulled the coverings up to my ears and turned my face to the wall; for indeed I was at the end both of my patience and my strength. I had had two days' running full of disagreeable incidents, and Menzies-Legh's fatal drop of milk seemed at last to have fallen into the brightness of my original strong tea. I ached enough to make his prophesied rheumatism a very near peril, and was not at all sure as I lay there that it had not already begun its work upon me, beginning it with an alarming promise of system and thoroughness at the very beginning, *i. e.*, my feet.

"Poor Otto," said Edelgard, getting up and laying her hand on my forehead; adding, after a moment, "It is nice and cool."

"Cool? I should think so," said I shivering. "I am frozen."

She got a rug out of the yellow box and laid it over me, tucking in the side.

"So tired?" she said presently, as she tidied up my clothes.

"Ill," I murmured.

"What is it?"

"Oh, leave me, leave me. You do not really care. Leave me."

At this she paused in her occupation to gaze, I fancy, at my back as I lay resolutely turned away.

"It is very early to go to bed," she said after a while.

"Not when a man is ill."

"It isn't seven yet."

"Oh, do not, I beg you, argue with me. If you cannot have sympathy you can at least leave me. It is all I ask."

This silenced her, and she moved about the van more careful not to sway it, so that presently I was able to fall into an exhausted sleep.

How long this lasted I could not on suddenly waking tell, but everything had grown dark and Edelgard, as I could hear, was asleep above me. Something had wrenched me out of the depths of slumber in which I was sunk and had brought me up again with a jerk to that surface known to us as sentient life. You are aware, my friends, being also living beings with all the experiences connected with such a condition behind you, you are aware what such a jerking is. It seems to be a series of flashes. The first flash reminds you (with an immense shock) that you are not as you for one comfortable instant supposed in your own safe familiar bed at home; the second brings back the impression of the loneliness and weirdness of Frogs' Hole Farm (or its, in your case, local equivalent) that you received while yet it was day; the third makes you realize with a clutching at your heart that *something* happened before you woke up, and that *something* is presently going to happen again. You lie awake waiting for it, and the entire surface of your body becomes as you wait uniformly damp. The sound of a person breathing regularly in the apartment does but emphasize your loneliness. I confess I was unable to reach out for matches and strike a light, unable to do anything under that strong impression that something had happened except remain motionless beneath the bed-coverings. This was no shame to me, my friends. Face me with cannon, and I have the courage of any man living, but place me on the edge of the supernatural and I can only stay beneath the bedclothes and grow most lamentably damp. Such a thin skin of wood divided me from the night outside. Any one could push back the window standing out there; any one ordinarily tall would then have his head and shoulders practically inside the caravan. And there was no dog to warn us or to frighten such a wretch away. And all my money was beneath my mattress, the worst place possible to put it in if what you want is not to be personally disturbed. What was it I had heard? What was it that called me up from the depths of unconsciousness? As the moments passed—and except for Edelgard's regular breathing there was only an awful emptiness and absence of sound—I tried to persuade myself it was just the sausages having been so pink at dinner; and the tenseness of my terror had begun slowly to relax when I was smitten stark again—and by what, my friends? *By the tuning of a violin.*

Now consider, you who frequent concerts and see nothing disturbing in this sound, consider our situation. Consider the remoteness from the highway of Frogs' Hole Farm; how you had, in order to reach it, to follow the prolonged convolutions of a lane; how you must then come by a cart track along the edge of a hop-field; how the house lay alone and empty in a hollow, deserted, forlorn, untidy, out of repair. Consider further that none of our party had brought a violin and none, to judge from the absence in their conversation of any allusions to such an instrument, played on it. No one knows who has not heard one tuned under the above conditions the blankness of the horror it can strike into one's heart. I listened, stiff with fear. It was tuned with a care and at a length that convinced me that the spirit turning its knobs must be of a quite unusual musical talent, possessed of an acutely sensitive ear. How came it that no one else heard it? Was it possible—I curdled at the thought—that only myself of the party had been chosen by the powers at work for this ghastly privilege? When the thing broke into a wild dance, and a great and rhythmical stamping of feet began apparently quite near and yet equally apparently on boards, I was seized with a panic that relaxed my stiffness into action and enabled me to thump the underneath of Edelgard's mattress with both my fists, and thump and thump with a desperate vigour that did at last rouse her.

Being half asleep she was more true to my careful training than when perfectly awake, and on hearing my shouts she unhesitatingly tumbled out of her berth and leaning into mine asked me with some anxiety what the matter was.

"The matter? Do you not hear?" I said, clutching her arm with one hand and holding up the other to enjoin silence.

She woke up entirely.

"Why, what in the world———" she said. Then pulling a window curtain aside she peeped out. "There's only the Ailsa there," she said, "dark and quiet. And only the Ilsa here," she added, peeping through the opposite curtain, "dark and quiet."

I looked at her, marvelling at the want of imagination in women that renders it possible for them to go on being stolid in the presence of what seemed undoubtedly the supernatural. Unconsciously this stolidity, however, made me feel more like myself; but when on her going to the door and unbolting it and looking out she made an exclamation and hastily shut it again, I sank back on my pillow once more *hors de combat*, so great was the shock. Face me, I say, with cannon, and I can do anything but expect nothing of me if it is ghosts.

"Otto," she whispered, holding the door, "come and look."

I could not speak.

"Get up and come and look," she whispered again.

Well my friends I had to, or lose forever my moral hold of and headship over her. Besides, I was drawn somehow to the fatal door. How I got out of my berth and along the cold floor of the caravan to the end I cannot conceive. I was obliged to help myself along, I remember, by sliding my hand over the surface of the yellow box. I muttered, I remember, "I am ill—I am ill," and truly never did a man feel more so. And when I got to the door and looked through the crack she opened, what did I see?

I saw the whole of the lower windows of the farmhouse ablaze with candles.

CHAPTER XVIII

MY hearers will I hope appreciate the frankness with which I show them all my sides, good and bad. I do so with my eyes open, aware that some of you may very possibly think less well of me for having been, for instance, such a prey to supernatural dread. Allow me, however, to point out that if you do you are wrong. You suffer from a confusion of thought. And I will show you why. My wife, you will have noticed, had on the occasion described few or no fears. Did this prove courage? Certainly not. It merely proved the thicker spiritual skin of woman. Quite without that finer sensibility that has made men able to produce works of genius while women have been able only to produce (a merely mechanical process) young, she felt nothing apparently but a bovine surprise. Clearly, if you have no imagination neither can you have any fears. A dead man is not frightened. An almost dead man does not care much either. The less dead a man is the more do possible combinations suggest themselves to him. It is imagination and sensibility, or the want of them, that removes you further or brings you nearer to the animals. Consequently (I trust I am being followed?) when imagination and sensibility are busiest, as they were during those moments I lay waiting and listening in my berth, you reach the highest point of aloofness from the superiority to the brute creation; your vitality is at its greatest; you are, in a word, if I may be permitted to coin an epigram, *least dead*. Therefore, my friends, it is plain that at that very moment when you (possibly) may have thought I was showing my weakest side I was doing the exact opposite, and you will not, having intelligently followed the argument, say at the end of it as my poor little wife did, "But how?"

I do not wish, however, to leave you longer under the impression that the deserted farmhouse was haunted. It may have been of course, but it was not on that night of last August. What was happening was that a party from the parsonage—a holiday party of young and rather inclined to be noisy people, which had overflowed the bounds of the accommodation there—was utilizing the long, empty front room as an impromptu (I believe that is the expression) ball-room. The farm belonged to the pastor—observe the fatness of these British ecclesiastics—and it was the practice of his family during the holidays to come down sometimes in the evening and dance in it. All this I found out after Edelgard had dressed and gone across to see for herself what the lights and stamping meant. She insisted on doing so in spite of my warnings, and came back after a long interval to tell me the above, her face flushed and her eyes bright, for she had seized the opportunity, regardless of what I might be feeling waiting alone, to dance too.

"You danced too?" I exclaimed.

"Do come, Otto. It is such fun," said she.

"With whom did you dance, may I inquire?" I asked, for the thought of the Baroness von Ottringel dancing with the first comer in a foreign farm was of course most disagreeable to me.

"Mr. Jellaby," said she. "Do come."

"Jellaby? What is he doing there?"

"Dancing. And so is everybody. They are all there. That's why their caravans were so quiet. Do come."

And she ran out again, a childishly eager expression on her face, into the night.

"Edelgard!" I called.

But though she must have heard me she did not come back.

Relieved, puzzled, vexed, and curious together, I did get up and dress, and on lighting a candle and looking at my watch I was astonished to find that it was only a quarter to ten. For a moment I could not credit my eyes, and I shook the watch and held it to my ears, but it was going, as steadily as usual, and all I could do was to reflect as I dressed on what may happen to you if you go to bed and to sleep at seven o'clock.

And how soundly I must have done it. But of course I was unusually weary, and not feeling at all well. Two hours' excellent sleep, however, had done wonders for me so great are my recuperative powers, and I must say I could not help smiling as I crossed the yard and went up to the house at the remembrance of Menzies-Legh's glass of tea. He would not see much milk about me now, thought I, as I strode, giving my moustache ends a final upward push and guided by the music, into the room in which they were dancing.

The dance came to an end as I entered, and a sudden hush seemed to fall upon the company. It was composed of boys and young girls attired in evening garments next to which the clothes of the caravaners, weather-beaten children of the road, looked odd and grimy indeed. The tender lady, it is true, had put on a white and cobwebby kind of blouse, which together with her short walking skirt and the innocent droop of her fair hair about her little ears made her look at the most eighteen, and Mrs. Menzies-Legh had tricked herself out in white too, producing indeed for our admiration a white skirt as well as a white blouse, and achieving at the most by these efforts an air of (no doubt spurious) cleanliness; but the others were still all spattered and disfigured by the muddy accumulations of the past day.

Though they stopped dancing as I came in I had time to receive a photograph on my mind's eye of the various members of our party: of Jellaby, loose-collared and wispy-haired, gyrating with poor Frau von Eckthum, of Edelgard, flushed with childish enjoyment, in the grip of a boy who might very well have been her own if I had married her a few years sooner and if it were conceivable that I could ever have produced anything so undeveloped and half-grown, and of, if you please, Menzies-Legh in all his elderliness, dancing with an object the short voluminousness of whose clothing proclaimed a condition of unripeness even greater than that of the two fledglings—dancing, in a word, with a child.

That he should dance at all was, you will agree, sufficiently unworthy but at least if he must make himself publicly foolish he might have done it with some one more suited to his years, some one of the age of the lady, for instance—singularly unlike one's idea of a ghost—standing at the upper end of the room playing the violin that had half an hour previously been so incomprehensible to me.

On seeing me enter he stopped dead, and his face resumed the familiar look of lowering gloom. The other couples followed his example, and the violin, after a brief hesitation, whined away into passivity.

"Capital," said I heartily to Menzies-Legh, who happened to have been in the act of dancing past the door I came in by. "Capital. Enjoy yourself, my friend. You are doing admirably well for what you told me is a weed. In a German ball-room you would, I assure you, create an immense sensation, for it is not the custom there for gentlemen over thirty—which," I amended, bowing, "I may be entirely wrong in presuming that you are—for gentlemen over thirty——"

But he interrupted me to remark with the intelligence that characterized him (after all, what ailed the man was, I believe, principally stupidity) that this was not a German ball-room.

"Ah," said I, "you are right there, my friend. That indeed is what you English call a different pair of shoes. If it were, do you know where the gentlemen over thirty would be?"

He spoiled the neat answer I had all ready of "Not there" by, instead of seeking information, observing with his customary boorishness, "Confound the gentlemen over thirty," and walking his long-stockinged partner away.

"Otto," whispered my wife, hurrying up, "you must come and be introduced to the people who are kindly letting us dance here."

"Not unless they are of decent birth," I said firmly.

"Whether they are or not you must come," said she. "The lady who is playing is———"

"I know, I know, she is a ghost," said I, unable to forbear smiling at my own jest; and I think my hearers will agree that a man who can make fun of himself may certainly be said to be at least fairly equipped with a sense of humour.

Edelgard stared. "She is the pastor's wife," she said. "It is her party. It is so kind of her to let us in. You must come and be introduced."

"She is a ghost," I persisted, greatly diverted by the notion, for I felt a reaction of cheerfulness, and never was a lady more substantial than the one with the violin; "she is a ghost, and a highly unattractive specimen of the sect. Dear wife, only ghosts should be introduced to other ghosts. I am flesh and blood, and will therefore go instead and release the little Eckthum from the flesh and blood persistencies of Jellaby."

"But Otto, you must come," said Edelgard, laying her hand on my arm as I prepared to move in the direction of the charming victim; "you can't be rude. She is your hostess———"

"She is my ghostess," said I, very divertingly I thought; so divertingly that I was seized by a barely controllable desire to indulge in open mirth.

Edelgard, however, with the blank incomprehension of the droll so often to be observed in women, did not so much as smile.

"Otto," said she, "you absolutely *must*———"

"Must, dear wife," said I with returning gravity, "is a word no woman of tact ever lets her husband hear. I see no must why I, being who I am, should request an introduction to a Frau Pastor. I would not in Storchwerder. Still less will I at Frog's Hole Farm."

"But you are her guest———"

"I am not. I came."

"But it is so nice of her to allow you to come."

"It is not niceness. She is delighted at the honour."

"But Otto, you simply *can't*———"

I was about to move off definitely to the corner where Frau von Eckthum sat helpless in the talons of Jellaby when who should enter the door just in front of which Edelgard was wrangling but the creature I had last parted from on unfriendly terms in the church a few hours before.

Attired this time from chin to boots in a long and narrow buttoned-down black garment suggestive of that of the Pope's priests, with a gold cross dangling on his chest, his eye immediately caught mine and the genial smile of the party-giver with which he had come in died away. Evidently he had been there earlier, for Edelgard as though she were well acquainted with him darted forward (where, alas, remained the dignity of the well-born?) and very officiously introduced me to him. Me to him, observe.

"Let me," said my wife, "introduce my husband, Baron Ottringel."

And she did.

It was of course the pastor who ought to have been introduced to me on such neutral ground as an impromptu ball-room, but Edelgard had, as the caravan tour lengthened, acquired the habit of using the presence of a third person in order to do as she chose, with no reference whatever to my known wishes. This is a habit specially annoying to a man of my disposition, peppery perhaps, but essentially *bon enfant*, who likes to get his cautions and reprimands over and done with and forgotten, rather than be forced to allow them to accumulate and brood over them indefinitely.

Rendered helpless by my own good breeding—a quality which leads to many a discomfort in life—I was accordingly introduced for all the world as though I were the inferior, and could only show my sensibility of the fact by a conspicuous stiffening.

"Otto thinks it is so very kind of you to let us come in," said Edelgard, all smiles and with an augmentation of officiousness and defiance of me that was incredible.

"I am glad you were able to," replied the pastor looking at me, politeness in his voice and chill in his eye. It was plain the creature was still angry because, in church, I would not pray.

"You are very good," said I, bowing with at least an equal chill.

"Otto wishes," continued the shameless Edelgard, reckless of the private hours with me ahead, "to be introduced to your—to Mrs.—Mrs.——"

"Raggett," supplied the pastor.

And I would certainly have been dragged up then and there to the round red ghost at the top of the room while Edelgard, no doubt, triumphed in the background, if it had not itself come to the rescue by striking up another tune on its fiddle.

"Presently," said the pastor, now become crystallized for me into Raggett. "Presently. Then with pleasure."

And his glassy eye, fixed on mine, had little of pleasure in it.

At this point Edelgard danced away with Jellaby from under my very nose. I made an instinctive movement toward the slender figure alone in the corner, but even as I moved a half-grown boy secured her and hurried her off among the dancers. Looking round, I saw no one else I could go and talk to; even Mrs. Menzies-Legh was not available. There was nothing for it, therefore, but unadulterated Raggett.

"It is nice," observed this person, watching the dancers—he had a hooky profile as well as a glassy eye—"to see young people enjoying themselves."

I bowed, determined to keep within the limits of strict iciness; but as Jellaby and my wife whirled past I could not forbear adding:

"Especially when the young people are so mature that they are fully aware of the extent of their own enjoyment."

"Yes," said he; without, however, any real responsiveness.

"It is only," said I, "when a woman is mature, and more than mature, that she begins to enjoy being young."

"Yes," said he; still with no real responsiveness.

"You may possibly," said I, nettled by this indifference, "regard that as a paradox."

"No," said he.

"It is, however," said I more loudly, "not one."

"No," said he.

"It is on the contrary," said I still louder, "a rather subtle but undeniable truth."

"Yes," said he; and I then perceived that he was not listening.

I do not know what my hearers feel, but I fancy they feel with me that when a gentleman of birth and position is amiable enough to talk to a person of neither it is particularly galling to discover that that person is so unable to grasp the true aspect of the situation as to neglect even to follow the conversation. Good breeding (as I have before remarked, a great hinderer) prevents one's explaining who one is and emphasizing who the other person is and doing then and there a sum of subtraction between one's own value and his and offering him the result for his closer inspection, so what is one to do? Stiffen and go dumb, I suppose. Good breeding allows no more. Alas, there are many and heavy drawbacks to being a gentleman.

Raggett had evidently not been listening to a word I said, for after his last abstracted "Yes," he suddenly turned the glassiness of his eye full upon me.

"I did not know," he said, "when I saw you in church——"

Really the breeding that could go back to the church and what happened there was too bad for words. My impulse was to stop him by saying "Shall we dance?" but I was too uncertain of the extent, nay of the existence, of his powers of seeing fun to venture.

"——that you were not English, or I should not have asked——"

"Sir," I interrupted, endeavouring to get him at all cost out of the church, "who, after all, *is* English?"

He looked surprised. "Well," said he, "I am."

"Why, you do not know. You cannot possibly be certain. Go back a thousand years and, as I lately read in an ingenious but none the less probably right book, the whole of Europe was filled with your fathers and mothers. Starting with your two parents and four grandparents and going backward multiplying as you go, the sixteen great-grandparents are already almost unmanageable, and a century or two further back you find them irrepressibly overflowing your little island and spreading themselves across Europe as thickly and as adhesively as so much jam, until in days a trifle more remote not a person living of white skin but was your father, unless he was your mother. Take," I continued, as he showed signs of wanting to interrupt—"take any example you choose, you will find the same inextricable confusion everywhere. And not only physically—spiritually. Take any example. Anything at random. Take our late lamented Kaiser Friedrich, who married a daughter of your royal house. It is our custom to regard and even to call our Kaiser and Kaiserin the Father and Mother of the nation. The entire nation therefore is, in a spiritual sense, half English. So, accordingly, am I. So, accordingly, to push the point a step further, you become their nephew, and therefore a quarter German—a spiritual German quarter, even as I am a spiritual English half. There is no end to the confusion. Have you observed, sir, that the moment one begins to think everything does become confused?"

"Are you not dancing?" said he, fidgetting and looking about him.

I think one is often angry with people because, having assumed on first acquaintance that they are on one's own level of intelligence, their speech and actions presently prove that they are not. This is unjust; but, like most unjust things, natural. I, however, as a reasonable man do my best to fight against it, and on Raggett's asking this question for all response to the opportunity I gave him of embarking on an interesting discussion, I checked my natural annoyance by realizing that he was what Menzies-Legh probably was, merely stupid. Stupidity, my hearers will agree, is of various kinds, and one kind is want of interest in what is interesting. Of course this particular stupid was hopelessly ill-bred besides, for what can be more so than meeting a series of, to put them at their lowest, suggestive remarks by inquiring if one is not dancing?

"My dear sir," I said, preserving my own manners at least, "in my country it is not the custom for married gentlemen over thirty to dance. Perhaps you were paying me the compliment (often, I must say, paid me before) of supposing I am not yet that age, but I assure you that I am. Nor do ladies continue to dance in our country once their early youth is past and their outlines become—shall we say, bolder? Seats are then provided for them round the walls, and on them they remain in suitable passivity until the oasis afforded by the Lancers is reached, when the elder gentlemen pour gallantly out of the room in which they play cards all the evening and lead them through its intricacies with the ceremony that satisfies Society's sense of the becoming. In this country, on the contrary——"

"Really," he interrupted, his habit of fidgeting more pronounced than ever, "you talk English with such a flow and volume that after all you very well might have joined——"

I now saw that the man was a fanatic, a type of unbalanced person I have always particularly disliked. Good breeding is little if at all appreciated by fanatics, and I might have been excused if, at this point, I had flung mine to the winds. I did not do so, however, but merely interrupted him in my turn by informing him with cold courteousness that I was a Lutheran.

"And Lutherans," I added, "do not pray. At least, not audibly, and certainly never in duets. More," I continued, putting up my hand as he opened his mouth to speak, "more. I am a philosopher, and the prayers of a philosopher cannot be confined within the limits of any formula. Formulas are for the undeveloped. You tie a child into its chair lest, untied, it should fall disastrously to the floor. You tie the undeveloped adult to a creed lest, untied, he should fall goodness really knows where. The grown man, of full stature in mind as well as body, requires no tying. His whole life is his creed. Nothing cut and dried, nothing blatant, nothing gaudily apparent to the outside world, but a subtle saturation, a continual soaking——"

"Excuse me," said he, "one of those candles is guttering."

And he hurried across the room with an expedition I would not have thought possible in a man so gray and glassy to where, in the windows, the illuminating rows of candles had been placed.

Nor did he come back, I am glad to say, for I found him terribly fatiguing; and I remained alone, leaning against the wall by the door.

Down at the further end of the room danced my gentle friend, and also her sister; also all the other members of our party except Menzies-Legh who, recalled to decency by my good-natured shafts, spent the rest of his time soberly either helping the pastor pinch off candle-wicks or turning over the ghost's music for it.

Desiring to watch Frau von Eckthum more conveniently (for I assure you it was a pretty sight to see her grace, and how the same tune that made my wife whirl moved her to nothing more ruffling than an appearance of being wafted) and also in order to be at hand should Jellaby become too tactless, I went down to where our party seemed to be gathered in a knot and took up my position near them against another portion of the wall.

I had hardly done so before they seemed to have melted away to the upper end.

As they did not come back I presently strolled after them. They then appeared to melt back again to the bottom.

It was very odd. It was almost like an optical illusion. When I went up, they went down; when I went down, they went up. I felt at last as one may feel who plays at see-saw, and began to doubt whether I were really on firm ground—on *terra cotta*, as I (amusingly, I thought) called it to Edelgard when we alighted from the steamer at Queenboro', endeavouring to restore her spirits and make her laugh. (Quite in vain I may add, which inclined me to wonder, I remember, whether the illiteracy which is one of the leading characteristics of people's wives had made it impossible for her to understand even so simple a classical play on words as that. In the train I realized that it was not illiteracy but the crossing; and I will say for Edelgard that up to the time the English spirit of criticism got, like a devastating microbe, hold of her German womanliness, she had invariably laughed when I chose to jest.)

But gradually the profitless see-sawing began to tire me. The dance ended, another began, and still my little white-bloused friend had not once been within reach. I made a determined effort to get to her in the pauses between the dances in order to offer to break the German rule on her behalf and give her one dance (for I fancy she was vexed that I did not) and also to help her out of the clutches of Jellaby, but I might as well have tried to dance with and help a moonbeam. She was here, she was there, she was everywhere, except where I happened to be. Once I had almost achieved success when, just as I was sure of her, she ran up to the ghost resting at that moment from its labours and embarked in an apparently endless and absorbing discussion with it, deaf and blind to all beside; and as I had made up my mind that nothing would induce me to extend my Raggett acquaintance by causing myself to be introduced to the psychical phenomenon bearing that name, I was forced to retreat.

Moodily, though. My first hilarity was extinguished. *Bon enfant* though I am I cannot go on being *bon enfant* forever—I must have, so to speak, the encouragement of a bottle at intervals; and I was thinking of taking Edelgard away and giving her, before the others returned to their caravans, a brief description of what maturity combined with calf-like enjoyment looks like to bystanders, when Mrs. Menzies-Legh passing on the arm of a partner caught sight of my face, let her partner go, and came up to me.

"I suppose," she said (and she had at least the grace to hesitate), "it would be no good asking—asking you to—dance?"

I stared at her in undisguised astonishment.

"Are you not dreadfully bored, standing there alone?" she said, as I did not answer. "Won't you—" (again she had the grace to hesitate)—"won't you—dance?"

Pointedly, and still staring amazed, I inquired of her with whom, for really I could hardly believe——

"With me, if—if you will," said she, a rather lame attempt at a smile and a distinctly anxious look in her eyes showing that at least it was only a momentary aberration.

Momentary or not, however, I am not the man to smile with feigned gratification when what is needed is rebuke, especially in the case of this lady who of all others needed one so often and so badly.

"Why," I exclaimed, not caring to conceal my opinion, "why—this is matriarchy!"

And turning on my heel I made my way at once to my wife, stopped her whirlings, drew her away from her partner's arm (Jellaby's, by the way), made her take her husband's and without a word led her out of the room.

But, as I passed the door I saw the look of (I should think pretended) astonishment of Mrs. Menzies-Legh's face give way to the appearance of the dimple, to a sudden screwing together of the upper and lower eyelashes, and my friends will be able to form a notion of how complete was the havoc England had wrought in all she had been taught to understand and reverence in her youth when I tell them that what she was manifestly trying not to do was to laugh.

CHAPTER XIX

ESSENTIALLY, as I have already pointed out, *bon enfant*, I seldom let a bad yesterday spoil a promising to-day; and when on peeping through my curtains next morning I saw the sun had turned our forbidding camp of the night before into a bland warm place across which birds darted singing, a cheery whistle formed itself on my lips and I became aware of that inward satisfaction our neighbours (to whom we owe, I frankly acknowledge, much besides Alsace and Lorraine) have aptly named the *joie de vivre*.

Left to myself this *joie* would undoubtedly always continue uninterruptedly throughout the day. The greater then, say I, the responsibility of those who damp it. Indeed, the responsibility resting on the shoulders of the people who cross one's path during the day is far more tremendous than they in the thickness of their skins imagine. I will not, however, at present go into that, having gradually in the course of writing this become aware that what I shall probably do next will be to collect and embody all my more metaphysical side into a volume to itself with plenty of room in it, and will here, then, merely ask my hearers to behold me whistling in my caravan on that bright August morning, whistling, and ready, as every sound man should be, to leave the annoyances of yesterday beneath their own dust and begin the new day in the spirit of "Who knows but before nightfall I shall have conquered the world?"

My mother (a remarkable woman) used to tell me it was a good plan to start like that, and indeed I believe the results by nightfall would be surprisingly encouraging if only other people would leave one alone. For, as they meet you, each one by his behaviour takes away a further portion of that which in the morning was so undimmed. Why, sometimes just Edelgard at breakfast has by herself torn off the whole stock of it at once; and generally by dinner there is but little left. It is true that occasionally after dinner a fresh wave of it sets in, but sleep absorbs that before it has had time, as the colloquialists would say, so much as to turn round.

My hearers, then, without my going further into this, must conceive me whistling and full of French *joie* in the subdued sunlight of the Elsa's curtained interior on that bright summer morning at Frogs' Hole Farm.

The floor sloped, for during the night the Elsa's left hind wheel had sunk into an uncobbled portion of the yard where the soft mud offered no resistance, but even the prospect of having to dig this out before we could start did not depress me. I thought I had noticed my head sinking lower and lower during my dreams, and after having, half asleep, endeavoured to correct this impression by means of rolling up my day clothes and putting them beneath my pillow and finding that it made no difference, I decided it must be a nightmare and let well alone. In the morning, on waking after Edelgard's departure, I realized what had happened, and if any of you ever caravan you had better see when you go to bed that all four of your wheels are on that which I called at Queenboro' *terra cotta* (you will remember I explained why it was my wife was unable to be amused) or you will have some pretty work cut out for you next morning.

Even this prospect, however, did not, as I say, depress me. Dumb objects like caravans have no such power, and as nobody not dumb had yet crossed my path I was still, so to speak, untarnished. I had even made up my mind to forget the half-hour with Edelgard the previous night after the ball, and since a willingness to forget is the same thing as a willingness to forgive I think you will all agree that I began that day very well.

Descending to breakfast, I experienced a slight shock (the first breath of tarnish) on finding no one but Mrs. Menzies-Legh and the nondescripts there. Mrs. Menzies-Legh, however, though no doubt feeling privately awkward managed to behave as though nothing had happened, hoped I had slept well, and brought my coffee. She did not talk as much as usual, but attended to my wants with an assiduousness that pointed to her being, after all, ashamed.

I inquired of her with the dignity that means determined distance where the others were, and she said gone for a walk.

She remarked on the beauty of the day, and I replied, "It is indeed."

She then said, slightly sighing, that if only the weather had been like that from the first the tour would have been so much more enjoyable.

On which I observed, with reserved yet easy conversation, that the greater part still lay before us, and who knew but that from then on it was not going to be fine?

At this she looked at me in silence, her head poised slightly on one side, seriously and pensively, as she had done among the Bodiam ruins;

then opened her mouth as though to speak, but thinking better of it got up instead and fetched me more food.

At last, thought I, she was learning the right way to set about pleasing; and I could not prevent a feeling of gratification at the success of my method with her. There was an unusually good breakfast too, which increased this feeling—eggs and bacon, a combined luxury not before seen on our table. The fledglings hung over the stove with heated cheeks preparing relays of it under Mrs. Menzies-Legh's directions, who, while she directed, held the coffee-pot in her arms to keep it warm. She explained she did so for my second cup. I might and indeed I would have suspected that she did so not to keep the coffee but her arms warm, if it had not been such a grilling day. Heat quivered in a blue haze over the hop-poles of the adjacent field. The sunless farmhouse looked invitingly cool and shady now that the surrounding hill-tops were one glare of light. To hold warm coffee in one's arms on such a morning could not possibly show anything but a meritorious desire to make amends; and as I am not a man to do what the scriptural call quench the smoking flax, and yet not a man to forgive too quickly recently audacious ladies, I dexterously mingled extreme politeness with an unshakable reserve.

But I did not care to prolong what was practically a *tête-à-tête* one moment more than necessary, and could not but at last perceive in her persistent replenishings of my cup and plate the exactly contrary desire in the lady. So I got up with a courteously declining, "No, no—a reasonable man knows when to leave off," murmured something about seeing to things, bowed, and withdrew.

Where I withdrew to was the hop-field and a cigar.

I lay down in the shade of these green promises of beer in a corner secure from observation, and reflected that if the others could waste time taking supererogatory exercise I might surely be allowed an interval of calm; and as there are no mosquitoes in England, at least none that I ever saw, it really was not unpleasant for once to contemplate nature from the ground. But I must confess I was slightly nettled by the way the rest of the party had gone off without waiting to see whether I would not like to go too. At first, busied by breakfast, I had not thought of this. Presently, in the hop-field, it entered my mind, and though I would not have walked far with them it would have been pleasant to let the rest go on ahead and remain myself in some cool corner talking to my gentle but lately so elusive friend.

I must say also that I felt no little surprise that Edelgard should gad away in such a manner before our caravan had been tidied up and after what I had said to her the last thing the night before. Did she then think, in her exuberant defiance, that I would turn to and make our beds for her?

My cigar being finished I lay awhile thinking of these things, fanned by a gentle breeze. Country sounds, at a distance to make them agreeable, gradually soothed ear and brain. A cock crowed just far enough away. A lark sang muffled by space. The bells of an invisible church—Raggett's, probably—began a deadened and melodious ringing. Well, I was not going; I smiled as I thought of Raggett and the eagle, forced to make the best of things by themselves. All round me was a hum and a warmth that was irresistible. I did not resist it. My head dropped; my limbs relaxed; and I fell into a doze.

This doze was, as it turned out, extremely *à propos*, for by the time it was over and I had once more become conscious, the morning was well advanced and the caravaners had had ample time to get back from their walk and through their work. Sauntering in among them I found everything ready for a start except the Elsa, which, still with its left hind wheel sunk in the soil, was being doctored by Menzies-Legh, Jellaby, and old James.

"Hullo," said Jellaby, looking up in the midst of his heated pushing and pulling as I appeared, "been enjoying yourself?"

Menzies-Legh did not even look up, but continued his efforts with drops of moisture on his saturnine brow.

Well, here my experience as an artillery officer accustomed to getting gun-carriages out of predicaments enabled me at once to assume authority, and drawing up a camp stool I gave them directions as they worked. They did not, it is true, listen much, thinking as English people so invariably do that they knew better, but by not listening they merely added another half-hour to their labour, and as it was fine and warm and sitting superintending them much less arduous than marching, I had no real objection.

I told Menzies-Legh this at the time, but he did not answer, so I told him again when we were on the road about the half-hour he might have saved if he had worked on my plan. He seemed to be in a more than usually bad temper, for he only shrugged his shoulders and looked glum; and my hearers will agree that Mrs. Menzies-Legh's John was not a possession for England to be specially proud of.

We journeyed that day toward Canterbury, a town you, my friends, may or may not have heard of. That it is an English town I need not say, for if it were not would we have been going there? And it is chiefly noted, I remembered, for its archbishop.

This gentleman, I was told by Jellaby on my questioning him, walks directly behind the King's eldest son, and in front of all the nobles in processions. He is a pastor, but how greatly glorified! He is the final expansion, the last word, of that which in the bud was only a curate. Every English curate, like Buonaparte's soldiers are said to have done, carries in his handbag the mitre of an archbishop. I can only regard it as a blessing that our Church has not got them, for I for one would find it difficult with this possibility in view ever to be really natural to a curate. As it is I am perfectly natural. With absolute simplicity I show ours his place and keep him to it; and I am equally simple with our Superintendents and General Superintendents, the nearest approach our pure and frugal Church goes to bishops and archbishops. There is nothing glorified about them. They are just respectable elderly men, with God-fearing wives who prepare their dinner for them day by day. "And, Jellaby," said I, "can as much be said for the wives of your archbishops?"

"No," said he.

"Another point, then," said I, with the jesting manner one uses to gild unpalatable truth, "on which we Germans are ahead."

Jellaby pushed his wisp of hair back and mopped his forehead. From my position at my horse's head I had called to him as he was walking quickly past me, for I perceived he had my poor gentle little friend in tow and was once again inflicting his society on her. He could not, however, refuse to linger on my addressing him, and I took care to ask him so many questions about Canterbury and its ecclesiastical meaning that Frau von Eckthum was able to have a little rest.

A faint flush showed she understood and appreciated. No longer obliged to exert herself conversationally, as I had observed she was doing when they passed, she dropped into her usual calm and merely listened attentively to all I had to say. But we had hardly begun before Mrs.

Menzies-Legh, who was in front, happened to look round, and seeing us immediately added her company to what was already more than company enough, and put a stop to anything approaching real conversation by herself holding forth. No one wanted to hear her; least of all myself, to whom she chiefly addressed her remarks. The others, indeed, were able to presently slip away, which they did to the rear of our column, I think, for I did not see them again; but I, forced to lead my horse, was helpless.

I leave it to you, my friends, to decide what strictures should be passed on such persistency. I cannot help feeling that it was greatly to my credit that I managed to keep within bounds of politeness under such circumstances. One thing, however, is eternally sure: the more a lady pursues, the more a gentleman withdraws, and accordingly those ladies who throw feminine decorum to the winds only defeat their own ends.

I said this—slightly veiled—to Mrs. Menzies-Legh that morning, taking an opportunity her restless and leaping conversation offered to administer the little lesson. No veils, however, were thin enough for her to see through, and instead of becoming red and startled she looked at me through her eyelashes with an air of pretended innocence and said, "But, Baron dear, what *is* feminine decorum?"

As though feminine decorum or modesty or virtue were things that could be explained in any words decent enough to fit them for a gentleman to use to a lady!

That was a tiring day. Canterbury is a tiring place; at least it would be if you let it. I did not, however, let it tire me. And such a hot place! It is a steaming town with the sun beating down on it, and full of buildings and antiquities one is told one must be longing to look at. After a day's march in the dust it is not antiquities one longs for, and I watched with some contempt the same hypocritical attitude take possession of the party that had distinguished it at Bodiam.

We arrived there about four, and Menzies-Legh pitched on an exceedingly ugly camping ground on a slope just outside the city, with villa residences so near that their inhabitants could observe us, if they had telescopes, from their windows. It was a field from which the corn had been cut, and the hard straw remaining hurt one's weary feet; nor had it any advantages that I could see, though the others spoke of the view. This, if you please, consisted of the roofs of the houses in the town and a cathedral rising from their midst in a network of scaffolding. I pointed this out to them as they stood staring, but Menzies-Legh was quite unshaken in his determination to stay just on that spot, in spite of there being a railway line running along the bottom of the field and a station with all its noises within a stone's throw. I thought it odd to have come to a town at all, for till then the party had been unanimous in its desire to avoid even villages, but on my remarking on this they murmured something about the cathedral, as though the building below, or rather the mass of scaffolding, were enough to excuse the most inconsistent conduct.

The heat of that shadeless stubblefield was indescribable. It did not possess a tree. At the bottom was, as I have said, the railway. At the top, just above where we were, a market garden, a thing of vegetables, whose aim is to have as few shadows as possible. Languidly the party made preparations for settling down. Languidly and after a long delay Menzies-Legh dragged out the stew-pot. In spite of the heat I was as hungry as a man ought to be who, at four o'clock, has not yet dined, and as I watched the drooping caravaners listlessly preparing the potatoes and cabbages and boiled bacon that I now knew so very thoroughly, this having been our meal (except once or twice when we had chickens, or, in extremity, underdone sausages) since the beginning of the tour, a brilliant thought illuminated the gloom of my brain: Why not slip away unnoticed, and down in the town cause myself to be served in the dining-room of an hotel with freshly roasted meat and generous wine?

Very cautiously I raised myself from the hard hot stubble.

Casually I glanced at the view.

With an air of preoccupation I went behind the Elsa, the first move toward freedom, as though to fetch some accessory of the meal from our larder.

"Do you want anything, Otto?" asked my officious and tactless wife trotting after me—a thing she never does when I do want anything.

Naturally I was a little snappish: but then if she had left me alone would I have snapped? Wives are great forcers of faults upon a man. So I snapped; and she departed, chidden.

Looking about me, up at the sky, and round the horizon, as though intent on thoughts of weather, I inconspicuously edged toward the market garden and the gate. With a man in the garden searching for slugs I spent a moment or two conversing, and then, a backward glance having assured me the caravaners were still drooping in listless preparation round the stew-pot, I sauntered, humming, through the gate.

Immediately I ran into Jellaby, who, a bucket of water in each hand, was panting along the road.

"Hullo, Baron," he gasped; "enjoying yourself?"

"I am going," said I with much presence of mind combined with the seriousness that repudiates any idea of enjoyment, "to buy some matches. Ours are running short."

"Oh," said he, plumping down his buckets and fumbling among the folds of his flappy clothes, "I can lend you some. Here you are."

And he held out a box.

"Jellaby," said I, "what is one box to a whole—shall we call it household? My wife requires many matches. She is constantly striking them. It is her husband's duty to see that she has enough. Keep yours. And farewell."

And walking at a pace that prohibited pursuit by a man with buckets I left him.

I have had so many dinners in dining-rooms since that one at Canterbury, ordered repasts without grease and that kept hot, that the wonder of it has lost in my memory much of its first brightness. You, my hearers, who dine as I now do regularly and well, would hardly if I could still describe be able to enter into my feelings. I found a cool room in an inn with the pleasantly un-English name *Fleur de Lys*, and a sympathetic waiter who fell in at once with my views about fresh air and shut all the windows. I had a newspaper, and I sipped a cognac while the meal was preparing. I ordered everything on the list except bacon, chickens, and sausages. I also would not eat potatoes, and declined, as a vegetable, cabbage. I drank much wine, full-bodied and generous, but I refused after dinner to drink coffee.

Filled and hallowed, once more in thorough tune with myself and life and ready to take any further experiences the day might bring with unruffled geniality, I left toward dusk the temple that had thus blest me (after debating within myself whether it would not be prudent having regard to the future in further lanes and fields to sup first, and regretfully realizing that I could not), and leisurely made my way across the street to that other temple, whose bells announced the inevitable service.

My decision to peep cautiously in and see whether the parson were alone before definitely committing myself to a pew was unnecessary, first because there were no pews but a mighty emptiness, and secondly because, along the dusk of this emptiness, groups of persons made their way to a vast flight of steps dividing the place into two and leading up to a region, into which they disappeared, of glimmering lights. Too clever now by far to go where there were lights and praying might be demanded of me, I wandered on tiptoe among the gathering shadows at the other end. It grew quickly darker among the towering pillars and dim, painted windows. The bells left off; the organ began to rumble about; and a distant voice, with a family likeness to that of Raggett, sing-songed something long. It had no ups and downs, no breaks; it was a drawn out thread of sound, thin and sweet like a trickle of liquid sugar. Then many voices took up the sing-song, broadening it out from a thread to a band. Then came the single trickle again; and so they went on alternately, while I, hidden among the pillars, listened very well pleased.

When the organ began, and an endless singing and repeating of the same tune, I cautiously advanced nearer in search of something to sit on. To the right of the steps I found what I wanted, an empty space in itself as big as our biggest church in Storchwerder but small in comparison to the rest, with immense windows full of the painted glass that becomes so confused and meaningless in the dusk, no lights, and here and there a chair or two.

I sat down at the foot of a huge pillar in this dark and unobserved corner, while the organ above me and the singing voices filled the spaces of the roof with their slumber-inciting repetitions. Presently, as a tired and comfortable man would do, I fell asleep, and was only wakened by the subdued murmur just round the edge of the pillar of two people talking, and I instantly, almost before my eyes opened, recognized that it was Frau von Eckthum and Jellaby.

They were apparently sitting on some chairs I had noticed as I came round to the greater obscurity of mine. They were so close that it was practically into my ear that they spoke. The singing was finished, and I fancy the congregation had dispersed, for the organ was playing softly and the glimmer of lights had gone out.

My ears are as quick as any man's, and I was greatly amused at the situation. "Now," thought I, "I shall hear what sort of stuff Jellaby inflicts on patient and inexperienced ladies."

It also occurred to me that it would be interesting to hear how she talked to him, and so discover whether the libel were true that except in my presence she chatted and was jocular. Jocular? Can anything be less what one wishes in the woman one admires? Of course she was not, and Mrs. Menzies-Legh was only (very naturally) jealous. I therefore sat quite still, and became extremely alert and wide awake.

They were certainly not laughing. That, however, may have been the cathedral—not that men of Jellaby's stamp have even a rudimentary sense of reverence and decency—but anyhow part of the libel was disposed of, for the gentle lady was serious. She was, it is true, a good deal more fluent than I knew her, but she seemed moved by some strong emotion which no doubt accounted for that. What I could not account for was her displaying emotion to a person like Jellaby. The first thing, for instance, that I heard her say was, "It is all my fault." And her voice vibrated with penitence.

"Oh, but it wasn't, you know," said Jellaby.

"Yes, it was. And I feel I ought to take a double share of the burden, and instead I don't take any."

Burden? What burden could the tender lady possibly have to bear that would not gladly be borne for her by many a masculine shoulder, including mine? I was about to put my head round the pillar's edge to assure her of this when she began to speak again.

"I did try—at first," she said. "But I—I simply *can't*. So I shift it on to Di."

Di, my friends, is Mrs. Menzies-Legh, christened with prophetic paganism Diana.

"An extremely sensible thing to do," thought I, remembering the wiriness of Di.

"She is very wonderful," said Jellaby.

"Yes," I silently agreed, "most."

"She is an angel," said her (I suppose naturally) partial sister, whose sentiments were besides, no doubt, at that moment coloured by the surroundings in which she found herself. But I could not help being entertained by this example of lovable blindness.

"It is so sweetly good of her to keep him off us," continued Frau von Eckthum. "She does it so kindly. So unselfishly. What can it be like to have such a husband?"

"Ah," thought I, a light illuminating my mind, "they are talking of our friend John. Naturally his charming sister-in-law cannot bear him. Nor should she be called upon to do so. To bear her husband is solely a wife's affair."

"What *can* it be like?" repeated Frau von Eckthum, in the voice of one vainly trying to realize something beyond words bad.

"I can't think," said Jellaby, basely, I thought, for he professed much outward friendship for John.

"Of course she is amused—in a way," continued Frau von Eckthum, "but that sort of amusement soon palls, doesn't it?"

"Extraordinarily soon," said Jellaby.

"Before it has so much as begun," thought I, recollecting the man's sallow, solemn visage. But then it is no part of a wife's functions to be amused.

"And she is really sorry for him," said Frau von Eckthum.

"Indeed?" thought I, entertained by the patronizing attitude implied.

"She says," continued her gentle sister, "that his loneliness, whether he knows it or not, makes her ache."

Well, I did not mind Mrs. Menzies-Legh aching, so thought nothing definite there.

"She doesn't want him to notice we get out of his way—she is afraid he might be hurt. Do you think he would be?"

"No," said Jellaby. "Pure leather."

I agreed, though once again surprised at Jellaby's baseness.

"I can't think," continued Frau von Eckthum—"I suppose it's because I am so bad—but I really cannot think how she can endure him, and in such doses."

"He is undoubtedly," said Jellaby, "a very grievous bounder."

"What," I wondered, "is a bounder?" But I applauded Jellaby's sentiment nevertheless, for there was no mistaking its nature, though his baseness was really amazing.

"It must be because Di has such a vivid imagination," continued her sister musingly. "She sees what he might have been, what he probably was meant to be——"

"And what he would still be," put in Jellaby, "if only he would allow his nice wife to influence him a little."

"But John," thought I, "in that is right. Let us be fair and admit his good sides. A wife should never, under any circumstances, be allowed allowed——"

Then, suddenly struck by the point of view, by the feminine idea (Socialists have the minds of women) of a man's being restored to what he was primarily intended to be when he issued newly-made (as poets and parsons would say) from the hands of his Maker through the manipulations of Mrs. Menzies-Legh, my sense of humour played me a nasty trick (for I would have liked to have heard more) and I found myself bursting into a loud chuckle.

"What's that?" exclaimed Jellaby, jumping up.

He soon saw what it was, for I immediately put my head round the edge of the pillar.

They both stared at me in a strange alarm.

"Pray do not suppose," I said, smiling reassuringly, "that I am a ghost."

They stared without a word.

"You look as though I might be."

They went on staring.

"I could not help, as I sat here, hearing what you were saying."

They stared as speechless as though they had been caught killing somebody.

"I really am not a spirit," said I, getting up. "Look—do I look like one?"

And striking a match I playfully passed it backward and forward across my features.

But its light at the same time showed me a flush of the most attractive and vivid crimson on Frau von Eckthum's face, colouring it from her hair to her throat. She looked so beautiful like that, she who was ordinarily white, that immediately lighting another I gazed at her in undisguised admiration.

"Pardon me," I said, holding it very near her while her eyes, fixed on mine, still seemed full of superstitious terror, "pardon me, but I must as a man and a judge look at you."

Jellaby, however, unforgivably ill-bred as ever, knocked the match out of my hand and stamped on it. "Look here, Baron," he said with unusual heat, "I am very sorry—as sorry as you like, but you really mustn't hold matches in front of somebody's face."

"Why sorry, Jellaby?" I inquired mildly, for I was not going to have a scene. "I do not mind about the match. I have more."

"Sorry, of course, that you should have heard———"

"Every word, Jellaby," said I.

"I tell you I'm frightfully sorry—I can't tell you how sorry———"

"You may be assured," said I, "that I will be discreet."

He stared, with a face of stupid surprise.

"Discreet?" said he.

"Discreet, Jellaby. And it may be a relief to you to know," I continued, "that I heartily endorse your opinion."

Jellaby's mouth dropped open.

"Every word of it."

Jellaby's mouth remained open.

"Even the word bounder, which I did not understand but which, I gathered from your previous remarks, is a very suitable expression."

Jellaby's mouth remained open.

I waited a moment, then seeing that it would not shut and that I had really apparently shattered their nerves beyond readjustment by so suddenly popping round on them in that ghostly place, I thought it best to change the subject, promising myself to return to it another time.

So I picked up my hat and stick from the chair I had vacated—Jellaby peered round the pillar at this piece of furniture with his unshut mouth still denoting unaccountable shock—bowed, and offered my arm to Frau von Eckthum.

"It is late," said I with tender courtliness, "and I observe an official approaching us with keys. If we do not return to the camp we shall have your sister setting out, probably on angelic wings"—she started—"in search of you. Let me, dear lady, conduct you back to her. Nay, nay, you need have no fears—I really can keep a secret."

With her eyes fixed on mine, and that strange look of perfect fright in them, she got up slowly and put her hand on my proffered arm.

I led her away with careful tenderness.

Jellaby, I believe, followed in the distance.

CHAPTER XX

LIFE is a strange thing, and full of surprises. The day before, you think you know what will happen on the morrow, and on the morrow you find you did not. Light as you may the candle of your common sense, and peer as you may by its shining into the future, if you see anything at all it turns out to have been, after all, something else. We are surrounded by tricks, by illusions, by fluidities. Even when the natural world behaves pretty much as experience has led us to expect, the unnatural world, by which I mean (and I say it is a fair description) human beings, does nothing of the sort. My ripe conclusion, carefully weighed and unattackably mellow, is that all one's study, all one's thought, all one's experience, all one's philosophy, lead to this: that you cannot account for anything. Do you, my friends, interrupt me here with a query? My answer to it is: Wait.

The morning after the occurrences just described I overslept myself, and on emerging about ten o'clock in search of what I hoped would still be breakfast I found the table tidily set out, the stove alight, and keeping coffee warm, ham in slices on a dish, three eggs waiting to be transferred to an expectant saucepan, and not a single caravaner in sight except Menzies-Legh.

Him, of course, I now pitied. For to have a treacherous friend, and a sister-in law of whom you are fond but who in her heart cannot endure you, to be under the delusion that the one is sincere and the other loving, is to become a fit object for pity; and since no one can at the same time both pity and hate, I was not nearly so much annoyed as I otherwise would have been at finding my glum-faced friend was to keep me company. Annoyed, did I say? Why, I was not annoyed at all. For though I might pity I was also secretly amused, and further, the feeling that I now had a little private understanding with Frau von Eckthum exhilarated me into more than my usual share of good humour.

He was sitting smoking; and when I appeared, fresh, and rested, and cheery, round the corner of the Elsa, he not only immediately said good morning, but added an inquiry as to whether I did not think it a beautiful day; then he got up, went across to the stove, put the eggs in the saucepan, and fetched the coffee-pot.

This was very surprising. I tell you, my friends, the moods of persons who caravan are as many and as incalculable as the grains of sand on the seashore. If you doubt it, go and do it. But you cannot reasonably doubt it after listening to the narrative. Have I not told you in the course of it how the party's spirits were up in the skies one hour, and down on the ground the next; how their gaiety some days at breakfast was childish in its folly, and their silence on others depressing; how they quoted poetry and played at Blind Man's Buff in the morning, and in the afternoon dragged their feet without speaking through the mud; how they talked far too much sometimes, and then, when I wished to, would not talk at all; how they were suddenly polite and attentive, and then as suddenly forgot I could possibly want anything; how the wet did not damp their hilarity one day, and no amount of sunshine coax it forth the next? But of all their moods this of Menzies-Legh's in the field above Canterbury was the one that surprised me most.

You see, he was naturally so very glum. True at the beginning there had been gleams of light but they soon became extinguished. True, also, at Frogs' Hole Farm, when demonstrating truths by means of tea in glasses, he had been for a short while pleasant—only, however, to plunge immediately and all the deeper into gloom and ill-temper. Gloom and ill-temper was his normal state; and to see him attending to my wants, doing it with unmistakable assiduity, actively courteous, was astonishing. I was astonished. But my breeding enabled me to behave as though it were the most ordinary thing in the world, and I accepted sugar from him and allowed him to cut my bread with the blank expression on my face of him who sees nothing unusual or interesting anywhere, which is, I take it, the expression of the perfect gentleman. When at length my plate was surrounded by specimens of all the comforts available, and I had begun to eat, he sat down again, and leaning his elbow on the table and fixing his eyes on the city already sweltering in heat and vapour below, resumed his pipe.

A train puffed out of the station along the line at the bottom of our field, jerking up slow masses of white steam into the hot, motionless air.

"There goes Jellaby's train," said Menzies-Legh.

"Jellaby's what?" said I, cracking an egg.

"Train," said he.

"Why, what has he got to do with trains?" I asked, supposing with the vagueness of want of interest, that Jellaby, as well as being a Socialist, was a railway director and kept a particular train as another person would keep a pet.

"He's in it," said Menzies-Legh.

I looked up from my egg at Menzies-Legh's profile.

"What?" said I.

"In it," said he. "Obliged to go."

"What—Jellaby gone? First Lord Sidge, and now Jellaby?"

Naturally I was surprised, for I had heard and noticed nothing of this. Also the way one after the other left without saying good-bye seemed to me inconsiderate—at least that: probably more.

"Yes," said Menzies-Legh. "We are—we are very sorry."

I could not, however, honestly join in any sorrow over Jellaby, so merely remarked that the party was shrinking.

"Yes," said Menzies-Legh, "that's rather our feeling too."

"But why has Jellaby———?"

"Oh, well, you know, public man. Parliament. And all that."

"Does your Parliament reassemble so shortly?"

"Oh, well, soon enough. You have to prepare, you know. Collect your wits, and that sort of thing."

"Ah, yes. Jellaby should not leave that to the last minute. But he might," I added with a slight frown, "have taken leave of me according to the customs of good society. Manners are manners, after all is said and done."

"He was in a great hurry," said Menzies-Legh.

There was a silence, during which Menzies-Legh smoked and I breakfasted. Once or twice he cleared his throat as though about to say something, but when I looked up prepared to listen he continued his pipe and his staring at the city in the sun below.

"Where are the ladies?" I inquired, when the first edge of my appetite had been blunted and I had leisure to look about me.

Menzies-Legh shifted his legs, which had been crossed.

"They went to the station with Jellaby to see the last of him," said he.

"Indeed. All of them?"

"I believe so."

Jellaby then, though he could not have the courtesy to say good-bye to me, could take a prolonged farewell of my wife and of the other members of our party.

"He is not what we in our country would call a gentleman," I said, after a silence during which I finished the third egg and regretted there were no more.

"Who is not?" asked Menzies-Legh.

"Jellaby. No doubt the term bounder would apply to him quite as well as to other people."

Menzies-Legh turned his sallow visage to me. "He's a great friend of mine," he said, the familiar scowl weighing down his eyebrows.

I could not help smiling and shaking my head at that, all I had heard the night before so very fresh in my memory.

"Ah, my dear sir," I said, "be careful how you trust your great friends. Do not give way too lavishly to confidence. Belief in them is all very well, but it should not go beyond the limits of reason."

"He's a great friend of mine," repeated Menzies-Legh, raising his voice.

"I wish then," said I, "you would tell me what a bounder is."

He glowered at me a moment from beneath black brows. Then he said more quietly:

"I'm not a slang dictionary. Suppose we talk seriously."

"Certainly," said I, reaching out for the jam.

He cleared his throat. "I got a lot of letters and telegrams last night," he said.

"How did you manage that?" I asked.

"They were waiting for me at the post-office here. I had telegraphed for them to be forwarded. And I'm afraid—I'm sorry, but it's inevitable—we shall have to be off."

"Off what?" said I, for a few of the more intimate English idioms still remained for me to master.

"Off," said he. "Go. Leave this."

"Oh," said I. "Well, we are used to that. This tour, my dear sir, is surely the very essence of what you call being off. Where do we go next? I trust to a place with trees in it."

"You don't understand, Baron. We don't go anywhere next as far as the caravans are concerned. My wife and I are obliged to go home."

I was, of course, surprised. "We are, indeed," said I, after a moment, "shrinking rapidly."

Then the thought of being rid of Mrs. Menzies-Legh and her John and Jellaby at, so to speak, one swoop, and continuing the tour purged of these baser elements with the tender lady entirely in our charge, made me unable to repress a smile of satisfaction.

Menzies-Legh looked in his turn surprised. "I am glad," he said, "that you don't mind."

"My dear sir," I said courteously, "of course I mind, and we shall miss you and your—er—er—" it was difficult on the spur of the moment to find an adjective, but Frau von Eckthum's praises of her sister the night before coming into my mind I popped in the word suggested suggested—"angelic wife——"

He stared—ungratefully I thought, considering the effort it had been.

"But," I continued, "you may be very sure we shall take every care of your sister-in-law, and return her safe and well into your hands on September the first, which is the date my contract with the owner of the Elsa expires."

"I'm afraid," said he, "I wasn't clear. We all go. Betti included, and Jumps and Jane too. I'm very sorry," he interrupted, as I opened my mouth, "very sorry indeed that things should have turned out so unexpectedly, but it is absolutely impossible for us to go on. Out of the question."

And he set his jaws, and shut his mouth into a mere line of opposition and finality.

Well, my friends, what do you say to that? What do you think of this example of the surprises life has in store for one? And, incidentally, what do you think of human nature? Especially of human nature when it caravans? And still more especially of human nature that is also English? Not without reason do our neighbours label the accursèd island *perfide*

Albion. It is true I am not clear about the *Albion*, but I am very clear about the *perfide*.

"Do you mean to tell me," I said, leaning toward him across the table and forcing him to meet my gaze, "that your sister-in-law *wishes* to go with you?"

"She does," said he.

"Then, sir——" I began, amazement and indignation struggling together within me.

"I tell you, Baron," he interrupted, "we are very sorry things have turned out like this. My wife is most genuinely distressed. But she too sees the impossibility—unforeseen complications demand we should go home."

"Sir——" I again began.

"My dear Baron," he again interrupted, "it needn't in the least interfere with you. Old James will stay with you if you and the Baroness would like to go on."

"Sir, I have paid for a month, and have only had a week."

"Well, go on and finish your month. Nobody is preventing you."

"But I was persuaded to join the tour on the understanding that it was a party—that we were all to be together—four weeks together——"

"My dear fellow," said he (never had I been addressed as that before), "you talk as if it were a business arrangement, a buying and selling, as if we were bound by a contract, under agreement——"

"Your sister-in-law inveigled me into it," I exclaimed, emphasizing what I said by regular beats on the table with my forefinger, "on the definite understanding that it was to be a party and she—was—to be—a—member of it."

"Pooh, my dear Baron—Betti's definite understandings. She's in love, and when a woman's that it's no earthly use——"

"What?" said I, startled for a moment out of all self-possession.

"Well?" he said, looking at me in surprise. "Why not? She's young. Or do you consider it improper for widows——"

"Improper? Natural, sir—natural. How long——?"

"Oh, before the tour even started. And propinquity, seeing each other every day—well," he finished suddenly, "one mustn't talk about it, you know."

But you, my friends, what do you say to that? What do you think of this second example of the surprises life has in store for us? I have been in two minds as to whether I would tell you this one at all, but to a law-abiding man, calm and objective as I know myself to be and as you by now must know me too, such an incident though pleasurable could not in any way affect or alter my conduct. Strictly Menzies-Legh was to be censured for mentioning it; however that, I suppose, was what Jellaby called the bounder coming out in him, and I perceived that whatever they exactly may be bounders have their uses. I repeat, I make no attempt to deny that it was a pleasurable incident, and although I am aware Storchwerder never liked her (chiefly, I firmly believe, because she would not ask it to her dinners) I am convinced that not one of you, my friends, and I say it straight in your faces, but would have been glad to stand at that moment in my shoes. I did not forget I was a husband, but you can be a husband and yet remain a man. I think I behaved very creditably. Only for an instant was there the least little lapse from complete self-possession. Immediately I became and remained perfectly calm. Edelgard; duty; my position in life; my beliefs; I remembered them all. It also occurred to me (but I could not well tell Menzies-Legh) that having regard to the behaviour throughout the tour of his wife it was evident these things ran in families. I could not tell him, but I felt myself inwardly in every way tickled. All I could do, indeed all I did do, was to say "Strange, strange world," and get up from my chair because I found myself unable to continue sitting in it.

"But what do you propose to do?" Menzies-Legh asked, after he had watched me taking a hasty turn or two up and down in the sun.

"Behave," said I, stopping in front of him, "as an officer and a gentleman."

He stared. Then he got up and said with a touch of impatience—a most unreliable person as regards temper: "Yes, yes—no doubt. But what shall I tell old James about your caravan? Are you going on or not? If not, he'll pilot it home for you. I'm afraid I must know soon. I haven't much time. I must get away to-day."

"What? To-day?"

"I must. I'm very sorry. Obliged to, you know——"

"And the Ailsa?"

"Oh, that's all arranged. I telegraphed last night for one of the grooms. He'll be down in an hour or two and take charge of it back to Panthers."

"And the Ilsa?"

"He'll take that too."

"No, my dear sir," said I firmly. "You leave the Ilsa in our charge—it and its contents."

"Eh?" said he.

"It and its contents—human and otherwise."

"Nonsense, Baron. What on earth would you do with Jane and Jumps? They're going up to town with me by train. And my wife and Betti—oh, yes, by the way, my wife gave me instructions to tell you how very sorry she was not to be able to say good-bye to you. I assure you she was really greatly distressed, but she and Betti are motoring up to London and felt they ought to start as early as possible——"

"But—motoring? You said they had gone to the sta——"

"So they did. They saw Jellaby off, and then were picked up by a motor I ordered for them last night in the town, and went straight from there———"

I heard no more. He went on speaking, but I heard no more. The series of surprises had done their work, and I could attend to nothing further. I believe he continued to express regret and offer advice, but what he said fell on my ear with the indifferent trickling of water when one is not thirsty. At first anger, keen resentment, and disappointment surged within me, for why, I asked myself, did she not say good-bye? I walked up and down on the hot stubble, my hands deep in my pockets and myself deep in conflicting emotions, while Menzies-Legh supposing I was listening regretted and advised, asking myself why she did not say goodbye. Then, gradually, I could not but see that here was tact, here was delicacy, the right feeling of the truly feminine woman, and began to admire her all the more because she had not said it. By degrees composure stole upon me. Reason returned to my assistance. I could think, arrange, decide. And before Edelgard came back with the two children, mere heated *débris* of that which had lately been so complete, what I had decided with the clear-headed rapidity of the practical and sensible man was to give up the Elsa, lose my money, and go home. Home after all is the best place when life begins to wobble; and home in this case was very near the Eckthum property—I only had to borrow a vehicle, or even in extremity take a *droschke*, and there I was. There too the delightful lady must sooner or later be, and I would at least see her from time to time, whereas in England among her English relations she was entirely and hopelessly cut off.

Thus it was, my friends, that I did not see Frau von Eckthum again. Thus it was our caravaning came to an untimely end.

You can figure to yourselves what kind of reflections a man inclined to philosophize would reflect as the reduced party hastily packed, in the heat and glare of the summer morning, that which they had unpacked a week previously amid howling winds and hail showers in the yard at Panthers. Nature then had frowned, but vainly, on our merriment. Nature now was smiling, equally vainly on our fragments. One brief week; and what had happened? Rather, I should say, what had not happened?

On the stubble I walked up and down lost in reflection, while Edelgard, helped (officiously I thought, but I did not care enough to mind) by Menzies-Legh, stuffed our belongings into bags. She had asked no questions. If she had I would not have answered them, being little in the mood as you can imagine to put up with wives. I just told her, on her return from seeing Jellaby off, of my decision to cross by that night's boat, and bade her get our things together. She said nothing, but at once began to pack. She did not even inquire why we were not going to look at London first, as we had originally planned. London? Who cared for London? My mood was not one in which a man bothers about London. With reference to that city it can best be described by the single monosyllable Tcha.

I will not linger over the packing, or relate how when it was finished Edelgard indulged in a prolonged farewell (with embraces, if you please) of the two uninteresting fledglings, in a fervent shaking of both Menzies-Legh's hands combined with an invitation—I heard it—to stay with us in Storchwerder, and the pressing upon old James in a remote corner of something that looked suspiciously like a portion of her dress-allowance; or how she then set out by my side for the station steeped in that which we call *Abschiedsstimmung*, old James preceding us with our luggage while the others took care for the last time of the camp; or with what abandonment of apparent affectionate regret she hung herself out of the train window as we presently passed along the bottom of the field and waved her handkerchief. Such rankness of sentiment could only make me shrug my shoulders, filled as I was by my own absorbing thoughts.

I did glance up, though, and there on the stubble, surrounded by every sort of litter, stood the three familiar brown vehicles blistering in the sun, with Menzies-Legh and the fledglings knee-deep in straw and saucepans and bags and other forlorn discomforts, watching us depart.

Strange how alien the whole thing seemed, how little connection it seemed to have with me now that the sparkling bubbles (if I may refer to Frau von Eckthum as bubbles) had disappeared and only the dregs were left. I could not help feeling glad, as I raised my hat in courteous acknowledgment of the frantic wavings of the fledglings, that I was finally out of all the mess.

Menzies-Legh gravely returned my salute; our train rounded a curve; and camp and caravaners disappeared at once and forever into the unrecallable past.

CHAPTER XXI

THUS our caravaning came to an end.

I could hardly believe it when I thought how at that hour of the day before I was lying beneath the hop-poles of Frogs' Hole Farm with the greater part, as I supposed, of the tour before me; I could hardly believe that here we were again, Edelgard and I, *tête-à-tête* in a railway carriage and with a future of, if I may coin a word, *tête-à-têteness* stretching uninterruptedly ahead as far as imagination could be induced to look. And not only just ordinary *tête-à-têteness*, but with the complication of one of the *têtes*, so to speak, being rankly rebellious and unwifely. How long would it take, I wondered, glancing at her as she sat in the corner opposite me, to bring her back to the reason in which she used before we came to England to take delight?

I glanced at her, and I found she was looking at me; and immediately on catching my eye she leaned forward and said:

"Otto, what was it you did?"

They were the first words she had spoken to me that day, and very naturally failing to see any point in them I requested her not to be subtle, which is courteous for senseless.

"Why," said she, not heeding this warning, "did the party break up? What was it you did?"

Were there ever such questions? But I recollected she could not dream how things really were, and therefore was not as much put out as I would otherwise have been at the characteristically wifely fashion of at once when anything seemed to be going wrong attributing it to her husband.

I therefore good-humouredly applied the Aunt Bockhügel remedy to her, and was willing to leave it at that if she had let me. She, however, preferred to quarrel. Without the least attempt to change the Bockhügel face she said, "My dear Otto—poor Aunt Bockhügel. Won't we leave her in peace? But tell me what it was you *did*."

Then I became vexed, for really the assumption of superiority, of the right to criticize and blame, went further than a reasonable man can permit. What I said as we journeyed up to London I will not here repeat; it has been said before and will be said often enough again so long as husbands have to have wives: but how about the responsibility resting on the wives? I remembered the cheerful mood I had been in on getting up, and felt no small degree of resentment at the manner in which my wife was trying to wipe it out. Give me a chance, and I am the kindest of men; take away my chance, and what can I do?

And so, my friends, as it were with a wrangle ended our sojourn on British soil. I lay down my pen, and become lost in many reflections as I think of all these things. Long ago have we settled down again to our ordinary Storchwerder life, with an Emilie instead of a Clothilde in the kitchen. Long ago we paid our calls announcing to our large circle that we were back. We have taken up the threads of duty, we have resumed regulated existence; and gradually as the weeks melt into months and the influence of Storchwerder presses more heavily upon her, I have observed that my wife shows an increasing tendency once more to find her level. I need not have worried; I need not have wondered how I could bring her to reason. Storchwerder is doing it. Its atmosphere and associations are very potent. They are being, I am thankful to say, too strong for Edelgard. After a few preliminary convulsions she began to cook my meals and look after my welfare as dutifully as before, and other effects no doubt will follow. At present she is more silent than before the tour, and does not laugh as readily as she used when I chance to be in a jesting mood; also at times a British microbe that has escaped the vigilance of those beneficent little creatures Science tells us are in our blood on the alert to devour intrusive foreigners crops up and causes her to comment on my sayings and doings rather *à la* Mrs. Menzies-Legh, but I frown her down or apply the Aunt Bockhügel, and in another few months I trust all will be exactly as it used to be. I myself am exactly as I used to be—a plain, outspoken, patriotic, Christian gentleman, going steadily along the path of duty, neither looking to the right nor to the left (if I did I should not see Frau von Eckthum for she is still in England), and using my humble abilities to do what I can for the glory of my country and my Emperor.

And now having finished the narrative there is nothing more to do but to buy a red pencil and put marks on it. Many, I fear, will be those marks. Unfortunate is the fact that you cannot be sincere without at the same time being indiscreet. But I trust that what remains will be treated by my hearers with the indulgence due to a man who has only been desirous of telling the whole truth, or in other words (and which amount, I take it, to precisely the same thing) of concealing nothing.

POST SCRIPTUM

A TERRIBLE thing has happened.

Finished a week ago and the invitations to come and listen already in the post, with the flat being cleaned in preparation and beer and sandwiches almost, as it were, on the threshold, I have been obliged to take my manuscript once more out of the locked drawer which conceals it from Edelgard's eyes in order to record a most lamentable occurrence.

My wife received a letter this morning from Mrs. Menzies-Legh informing her that Frau von Eckthum is about to be married to Jellaby.

No words can express the shock this has given me. No words can express my horror at such a union. Left to herself, helpless in the clutches of her English relatives, the gentle creature's very virtues—her pliability, her tender womanliness—have become the means of bringing about the catastrophe. She was influenced, persuaded, a prey. It is six months since she was handed over entirely to the Menzies-Leghs, six months of no doubt steady resistance, ending probably in her health breaking down and in her giving in. It hardly bears thinking of. A Briton. A Socialist. A man in flannel. No family. No money. And the most terrible opinions. My shock and horror are so great, so profound, that I have cancelled the invitations and will lock this up perhaps forever, certainly for some weeks; for how could I possibly read aloud the story of our harmonious and delightful intercourse with the tragic sequel public knowledge?

And my wife, when she read the letter at breakfast, clapped her hands and cried, "Isn't it splendid—oh, Otto, aren't you glad?"

THE END

Printed in Great Britain
by Amazon